Lady Lou th

Audre
Published by

© Copyright 2019 Audrey Harrison

Audrey Harrison asserts the moral right to be identified as the author of this work.

This novel is entirely a work of fiction. The names, characters and incidents portrayed in it are the work of the author's imagination. Any resemblance to actual persons, living or dead, events or localities is entirely coincidental, except the character of Lou who is inspired by Lou Harrington, a good friend.

This eBook is licensed for your personal enjoyment only. This eBook may not be re-sold or given away to other people.

Thank you for respecting the hard work of this author.

Find more about the author and contact details at the end of this book and the chance to obtain a free copy of The Unwilling Earl.

*

This book was proof read by Joan Kelley. Read more about Joan at the end of this story, but if you need her, you may reach her at oh1kelley@gmail.com.

Dedication

This book is dedicated to my very own Lady Lou, who I've considered a friend for the last ten years. You can find out more about Lou in the 'About this book section' at the end of the story. Lou, I hope you enjoy the story, although there is a lot of artistic licence in here!

Lady Lou the Highwayman

Glossary:

A Royal Scamp – a highwayman who robs civilly
Gentleman of the Road – a highwayman
High Road – a highwayman
High Pad/Rum Pad/Pad/Padder – a highwayman
Knight of the Road – a highwayman
Rank Rider – a highwayman
Scamp – a highwayman
Snaffler – a highwayman

Chapter 1
Hampstead Heath 1809

The shot rang out across the clear night, startling the four horses travelling at speed over the open heathland.

"Halt, and no one will die!" came the loud, gruff voice of the lone rider on a dappled grey steed when the carriage led by the fine thoroughbreds came to an ungainly standstill.

The coachman and footman travelling on the outside of the carriage were not foolish enough to attempt any imprudent heroics when two guns pointed in their direction. Jackson, the coachman wouldn't have been able to do anything, even if he'd wanted to as he had his hands full, trying to calm the normally exquisitely behaved animals.

The horseman dug his knees into the flank of his horse and slowly approached the now stationary carriage. He was dressed in a large black cloak, black gloves, tri-corn hat, and a dark cravat, which was being used to cover his face. The horses attached to the carriage expressed, by the rolling of their heads, their displeasure at being frightened and brought to a sudden halt, shaking their manes, and snorting indignantly. This was not how the high-quality beasts were used to being treated.

The highwayman noted that the coachman soon had the animals under control. His eyes took in everything about the scene whilst keeping his pistols pointed in the direction of the servants.

"If you are sensible, no one needs to be hurt. No fast movements, and your families won't be forced to go into mourning," came the rough voice, spoken through the dark cloth, which was wrapped across the lower features, revealing only the bright eyes that were observing and anticipating every movement.

The footman put his hands up in an effort to ensure there would be no misunderstanding about reaching for a weapon. Jackson was holding tightly onto the reins, desperately wanting to flick the leather to send the horses into a speedy getaway but knowing that a bullet could travel far faster than even four horses working together. He grappled to restrain his instinct to flee. He might want to escape, but he didn't want to die in the attempt.

"I want your blunt and your jewellery. I am not interested in who you are or what you're doing on the heath at this time of night," the attacker said, finally reaching the barouche door and pointing one of the guns underneath the hanging curtain into the now open window.

A female gasp was heard at the movement, but the material hid the occupants of the carriage.

The sound had come from Lady Helena Ashton. She had been persuaded by her brother and his friend to be the last ones leaving the ball they had attended. A game of cards had spiralled out of control, the bets increasing in size at an alarming pace, and neither gentleman had wanted to leave before they managed to make the purses of their fellow players a lot lighter. It was typical behaviour of the pair. Helena had become embroiled due to the lack of a female chaperone, from which other young ladies in society had the benefit. So far, she'd managed to persuade her brother that he was the best escort she could have, and as it would have meant introducing an older, more circumspect woman into their family, her brother had been easily convinced, but a chaperone would have insisted upon an earlier departure.

Lord Simon Ashton, the Earl of Garswood, and his friend, Lord Henry Roby, Earl of Ince, looked at each other as the tip of the pistol intruded into the plush vehicle.

"Give me your blunt before I force you to step outside. The decision is yours: blunt or carriage. It is a long walk to town, and there isn't only myself on the heath tonight, I promise you," came the menacing voice, offering an unattractive choice.

Simon touched his finger to his lips, looking at his sister, and took a pistol from the inner pocket of the opposite seat. He nodded to Henry and slowly began to open the door on the other side of the carriage from the robber. His movements were fast but careful. If he made the vehicle rock, their attacker would realise he was trying to deliver a counter-attack. Discovery would guarantee someone getting hurt, and he wasn't going to allow that to happen.

Henry took out a small purse of money from the pocket of his frock coat and slowly moved it through the curtain. "Don't shoot! We will give you whatever we have of value. There is no need for violence." His voice was unusually meek as he played the part of the frightened gent.

"Wise man," was the gruff response. "But I don't want any stupidity. Give me everything now, and I'll let you go. The quicker you are, the sooner you will be on your merry way."

"My friend has a necklace that is valuable, but is proving difficult to remove," Henry said amenably, sounding surprisingly calm for one who had a gun pointed at him.

The nose of the pistol was used to pull the curtain to one side, revealing Helena struggling with her necklace; that it was because her hands were shaking so much did not matter. She was aware she needed to delay handing over her valuables to let Simon do whatever he was planning. The thought that her brother was putting himself in danger didn't help as she tried to unfasten the clasp. Helena had never felt fear like this, and it was only by gritting her teeth that she prevented herself from crying out in terror.

The high pad eyed the necklace with approval. It would be worth the wait. A cascade of diamond droplets rested elegantly around Helena's neck. It was the perfect accessory for the more restrained dress of a debutante.

"Hurry!" The assailant cursed when Helena fumbled once more. "I haven't got all night!"

"I would say your time is up right about now," came Simon's clear cold voice before the second shot of the evening rang out into the moonlit night.

The masked horseman had time only to register surprise in his eyes before the force of the bullet hitting his body unseated him, and he fell to the ground. The placid, dappled grey was frightened enough to rear slightly at the unexpected movement before galloping away into the night.

Helena managed to stifle the scream she wanted to release, instead slumping against the plush interior of the carriage, feeling the weakening effects on her body of the terrifying few moments that had just passed.

Henry flung open the door nearest their attacker and jumped down. "Have you killed the damned cur?" he asked his friend.

"No. I aimed at the shoulder. I want to see this high road hang," Simon said fiercely.

"He's still alive then?" Helena asked, leaning towards the open door to try to see what was happening. She was not one for fainting fits but was definitely feeling more wobbly than normal as a result of the incident.

Simon bent down and felt for a pulse and placed a hand on the chest of the attacker to feel the body moving as it breathed in its unconscious state. He had never considered for a moment that they would face any danger on the heath. Highwaymen patrolled the area, but he was contemptuous enough to have dismissed them as a real threat. His arrogance had put them all at risk. He appeared his usual calm, uninterested self, but inside he was deeply disturbed.

"Shall I drive to the find the nearest magistrate, My Lord?" Jackson asked, leaning over the top of the carriage. He was still shaken from the experience and wished to flick the reins as soon as possible. Every second remaining in the open was a second too long in his opinion.

"No. He is out cold. We'll put him in the carriage. I'm not wasting any more time in this God-forsaken place. This thief spoke the truth when he said there will be others keen to take over where he left off," Simon said fiercely, admitting, inwardly at least, that he'd been a buffoon to travel on the roads so late at night.

He was angrier with himself than the situation; he'd been half-witted and had risked his sister, his friend, and his servants as a result. They should have commenced their journey home when the ball was coming to a close; his foolhardiness had put those under his care in danger.

The footman immediately jumped off his perch in order to help his master lift the offender into the carriage, but he paused when Simon stood over the body, hands on hips, a deeper frown than usual marring his expression. Simon was doubting what he'd felt, but the niggle wouldn't be pushed aside.

"My Lord?" the footman asked tentatively.

"What is it, Simon?" Helena asked her brother, still looking out of the open carriage door.

"Something's not right," Simon responded, still frowning. He bent and removed the hat and mask of their attacker. Helena and Henry watched as Simon crouched for a moment, loosening the neckerchief that had been so tightly fastened. He leaned back on his haunches, running a hand over his face.

"Simon?" Helena repeated in concern.

There was a pause before Simon looked at his sister and his friend. "I've just shot a woman," he said dully.

"A woman? No!" Helena gasped. She stepped out of the carriage, her curiosity overcoming the feelings of shock, which until that moment, had kept her glued to her seat.

"I'm pretty damned sure," Simon groaned. He was not one usually for cursing in his sister's company, but the fact that she did not respond at the outburst showed they were all too caught up in the strange situation to notice the expletive.

"She's still a thief," Henry reminded his friend.

"Maybe so, but what kind of dog am I that I shot first?" Simon responded. "We need to get her to a doctor."

"What about the magistrate?" Henry asked.

"She needs a doctor first. The magistrate can wait," Simon said firmly, his insides churning.

He stood in order to assist the footman in lifting the thief into the carriage. Glancing down at the now unmasked woman, he felt sick to his stomach. According to everyone in the *ton*, he was an unfeeling brute. His loyal sister was the only one who saw the real person underneath the façade. His cold, uncaring persona was an image he was keen to reinforce. He wasn't without a heart; it was more that Society, and people in general, left him feeling cold, so keeping them at a distance was his aim.

His own father had been aloof at the best of times; he had been a man without feelings or morals in Simon's opinion. Women had been paraded in front of Simon and Helena while they grew, all being their father's Cyprians. He would then invite them into his own circle to socialise with his wife. Simon had watched as everyone acted falsely, being openly welcoming yet critical when a back was turned. He'd hated his father's behaviour and the way his mother had never challenged it, but most of all he despised Society for their fickleness. Refusing to trust anyone in his circle, he had built an immovable block around his emotions and had allowed only Helena to remain in his heart.

Simon's gentlemanly code of conduct railed against inflicting harm on anyone of the weaker sex, and he helped lift the body into the carriage far gentler than he would have done only a few moments before.

The three original passengers climbed into the barouche in silence, the space suddenly feeling small and oppressive as the carriage moved off.

Chapter 2

The trio travelled without speaking for a while, all seated on the same side of the carriage, the thief having been laid on the opposite seat. She was dressed in black from head to toe, a cloak covering the male clothing she wore underneath. The hat had been left at the roadside, and although she wore a scarf over her hair, several long, wavy, red strands were freeing themselves. A slender face was revealed now that the face cloth had been removed. Her skin was startlingly white in contrast to the dark shirt she wore.

Simon had tied a pad of cloth to her shoulder in an effort to soak up the blood. Henry was right: She was a thief, but that did not stop the bile threatening to rise each time he looked at her. He had shot a woman, and every fibre of his gentlemanly body felt the wrongness of the act.

"When did you realise?" Helena asked.

Simon flushed slightly at the question. "The first hint was when I placed my hand on her chest to feel for signs of breathing, but I doubted the reality of what I had felt."

"Oh." It was Helena's turn to look discomfited. "She didn't sound like a woman!"

Henry looked at Simon with a smile on his face. "You have always been the luckiest of men!" he chortled.

Simon shot Henry a look that spoke all that he could not say in front of his sister. "I had rather not have shot a female. That's not how I get my thrills." Simon spoke the truth although he had felt a rush of adrenaline when he'd been climbing out of the carriage and sneaking around to the other side. The burst of excitement at the situation had been a refreshing change to feeling nothing.

"She was stealing from us," Henry pointed out reasonably, looking as relaxed as one could. No one seeing him would guess he'd just had a gun pointed at his chest. "She will still hang, so what's the difference if she is male or female?" Henry was six and twenty and spent much of his time involved in the more wanton side of life. Only his friendship with Simon kept him from completely disappearing from Society in search of permanent debauchery. His dark good looks made him look like the devil he acted, and he used his handsome features and sarcastic charm to gain access to as many women as were enticed by contrived angelic expressions and bad-boy actions. He was an unlikely friend for Simon, but in a way, it was because Henry was open with his opinions and behaviour; there were no hidden depths to him. There was an honesty to Henry's actions, even if Simon did not approve of everything he did.

"How can you be so brutal?" Helena exclaimed in shock. Only a year out of the schoolroom, at eighteen, she had the confidence of the young, who presumed they knew the ways of the world, only to find their experience sadly lacking. The only person she'd met who could unnerve her with a look or a word was Henry. They had an uneasy relationship. He always bordered on the darker side of life, and his more cynical teasing was beyond Helena's experience. As a result, he made her feel uncomfortable, to which she reacted badly.

"You wouldn't be so forgiving if one of those pistols had gone off," Henry snapped. He was old enough to treat a debutante more gently, but Helena always seemed to bring out the worst in him. He took issue with what he saw as her condemnation of him. Helena would have been surprised to know she had such an effect on Henry. To her mind, he did everything he could to taunt her whilst remaining annoyingly disdainful and smug. "She risked being hanged the moment she embarked on her scheme. I am not going to start feeling remorse just because she's a wench." He shrugged and folded his arms a little defensively. Helena's censure was regular and consistent.

Helena turned to her brother. "Why would a woman do such a thing?"

"I have no idea, but I'm determined to find out," Simon responded grimly. He didn't like being unsure or uncertain of any situation in which he found himself, and this whole situation had unnerved him. The sooner he regained his cold, unruffled demeanour the better.

*

Lou tried to remain still and passive as she rocked and rolled on the seat as the carriage moved at speed. She could weep with the pain in her shoulder, but she could not reveal that she was awake.

She had listened to the conversation with stirrings of hope; they were not going straight to the magistrate. There might be a chance of escape. She silently cursed. There *had* to be an opportunity to make off. The girls depended on her, and she would not fail them. But, oh! The pain! She had never felt anything like it, and it took all of her strength not to betray herself by casting up her accounts. No. She gritted her teeth; remaining still would hopefully give her the opportunity to choose her chance of freedom.

She tried to focus on what had happened to take her mind off the pain. She had never been so foolish before; her over-confidence had cost her dearly. She should have pulled the curtain back as soon as she approached the carriage. A curse threatened to escape her lips. Her self-assuredness had endangered the people who relied on her.

Dizziness overtook Lou when a particularly deep hole on the road made the carriage rock to one side, jolting her shoulder, and for once, she didn't fight it but allowed the blackness to engulf her.

Simon watched the colour drain from Lou's face when the carriage lurched. The action helped to increase his annoyance with the whole situation. He was not self-indulgent enough to assign himself unnecessary blame, but he had hurt someone, and it didn't rest easy with him. He had been foolish in the extreme to stay late and then to refuse the hospitality of the host to stay the night. His hauteur at the concerns of their hosts could have cost him the lives of his sister and his friend, something that would see him staring at the canopy of his bed long into the early hours.

The sooner they reached home the better.

*

The streets of London had never been so welcoming to the three conscious occupants within the carriage. When, eventually, the vehicle came to a halt outside number ten Half Moon Street, the footman landed nimbly on the pavement. Opening the door, he helped Helena down the steps before positioning himself to best help his master and friend move the injured woman out of the carriage.

They paused when Lou groaned in pain, but her eyes remained closed, and no one was sure if she had regained consciousness or not. Helena had given instructions that the doctor be sent for and a fire set in the largest guest room. It seemed ridiculous setting the finest guest room for someone who, not so long ago, had been pointing a gun at them, but Helena knew it would be easier to nurse her in the largest room.

The bustle surrounding their arrival eased only when Lou was placed on the bed. The housekeeper ushered everyone out of the room while she tended to the unexpected arrival in preparation for the doctor's attendance.

Simon waited in his study for the medical man to be sent in to him. Simon had to be somewhat honest in explaining what had happened, but he did not wish to announce to everyone the sorry details of the evening, so he explained only that there had been a robbery and shooting. By the time the doctor saw his patient, there was no evidence of her being a highwayman; all outer clothing had been removed.

Once the doctor had been taken to the bedchamber, Simon poured himself a large glass of brandy, placing the cool glass against his forehead. The excesses of the early evening had left a dull ache, which was probably worse than the hangover he'd have suffered if the journey had been uneventful.

By the time the doctor returned to the study after making the examination, Simon was ensconced in a chair in front of a crackling fire, letting the heat wash over him as he pondered what to do. He had shed his fine frock coat and loosened his perfectly folded cravat, feeling unusually constrained in his attire.

Henry had offered to stay around, but Simon was aware that Henry was more inclined to act on gut instinct, and for some reason, that would not do for this situation. Simon had wished him a cordial goodnight. Henry was always quick to offer his opinions, and after the evening's events, Simon was reluctant to have them clouding his own thoughts.

"My Lord." The medical man bowed.

"Doctor Rowson, how is the patient?" Simon asked, standing.

"She has been lucky. The bullet appears to have travelled straight through her shoulder, so there is no need for surgery," Doctor Rowson explained.

"That's something, I suppose," Simon said with unexpected relief. "I would appreciate your discretion with regard to our temporary house guest. We don't know the details of the robbery as yet, and I am loath to cause widespread panic." Simon wasn't sure why he'd decided to lie and make-out that the unknown woman had been the victim, but he thought it the best course of action.

"Of course," Doctor Rowson said. "I shall check on her in the morning. There's no need for me to stay for now. I have left laudanum with your housekeeper to top up the dose I have already administered. I doubt she'll regain consciousness during the night."

The doctor left the room, and Helena passed him in the hallway, entering the study after he left.

"Mrs Cox asked me if you have already informed the magistrate," Helena said to her brother.

"Ah, the staff have already been gossiping," Simon said with annoyance.

"Mrs Cox is hardly one to gossip," Helena responded diplomatically, defending the housekeeper.

Simon sighed. "I suppose so. I will inform on the rascal when I know she's out of danger."

"She is a criminal. Should we not be handing her over now?" Helena asked.

"Am I the only one slightly curious as to why a woman is taking to the heath and acting as a highwayman?" Simon asked with frustration.

"It is an extremely dangerous thing to embark on," Helena admitted.

"Which is the reason I want to know why she was doing it," Simon responded. It was unheard of for a woman to put herself in such a precarious position. Rivalry between highwaymen was rife; if they had found her, she would have been attacked in the most brutal way before being left for dead. Yet, she had looked small and fragile in the carriage. His instinct was telling him she didn't belong to the life she'd chosen, and it piqued his curiosity. "She will face the magistrate, but I want some answers first."

"Is she not likely to steal from us while we sleep?" Helena asked, normally one to go along with any of her brother's schemes, but the evening had rattled her.

"You're beginning to sound like Henry," Simon responded.

"I had rather be shot than be compared to that beast!" Helena said angrily.

Simon chuckled at his sister's outburst.

Helena sat in the chair opposite her sibling. She hadn't changed out of her finery, and her necklace glistened in the firelight. "You are going to take on this woman as one of your charitable causes, aren't you?" sister asked brother.

Simon smiled a little. "I've made a difference to some of the lives I've come into contact with." In an effort to try to feel something good, he donated a lot of his funds to the charities that existed to elevate the hardships of life. In his own way Simon was trying to prove that not everyone in Society was the same as his father. "But rest easy. I will not try to save her. I'm curious. That's all. A woman must be in dire need to do what she attempted to do. I doubt she has any redeeming characteristics. Once a criminal, always a criminal."

"And in our house!"

"I'll have a footman sleep outside your door if you are worried about your safety."

"I'm not," Helena sighed. "If I am being honest, I'm also a little curious. I'm rattled mainly of being in Henry's company for too long. He is the only one able to disconcert me with his constant ridiculing and chiding. He left the house still mocking me for needing my smelling salts in the carriage when I only used them a little!"

"You should be used to his ways by now, Helena," Simon said gently. "He doesn't mean half his taunts. He only says them because you react. If you ignored him, he would soon tire of tormenting you."

"Does he not mean them? He's so derisive of anything I say or do. It wasn't so bad when I saw him occasionally, but since my come out, I see him every day and have to dance with him at each ball we attend," Helena said with frustration.

Simon laughed. "You're the only girl on her first season who has ever complained about a consistent dance partner. And a titled one at that."

"When said partner spends the whole dance making quips, half of which I do not understand, it can be a long half hour!" Helena proclaimed.

"I'll have a word with him," Simon said with sympathy. He could be a devil himself, but never towards his sister. "I forget how young you are, my love. You have always seemed so grown-up, but Henry is a cad. I'll warn him to ease off with you. Perhaps it is time we organised a chaperone as your escort? She would protect you against the words of men like Henry more than I do."

"Oh, no!" Helena said quickly. "I like having you escort me around town. I'm having a rare old time of it compared to the other debutantes. They cannot move from their chaperone's sides and are watched even when they're dancing. You trust me to behave sensibly. Henry is the only blot on the landscape."

"A chaperone would have insisted we left the ball at a reasonable time," Simon said darkly.

"One lapse in judgement. That's all tonight was," Helena reasoned. The last thing she wanted was some distant, aged relative watching her every move; Simon was far more lenient. She was not foolish enough to get herself into a scrape, but she enjoyed having more freedom than her peers.

"You could have been hurt," Simon said quietly.

"But I wasn't, and now you have a puzzle to solve before you inform the magistrate," Helena said, feeling calmer now that she had voiced her vexation about Henry.

*

Once Helena left him, Simon closed the door on his study and walked up the marble stairs to the guest room. On entering, he nodded to Mrs Cox, the housekeeper.

"She sleeps deeply, My Lord. I doubt we'll hear anything from her for days, the amount of laudanum the doctor gave her. She's only a slight thing," Mrs Cox said.

Simon glowered at the unconscious form in the bed. She was indeed slight. In the lamplight of the room, he studied her face. It was petite and very pale, although the loss of blood probably added to the lack of colour. Freckles stood out over the bridge of her nose. Her hair, now unadorned, almost covered the pillow; it was wavy and the richest red Simon had ever seen. It made him think of woodnymphs. But then he shook himself. She hadn't acted like some sort of elf; she had been an out-and-out crook.

She was beautiful though. The crease mark of a frown marred the smoothness of her forehead. Simon wondered what had happened to her to make a permanent mark on one who was obviously young. For some reason, it bothered him that she'd suffered troubles in her life. No one so young should have worries enough to be always frowning, although he knew many had.

His own permanent furrow had etched itself on his face as soon as he'd realised what a farcical family he was connected to. He'd longed to support his mother, and even though they'd spoken about his father's mistresses, his mother had insisted there was nothing wrong with the arrangement. He'd never understood her reasoning, and it had created a distance between mother and son. He remembered that day. It was seared into his memory.

"We have a good home. What are we lacking?" Lady Ashton had asked her young son.

"A father who wants to be with us," the young Simon had responded without hesitation. He had been a sensitive boy who read a lot and was shy in company, more like his quiet mother than his gregarious father.

"Your father does want to be with us," his mother had pointed out.

"Only when one of his ladies is with him," Simon ground out.

"We can't be selfish," Lady Ashton said gently. "He is a good man. If he needs his entertainments from others, we have to accept that. Don't expect too much."

"Is this normal?" Simon asked.

"More than I thought when I married. We are not so unusual. Even the royal family flaunt their mistresses," Lady Ashton said. "Put aside any foolish ideas you might have about falling in love. Marriage is about joining families. Nothing more."

Simon had continued to watch and be shocked by his father's behaviour. He could see that it hurt his mother, whether she admitted it or not, and he hated his father for causing so much pain to someone he should've loved. Growing up in a toxic environment meant the young boy might not have been able to withdraw from Society, but he could protect his heart from further damage while he was forced to be a part of it.

He succeeded very well; only Helena was allowed into his heart once his parents had died. Helena guessed to some extent why he remained aloof and outwardly cold. She felt sorry that the brother she adored wouldn't open himself up to love or even trust anyone. She'd been younger, so she was less affected by their unusual home life. Perhaps she'd have felt differently if her parents were alive now, but they'd died, and the Cyprians had disappeared for good.

Simon brought himself to the present. "Was there anything in her clothing that would identify her?" he asked, expecting a negative answer.

"No. I have taken the liberty of having the clothing placed out of the room just in case she does wake," Mrs Cox responded.

"Good. Connor is to be the footman stationed outside the door all night. If you need anything, just shout. I suggest you leave the door slightly ajar," Simon said. He didn't think for one moment that any of his household was in danger, but after his foolishness earlier, he wasn't about to take any chances with those under his care.

"Thank you, My Lord. I'll notify you as soon as she wakes."

Chapter 3

Unfortunately for Simon, his curiosity about his unexpected guest was not to be satisfied as soon as he wished. An infection developed in the wound, and delirium from fever prevented any coherent communication with the woman for days.

On one of his regular visits to the sick room, he was surprised to see Helena tending the patient. She was dressed in a practical cotton day-dress, and her hair was secured for function rather than for fashion.

"Have the staff deserted their posts?" Simon asked.

"No. I didn't want it to become too burdensome for them when I'm perfectly capable of mopping a brow and soothing the ramblings of someone barely conscious," Helena said with a small smile.

"Is that a hint to me to take my turn as I brought her here in the first place?" Simon asked, raising an eyebrow.

"You tending someone in a sick room? Shudder at the thought!" Helena laughed. "I am more than capable of carrying out morning visits and attending an evening entertainment while still relieving Mrs Cox for a few hours."

"Don't wear yourself out," the protective brother advised.

"I am more likely to be worn out by boredom at the parties we attend," Helena said, wiping a cool cloth over the still woman.

"I expected you to enjoy your first season with relish," Simon said in surprise.

"I am. I did," Helena stated with a sigh. "Do you not find it a little tedious?"

"Tedious? In what respect?" Simon was surprised at Helena's words. She was a far different character than himself. He thought himself the cynical one whereas he would have described Helena as easier to please, more apt to accept her role in life.

"It is all the same. The same people at the same balls, the same card parties, the same theatre shows. I enjoyed it for the first month, but now... I can't ever imagine wanting to come back for a second season." Helena tried to explain, for the first time, her disillusionment at the Society she belonged to. It probably had more to do with the shock of the robbery. It had suddenly put things into clearer perspective for her.

"You'll have to marry some Lord who lives in the wilds of Wales and never visit London again," Simon grinned at his sister.

Helena smiled. "That is a far more tempting prospect than you could possibly realise."

"If you are unhappy, we don't need to stay in London. I am here purely for your benefit. As I've no intention of marrying for at least another ten years, if at all, I don't need to look to the marriage mart quite yet."

"Ten years! Why you'll be in your dotage by then!" Helena exclaimed.

Simon laughed. "Thank you for that, little sister. Don't start counting down my final years just yet."

The patient moaned, and Simon returned his gaze to the woman. "It would seem ironic if she dies without facing trial."

"Probably the more humane way to die," Helena said quietly.

Simon looked at his sister in surprise. "Why, Helena! A few days ago, you were all for dragging her to the magistrate. Now she's eliciting your sympathy?"

"I know I must appear inconsistent, but I think my first reaction was because of the upset of it all. I was so angry and afraid when the shot rang out. It just as easily could have been you," Helena said quietly.

Simon moved to his sister's side and planted a kiss on her cheek. "My aim was to get you out of danger. You are my last close relative, Helena, and so very precious to me."

Helena smiled at Simon. "I keep wondering: What would it take for me to do something so desperate as to hold-up a carriage on the heath in the middle of the night? I can't come to any satisfactory solutions."

"She is of a lower class than you. Don't try to understand her motivations although I admit to having some of the same questions. It will probably drive us both mad if we try to understand her," Simon said before leaving the room.

*

Simon returned to the sick room late in the night. Helena had retired hours before, and the house was still. A truckle bed had been set-up in the corner of the room, and Mrs Cox slept soundly on it. She hadn't wanted to put any of the maids in the room in case there was trouble when the occupant eventually awoke.

Simon had been drawn to the room. It looked as if their unexpected visitor was in a deep sleep, a positive when fighting a fever. Simon frowned. Why did he want her to survive the fever to then be hanged? Helena was correct. If she died this way, she wouldn't know anything about it. It was the most humane way to end her days.

He sighed as he watched her. Each moment she was in his house he was less angry at her actions and more curious as to who she was and why she'd done what she had. If there was a look the lower classes had, she didn't seem to have it. She just seemed slight and vulnerable, and it didn't rest easy that he'd played a part in her troubles. He felt an unconscious pull towards her, and it angered him that he should be so weak. She could have injured or killed the person he loved most in the world. She deserved to be punished. He stood frowning down at the sleeping form not quite convincing himself of his anger.

As quietly as he had entered the room, he retreated to his own chamber. He wondered if anyone was missing her. For some reason he was convinced she belonged to someone and knew instinctively she would be missed by those who knew her.

*

Helena repeated her visitations each afternoon, and after a few days, saw a difference in the patient. The fever seemed to have lessened. She was not fully lucid, but there seemed to be less delirium. Helena tried to soothe the agitation when it occurred.

Urgent mumbling brought Helena to the edge of the bed once more.

"Shh, don't fret. The doctor will be here soon," Helena soothed.

"Marianne, Heather," moaned the stranger, with a broad Scottish lilt.

Helena was astounded that the voice was so different than the one they'd heard on that night. "Is that your name?" she probed.

Two green eyes opened and blinked a few times at Helena, clearly trying to focus. Helena wasn't sure her sight was fully clear, but the stranger started to speak.

"Marianne. Heather. I need to go to them," the woman croaked.

"You are in no fit state to go anywhere," Helena responded.

The woman tried to lurch forward, wincing as she did, before falling backwards onto the pillows, clearly in pain. "I need to go."

"Let's take one step at a time, shall we? What is your name?" Helena asked.

The stranger glared at Helena but said nothing. The colour had drained from her face after she tried to move, making Helena think it wouldn't be long before she slipped back into unconsciousness.

"There's no point being silly about this. You are in no state to move anywhere. Why make things more difficult by not telling me your name? You've got to admit, you are in no position to argue. And it would make my life easier to know who you are," Helena said, matter-of-factly.

Helena received a glower that would have frightened most people, but she returned the scowl with an expression of slight amusement. She had to admire someone who was clearly at a disadvantage but still able to fight against her captor in a small way.

"Lou."

"Lou? Did I hear correctly? I've never heard that name before," Helena said.

"Lou. Just Lou," came the belligerent response.

"Well, just Lou, you've been unconscious for the best part of five days—"

"Five days! No! I must go!" Lou lurched forward once more, and Helena barely managed to prevent her from falling out of bed. The spirit might have been willing, but the physical capability was lacking, so Helena was able to push her backwards without much force.

"Will you stop this?" Helena asked in exasperation. "Nothing is so important that it cannot wait for another day or two."

"You don't understand," Lou ground out, once more glaring, but her weakness took the venom from the action.

"That's a certainty," Helena responded. "From the moment I met you, I have not understood any of what's happened. You certainly know how to make an impression!"

Lou managed an expression halfway between a grimace and a smile, but it lasted only a second before she became serious and disturbed once more. "Please let me go. They need me."

"Who does?" Helena asked. At Lou's gritted teeth at the question, Helena pushed more. "Marianne and Heather?"

Lou seemed to take in her surroundings before sighing. "Yes," she said quietly.

"Can I get a message to them? Let them know you are safe?" Helena offered. It seemed ridiculous that she was offering comfort to a criminal, but Lou was clearly agitated, and it wouldn't do her condition any good. Helena was no longer angry at the woman; she, like her brother, was now more curious about the stranger.

"No. I must go to them," Lou insisted.

Helena sighed. "We are not going to achieve anything other than tiring you out if you keep on with this single-minded attitude. You aren't well enough to move. Please do not mention it again."

"I'll box your ears!" Lou snarled.

"I would like to see you try!" Helena snapped back. She stood. "I'll leave you to your own devices. There will be a footman standing in the doorway ready to pick up your unconscious form when you try to escape. I do not see why I should put up with anymore of your nonsense!"

"You're a damned cur!" Lou snarled.

"This from a woman who tried to rob me by pointing a gun in my face! There is only one cur in this room, and it isn't me!" Helena snapped.

Lou closed her eyes with a sigh at Helena's words. "It hurts."

"I imagine it does," Helena responded, pausing. She felt like a parent waiting for a child to confess something and knew instinctively, she had to be patient.

"If I tell you where they are, will you give me your word you won't turn them in?" Lou asked, finally accepting that she needed help. If it wasn't so important to reach Marianne and Heather, she would never betray their whereabouts, but they'd been five days without her. She prayed they were still unharmed.

"Turn them in to whom?" Helena asked, genuinely puzzled.

"I tried to rob you. I know I am asking too much," Lou responded.

"Probably. But you're obviously concerned enough to trust someone who is holding you captive, so they must be important. Who are they, and where will I find them?"

"They're my responsibility," Lou ground out. Only the thought of Marianne and Heather falling into the hands of the worst kind of men forced Lou into trusting the woman whose house she was in. It was clear the young woman was a lady, which wasn't the best thing in the circumstances, but she would have to do. "Let them know I am well and will return as soon as I can."

"I'm afraid that will not be as easy as you think. You held up my brother's carriage; the magistrate is to be informed," Helena said. There was no point lying to the woman. She had committed a crime and needed to pay for it. The fact that neither brother nor sister seemed keen to inform on their strange guest was not reason to give her false hope. Helena didn't have authority over her brother's decisions.

Lou closed her eyes, but not before an expression of complete despair flitted across her face. "Then it's over," she said quietly. "All that effort and risk for nothing. He won in the end."

Helena frowned. Perhaps Simon had been right to be curious about Lou; there was obviously more to her than they knew. She softened towards her captive.

"Are they in some sort of trouble?" she asked gently.

"They might be since I've left them alone for so long," Lou admitted. "Please, would you check to see if they are safe? Tell them to use the funds to get out of London. I didn't realise quite how depraved it was until we arrived here, and then it was too late."

"Where are they?" Helena asked.

Lou grimaced before speaking. Helena suspected it was costing her a great deal to reveal what she had to.

"Number six Litcham Street. The basement rooms. It's in Kentish Town," Lou responded quietly. She took off a bracelet of tiny shells that had been tied firmly around her wrist. "Give Marianne this. She'll know you're telling the truth when you say I have sent you."

Helena accepted the bracelet and moved towards the door.

"There's just one other thing… " Lou started.

"Yes?" Helena responded.

"Don't go on your own. It is not the place for a lady," Lou finished grimly.

Helena remained silent, but with a nod of understanding, she left the bedchamber.

Lou closed her eyes in pain and desperation once Helena was out of sight. She had been arrogant to think the risk was worth taking, and because of that, Marianne and Heather would be left without her protection. Tears stung her eyes. She wasn't afraid about her own destiny, but she was afraid for them. What security had she given them? Cameron would never have agreed to their journey, and she could feel only shame, for now he would know how she'd let all of them down. She had been so confident that she knew best, that she needed no-one's assistance.

It had seemed a simple plan when she had brought them to London. Only now she realised and admitted what a fool she'd been.

Chapter 4

Helena entered Simon's study with a frown creasing her brow.

"What is it?" Simon asked, ever responsive to the needs of his sister.

"I think you were right to be curious about our attacker. She isn't what she seems to be."

"Oh?"

Helena told him of their conversation. "And another thing. She is definitely Scottish. Her accent is strong. Not the gruff voice we heard on the heath!"

"I suppose it makes sense to change your voice when in disguise," Simon said. "So, she has children? It makes it seem an even stranger choice of raising funds. Her sort usually sell their bodies to raise money."

"Perhaps she couldn't face it," Helena said tartly, not wanting to think about women so desperate they would have to resort to such horror.

"The children might be as a result of that occupation," Simon said.

"She was so concerned about them. I must go and check that they are well. It didn't sound as if they live in the most wholesome of areas," Helena mused.

"I'll go. I do not want you being put at further risk," Simon said forcefully.

"If they are young, which they must be, as she isn't much older than I am, they might be afraid at your appearance," Helena reasoned.

"You aren't going without me," Simon insisted, acknowledging Helena's reasoning.

"I would not dream of it. I think we should take at least two footmen as well. Who knows how they're living?"

*

Kentish Town wasn't one of the worst addresses in London, but as with all areas, once off the main thoroughfares, living conditions could change dramatically. Simon had covered his coat of arms on his carriage, and the driver and three footmen accompanied them. He was no coward but had learned the hard way to be less blasé about Helena's safety.

They turned into Litcham Street, and it was clear it wasn't the poorest street, but it barely ranked above the lowest addresses. The people living on this street were probably in a desperate battle to keep themselves from completely falling into the gutter. Helena and Simon exchanged a look of curiosity as the carriage came to a halt outside number six.

The brother and sister walked down the steps to the basement door with the footmen remaining at the top of the stairs ready to react should they be needed.

Simon knocked loudly on the door, but there was no response. He knocked again, and the door at street level opened. An old woman stepped out of the building and looked with interest at the visitors.

"Ye won't get any answer from them."

"We have important information to give," Helena responded.

"There has been no sight nor sound of 'um for days," the old woman continued.

"Thank you," Simon responded, nodding to one of the footmen who moved to the old woman and gave her a coin for her trouble. She nodded and moved down the steps, turning her back to them as she wandered down the street.

"Time to return home," Simon said, making a move to go up the basement stairs.

Helena hesitated. "If they're afraid and very young, they might have been taught not to answer the door. She obviously could not take them with her when she went out," she said.

"I'm not forcing the door," Simon responded.

"I'm not asking you to!" Helena harrumphed. She went close to the door and pressed her mouth as close to the corner as possible. "Marianne! Heather! I have news about Lou," she said, hopefully loud enough for the sound to travel beyond the wooden structure.

Helena wasn't sure if she heard a scraping behind the door, so she repeated her words. "Lou hasn't been well; she is staying at my home," she added to encourage whoever was behind the door.

This time both heard a movement indicating a lock was being drawn back on the door. Slowly the door opened, and a worried pair of green eyes peeped around the slit.

Helena didn't move but smiled in encouragement. "Hello! You must have been worried sick about Lou not returning home. She's had a fever, which is why it has taken us so long to visit you. Can we come in?"

"We are not to let anyone in, no matter who they are," came the lilting brogue of the young woman.

"Are you Marianne?" Helena asked.

"No."

"Ah, you must be Heather then," Helena continued. "I have something for Marianne." Helena rummaged in her reticule. "Perhaps this will help prove we are friends? Lou gave it to me to pass on to you to show that she'd sent me." Helena handed over the small bracelet.

The door slowly opened to reveal two young girls of around sixteen. Simon looked in surprise and frowned. This was not what he had been expecting. Nothing about this whole situation added up. It made him feel uneasy. All his suppositions appeared to be wrong.

He pushed his curiosity to the side for the moment and smiled encouragement to the girls. They looked worried and frightened in equal measure. "May we come in? Lou knows we are here."

The girls exchanged a worried look but opened the door to allow entry. Simon indicated that the footmen should remain at the top of the basement steps. There was no point terrifying the girls by having three burly footmen walk into their small home.

Helena walked into the room, smiling at the girls. "You must have been worried about Lou."

"We didn't know where to start looking for her," admitted the eldest. "I am afraid we can't offer you any refreshments. Lou never allowed us out without her escort. There is no food left in the house." A blush stained her cheeks at having to admit such a thing.

Helena shot a glance at her brother. Their attire was stained and worn, but it had once been fine; the quality of the material was unmistakable. "We don't need anything, thank you. So, which one is Marianne and which is Heather?"

"I'm Marianne," the one with dark auburn hair said. She was the slightly taller of the two, but their facial features were very similar. They were clearly sisters. "I'm Lady Marianne Drummond, lately of Glenloch Manor."

"Lady Marianne?" Simon asked in disbelief.

"Yes," Heather responded, a glint in her eyes. "We came to London to try to get an audience with our elder half-brother, but the fiend wouldn't help us!"

"Heather!" Marianne hissed. "We mustn't let our tongues loose! Remember what Lou said!"

"Who is your half-brother?" Simon asked.

"Lord Duncan Drummond, Earl of Glenmire. Duncan is our father's first wife's son," Heather said, defiantly glaring at her sister as she revealed their personal information.

Helena recognised the glare immediately and had to restrain the smile that threatened. "Lou is your full sister?"

"Yes, along with our brother Cameron," Marianne said, giving up any hope of keeping anything a secret while Heather was around.

"Where is he?" Simon asked.

"He's in Portugal with Wellesley," Heather supplied proudly. "Lou said Duncan would have never been brave enough to sell our estate in Scotland if Cameron had been around."

"For goodness sake, Heather! Why not tell everyone our woes?" Marianne snapped. She might be quieter than her sibling, but she was no simpering wallflower.

"I know of a Drummond, but only by reputation," Simon admitted, racking his brain for information.

"It won't be a good recollection. He might have position and a title, but he has little else to recommend him," Heather muttered.

Simon smiled at the young girl, amused at her spirit. "No. I don't think I am aware of much that makes him stand-out in Society."

"I wish he could hear that," Heather said with a smile. "He'd be mortified to find out that not everyone regards him as highly as he does himself!"

Simon's mouth twitched in appreciation. The girls were on their uppers, downtrodden as they were, but they had spirit.

A commotion at the top of the stairs interrupted the conversation. Heather immediately clung to Marianne, all bravado gone. Simon walked to the still-open door and looked up. A man was trying to get down the stairs but was being prevented access by the large footmen; he was clearly not pleased.

"They owes me money!" the stranger snapped.

Simon turned back to the frightened girls. "Do you?"

"He has been here every day since Lou disappeared. He says he's lost a horse," Heather said, seeming to have decided to trust Simon.

"A horse?" Simon asked, curious to know if the girls knew anything about Lou's night-time activity.

"Lou used to hire a horse to travel to and from her work. She said it was cheaper than a hackney," Marianne said quietly. "We don't know where she hired it from."

"Where did she work?" Simon asked.

"We don't really know. She said it was something to do with the *ton*, and it would help us to support ourselves until Cameron returned home, but she never really talked about it," Heather admitted. "Do you think he is telling the truth?" she asked Simon.

"I have no idea," Simon admitted honestly. He walked up the steps and spoke to the man. "What horse was it?"

"A fine, dappled grey mare. She's worth twenty pounds!" the man spat.

"I doubt that very much," Simon responded with derision, but the man had described the colour of the horse that bolted when Lou had been shot. "What did you charge per day to hire it?"

"One pound," the man said belligerently. "I'll not be out of pocket!"

"That is five days hire, plus the cost of the horse. I'll give you ten pounds, and I never want to see you here again," Simon said.

"That is robbery, that is! My horse was worth more than that!"

"That's all you are getting," Simon responded harshly. He knew full well the man was getting more than the horse was worth. "Take it or leave it."

The man muttered curses but held out his hand for the money. Simon thrust the amount in his hand and immediately turned away. On re-entering the room, Heather scrambled to a jar in a cupboard. She held out her hand to Simon.

"Here. We can pay for the horse. We hadn't any idea of what had happened to Lou, and she made us promise that we would not open the door, so we didn't know if he was lying when he was shouting and banging," Heather babbled, a blush tinging her cheeks.

"I do not want your money," Simon said, or whoever it belongs to, he thought grimly to himself.

"Ten pounds is a lot. You have to take it. Lou says we have to be self-reliant to survive. Relying on Duncan was a waste of time," Heather said.

"I do not want your money," Simon repeated.

"Keep it," Helena said, placing her hand gently on Heather's arm. She didn't want her brother saying something about where the money had come from. She was sure the girls knew nothing of what Lou had been doing.

"What happened to Lou?" Marianne asked.

"She fell off her horse near our carriage and was injured," Helena said quickly, not sure what Simon would reveal.

"Is she well?" Marianne asked, worriedly.

"She developed a fever, so we didn't know who she was but she's awake now, and although still not fully recovered, she can have short conversations before needing more rest. I am sure she'll be feeling more the thing in a day or two," Helena explained.

"Can we see her?" Heather asked.

"Of course," Helena responded. "I think you should bring your things and some of Lou's and stay with us for a while."

Simon didn't know whether to curse, laugh, or shout at Helena. They seemed to be becoming more embroiled in this strange family, and he wasn't sure it was the road he wanted to go down. Feeling guilty at injuring a woman was one thing; becoming a good Samaritan to a highway robber and her family was another.

"Are you sure?" Heather asked. She seemed to be more attuned to people's mood changes and looked at Simon worriedly.

"Yes," Simon ground out, scowling at Helena. He would have words with his sister later. She'd had the cheek to accuse him of taking on people he felt sorry for, and here she was doing exactly the same.

"Thank you!" Marianne said, immediately starting to gather things together.

Simon moved over to Helena while the girls collected their worldly-goods into one box, which didn't appear to hold much.

"Is this wise?" Simon whispered. "You criticised me for my actions! I think this is folly."

"We cannot leave them here. They make me look like a woman of the world! Who knows what would happen to them if they did venture out? If they remain here and are unprotected, they'll be forced to go outside. they have admitted there is no food. Simon, we cannot leave them to fend for themselves. It wouldn't be right," Helena whispered back.

"What are they going to do when the magistrate is called?" Simon asked.

"Are you still going to do that?" Helena asked in surprise.

"Do you think I shouldn't?" Simon asked.

"It is not as simple as it first appeared, is it?" Helena asked. "We didn't know the motivation behind the robbery then."

"It is still a robbery with a gun, which could have killed someone," Simon pointed out.

"I know, but she was obviously desperate," Helena reasoned.

"I would imagine that most criminals would argue the same," Simon pointed out. He smiled a little and held-up his hands at the glare he received from Helena. "Fine! I will admit it's more perplexing than I first thought. Though don't be dragged into feeling sorry for them, Helena. When all is said and done they are not your responsibility, and they do have family in London."

"How can we abandon them when their brother is fighting with Wellesley?" Helena said. "He is protecting a country against a tyrant, and his family is being treated appallingly by Lord Glenmire. Their own brother! It isn't right!"

"There're two sides to every family argument. Be careful," Simon cautioned, but he was pleased and proud that his sister felt so passionately about something. He'd met far too many young women who cared nothing beyond the latest on-dit, fashion, or some other frippery to know that thinking of others was not usual in their circle.

"You said yourself you have not heard anything good about him!"

"But the point is, I don't know him well enough to make an informed judgement," Simon responded.

Any further discussion was interrupted as Heather came to them. "We haven't got much, just one portmanteau between the three of us. I don't think Lou expected us to stay in London for long, and if it hadn't been for our prig of a brother, we would be back home by now!"

"Oh, Heather! Please keep your opinions to yourself!" Marianne appealed, to which she received an answering glare.

"They might as well know," Heather said defensively.

"Let's get you home," Helena said becoming efficient and deflecting a potential argument.

The footmen were called and the box lifted onto the rear of the carriage. The party clambered into the equipage and soon set-off at a smart pace.

"This is very kind of you," Marianne said shyly to Simon. She was definitely the quietest of the three sisters.

Simon nodded in acknowledgement but remained silent. He was conflicted and had been since he'd realised he'd shot their attacker. When he'd seen her that first night, something had changed within him. He had felt a pull of emotion he'd never experienced, and he was afraid of where it might lead. If he started pitying every lost cause, he was doomed to be a lot poorer in a very short space of time. His chastisement of Helena had only been because of concern on his part. They were already in too deeply, and the more time he spent in the company of this red-headed family, the less sure he was that they'd ever be the same again.

*

Lou awoke to see three pairs of eyes watching her closely. She opened her arms immediately to enfold Marianne and Heather. The gasp of pain the movement caused was noticed only by Helena.

"We have been so worried about you!" Marianne said, clinging to Lou.

"I'm sorry. I'm so sorry," Lou repeated over and over.

"It is fine. We were safe," Heather assured her sister, glossing over the fear the two girls had experienced over the days they'd thought they'd been abandoned.

"I want you to take the money and leave London. Send a letter to Cameron explaining everything. We should have done that straight away. He needs to return to Scotland and sort out a home for you," Lou said quickly.

"We can do it with you when you recover," Heather said quickly. "You'll soon be on your feet."

Lou didn't meet the gazes of her sisters. "It would be best if Cameron came. I was foolish in thinking I had all the answers."

Marianne sat on the edge of the bed. "This is not like you, Lou. You mustn't be feeling the thing. Are you very ill? You have never bowed to Cameron's superior knowledge before!"

Lou smiled slightly. "And look where it's got me," she said quietly.

"Marianne, Heather, I think Lou needs to rest now. Her shoulder is still causing her pain. We do not want another fever to develop," Helena said gently.

"Your shoulder? What happened to your shoulder?" Heather asked.

"I hurt it falling off the damned horse!" Lou said in the tone of voice that had both her sisters in no doubt that's exactly what had happened.

"You must rest then. May we come and visit her later?" Marianne asked Helena.

"Of course. Now, how about having something to eat before exploring the garden here for a bit of fresh air? You have been closed up too long," Helena said gently. "Mrs Cox will have something waiting for you in the drawing room. I'll be along soon, after I have made sure your sister is comfortable."

After kisses were exchanged, Lou and Helena were left alone.

"Thank you for bringing them," Lou said quietly.

"How old are they? They seem a lot younger than I, but then I feel that they can't be," Helena asked.

"They are seventeen. Twins. But as you can see, not identical," Lou admitted. "They've had a very sheltered life, so they appear younger than their years." She didn't know what had been revealed, but there was no point in lying at this stage.

"Is there only your brother who can care for them?"

"Yes."

"I am presuming you're Lady Lou, rather than 'Just Lou'," Helena said with a half-smile. Lou flashed her trademark glower at Helena, which the young woman ignored. "We know what your half-brother did. Well, some of it."

"Bloody Heather!" Lou snapped with exasperation. "It's a wonder she stayed inside at all. She is happy to talk to anyone and everyone."

Helena had blinked at the outburst but had already come to the conclusion that Lady Lou, whoever she was, wasn't your average lady of fashion.

"Don't be hard on her. They didn't let us through the door until I showed them your bracelet," Helena defended the girls, feeling quite protective of them even though she was so close in age to them. "Would your half-brother not take them in?"

"I wouldn't trust him with a dog, let alone my sisters!" Lou ground out. "He would sell them if there was a profit to make!"

"He sold your estate," Helena said quietly.

Lou flashed her a look, but then sighed. There was no point trying to keep her troubles hidden when Heather had already revealed them. "Our father left Cameron a medium-sized estate in Scotland. It was lovely, in the middle of a forest, surrounded by wildlife. We had a secure home there until we married, but then Duncan decided that he wanted the blunt the estate could provide."

"How could he sell it without your brother?"

"He said that father left Cameron an estate, but not necessarily that one. Which is ridiculous, as Father must have specified the estate he bequeathed Cameron. Duncan says that there will be one ready for Cameron when he returns from war, but I am absolutely convinced my half-brother is hoping Cameron will be killed whilst in Spain, and there will be no need to provide anything. He hadn't made any provision for us at all. We were to be cast out when the new owner moved in," Lou admitted.

"Surely you have some legacy yourselves?" Helena asked in shock.

"All held in trust until we are five and twenty or if we marry first. You won't win any prizes to guess who the guardian of the trusts is!" Lou said with derision.

"Lord Glenmire?" Helena said with a grimace.

"The one and only. I stupidly thought facing him would change things. He always was a coward when face to face, so I was convinced he would back down if I challenged him, but he has a witch of a wife now, and she's worse than he is. Apparently, they thought one of our distant relations would have provided a home for us until Cameron came home! I have never felt as angry in my life!" Lou admitted. Now that she'd started speaking to Helena, it seemed she couldn't stop. In some ways it was a relief because she'd kept so much to herself these past weeks. Always not wanting to upset her sisters, she'd kept her own fears hidden.

"I'm not surprised! I cannot believe a relation would treat anyone so ill!" Helena said astonished. "What did you do?"

"After I'd drawn his cork with a well-aimed punch, I left cursing them both to the devil," Lou said with some satisfaction.

"You didn't!"

"I had wanted to do it for years. He was always a sly dog, only out for himself. It was extremely satisfying," Lou admitted.

Helena laughed. "Your choice of occupation was a little extreme," she said tentatively.

Lou sighed and closed her eyes. "I thought it was so simple. I would get enough blunt to get us back home and support us until Cameron returned. I presumed the *ton* were all as weak-spirited as Duncan is."

"There are more like my brother than there are like yours," Helena admitted.

"Then I'm surprised I lived for so long," Lou admitted. Helena looked uncomfortable at the words. "Don't fret. I have accepted what must happen, but there's just one thing… "

"What?"

"Let me write a letter to Cameron and then I will send the girls away. We have an aunt who lives near Fort William. She is not particularly fond of visitors, but if she knows Cameron will return as soon as he can, she will let them stay. She won't be so heartless as to turn them out," Lou explained. "I am fully aware you do not owe me anything, but please do not let them be here when you call for the magistrate."

Helena rose. "I need to speak to my brother."

Chapter 5

Helena walked into Simon's study and closed the door behind her. She was a little perturbed to see Henry enjoying a glass of brandy with her brother. At first, she thought it best not to mention what she wanted to talk about, but then she realised that Henry was involved as well. Perhaps it was appropriate to speak to them both at once.

The men were seated in front of the fire, their usual position when putting the world to rights. Both were dressed in the height of fashion, shining boots, tight-fitting breeches, colourful waistcoats, and fine woollen frock coats. Each was considered handsome by their acquaintances and more so when standing in a ballroom together. The darkness of one contrasted with the paleness of the other to show each off to perfection.

Helena remained standing. The pair were known to be quick with a retort, usually of the cutting kind, although Simon would never be scathing towards his sister. Nevertheless, they were a pair to easily intimidate others when together, and Helena swallowed as she approached them. Standing, to give herself extra height and the courage to speak, she set her shoulders.

"We're going to forget the robbery ever happened," she started with a defiant tilt of her chin.

"What?" Henry asked in astonishment.

"The situation has changed. It would be destroying a family if we called the magistrate and let him take her away," Helena continued.

"She could have easily destroyed our family," Simon said gently, watching his sister closely. He'd been struggling for days with the decision to call the magistrate and was interested in why Helena had come to the same conclusion he had.

"But she did not, and there are extenuating circumstances that made her act in the way she did. I won't go along with any arrest."

"She's hoodwinked you!" Henry said. "Let me have ten minutes with her, and she will soon be admitting her crime!"

"She already admits it!" Helena ground out. "This is about more than a crime that took place. It is about a family that has been wronged by the person who should have been protecting them! Simon, we can't do it to them. It is worse than Lady Heather explained."

"Lady Heather?" Henry mocked. "They truly have got you fooled! They fed you some sort of Banbury story! You're greener than even I thought, Lady Helena!"

"Do you know I admire Lady Lou for punching her brother?" Helena almost shouted. "I would like to wipe that supercilious smile off your face!"

"You little cat!" Henry laughed. "Who would think what fire lies beneath that perfect exterior!"

"Henry," Simon warned. He wasn't one for being overly protective where Helena was concerned, but from what she'd confided in him, he knew she couldn't compete against Henry when he was in one of his moods.

"Garswood, you are such a bore sometimes!" Henry said.

"He's a gentleman!" Helena said, her cheeks flushed with indignation at Henry's words.

"My warning goes to you, too, Helena. There is no need for fall-outs between us, thank you. Our lives have been disrupted enough," Simon responded fairly.

"I won't be able to live with myself if we inform on her and those girls lose a sister. They have lost their father and their home, and their lives have been turned upside down. All the time while their brother is at war. It is enough," Helena appealed to her brother.

"I know," Simon said quietly.

"I don't believe this!" Henry spat. "Do I have a say in this decision? I was in the carriage as well!"

Simon smiled slightly at his friend. "You have been in more scrapes than this, and if past behaviour is anything to go by, it won't be the last. I had already decided not to take it further." Simon couldn't admit that, from the moment he'd seen her uncovered in the carriage, the will to see her punished had begun to dissolve.

"Oh, Simon, thank you!" Helena said, walking over to her brother and kissing him on the cheek. "I know it is the right decision!"

"Why not introduce them to Society while you're at it?" Henry asked sarcastically.

"Why not indeed? I will seek out Lady Marianne and Lady Heather and see if they have already been presented at court. I'm sure it can be arranged if they have not."

With a defiant look at Henry, Helena left the room.

"You could live to regret this," Henry said to Simon.

"Possibly. But it's the right thing to do," Simon responded.

*

Early in the evening Simon approached the bedchamber. Helena had relieved the staff of their responsibilities in caring for Lou as Marianne and Heather were keen to care for their sister. Once Helena had Simon's assurance there would be no further action, she had instructed the footmen they no longer needed to be on guard outside the bedroom.

Lou was alone, with her eyes closed. She looked so pale and fragile, but Simon was completely aware of how deceiving looks could be.

"Should you be alone in a bedchamber with me without a half a dozen footmen loitering?" Lou asked, her eyes still closed.

Simon half-smiled. "Probably not, but I am prepared to take the risk. I managed perfectly fine when you were fit and well, the first time we met."

Lou's eyes opened, and Simon was immediately pinned by a clear green he'd never seen before. "That was as a result of my assuming everyone in Society was like my buffoon of a brother. I will not make that assumption again."

"I'm suitably warned," Simon said with an amused smile.

"I need to send a letter to my brother advising him of what has happened," Lou said, hating that she needed to ask for help.

"There is no need. I sent an express as soon as we returned with your sisters," Simon admitted.

"You did what?" Lou bellowed.

Simon blinked in surprise at the forcefulness of Lou's words. "I thought it best to let him know what was happening."

"Yes. It is. Which is why I wanted to send him a letter!" Lou snapped. "You had no right interfering with my family's concerns! Who the devil do you think you are?"

"Lord Simon Ashton, Earl of Garswood, at your service, madam," Simon said with a mock bow. "And you gave me the right to interfere in your life the moment you stuck a gun in my face!" he snapped.

"Oh, for goodness sake! When are you going to stop rattling on about that?"

Simon stopped and looked at Lou in astonishment. "You're unbelievable. You could just say thank you, you know."

"Why on earth would I thank you? You have done nothing other than complicate matters since I had the misfortune of meeting you. If I were back home, I would run you through with a broadsword!" Lou snapped.

"A broadsword?" Simon laughed. "How archaic!"

"You won't be saying that when it is sticking in your chest!" Lou responded.

"It would only reach its target because I wouldn't respond. Why on earth would I want to injure — again — a member of the fairer sex?" Simon asked, knowing his words would infuriate the captive.

"You had better arrange for my hanging to be sooner rather than later if you want to sleep safely in your bed," Lou ground out, her eyes spitting daggers that she would have liked to have in her hands.

"It looks as if I am going to be putting myself at risk then. Along with my sister. We have agreed that the magistrate won't be called. No one was hurt, apart from you of course, but it is probably punishment enough for you to be stuck here for days on end. We can forget the whole episode as long as you disappear back to Scotland as soon as you're well enough to travel," Simon said, gaining some satisfaction at seeing the surprise his words caused.

"I am not going to hang?" Lou asked in disbelief.

"Not because of me. What foolish risks you take in the future, well, that's up to you." Simon shrugged. "I will leave you to plan the nefarious ways that I am going to meet my end."

Simon left the room, closing the door firmly behind him. It gave Lou the privacy she needed to compose herself. She thought she'd come to terms with the possibility of dying, but the weight that was lifted off her shoulders at Simon's words convinced her that she hadn't.

Blinking away tears, she would've sagged if she hadn't already been lying down. She wasn't going to die. Not yet, anyway. Being humble didn't come naturally to her. She'd had to be seen as stronger than she would have normally been expected to be, but she was humbled by Simon and Helena. She wasn't sure she could've been as magnanimous if their roles were reversed.

Lou smiled. Simon was a gentleman in every sense of the word. His expression when she'd mentioned running him through with a broadsword had been comical, and she laughed at the memory. Duncan would've run for the hills at her words, but Simon had laughed at her. She liked that.

*

Helena had persuaded Marianne and Heather to accompany her on a walk through Hyde Park. Lou felt well enough to sit in a chair and had encouraged her sisters to leave her be.

The three young ladies walked through the park. The sisters had worn their best dresses, which back home they would've worn at a ball, but their daytime attire was no longer good enough to be seen. Spencer jackets covered the short sleeves of the nicer of the dresses they owned, so they felt almost equal to the others promenading through the parkland.

"Your sister mentioned you have an aunt in Fort William. Is she your only relative other than your two brothers?" Helena asked.

"Yes. Duncan is married, although his wife is as horrible as he is!" Heather responded tartly.

"Heather! For goodness sake!" Marianne appealed in vain to her sister.

"I was always told not to lie," Heather responded in mock-seriousness.

Helena laughed. "I've always longed for a sister, but I am beginning to see the disadvantages!"

Heather smiled. "I am not as bad as Lou. Cameron despairs of her!"

"How long do you think it will be before he receives your brother's letter?" Marianne asked.

"I've no idea, but an express should reach him sooner rather than later," Helena admitted.

"It is lovely here," Marianne admitted. "Lou always said she wasn't bothered about having a season in London, but I wanted to."

"Was there no opportunity?" Helena asked.

"Duncan should have arranged it. His wife could have been our chaperone, but he said they had little time and less funds to do it," Heather responded, her words betraying her own longing.

"That is a shame, but believe me, it is not as fun as I'd thought it was going to be," Helena admitted.

"Really? But all those balls! All that finery!" Marianne said wistfully.

"Those were my thoughts before the start of the season, but in reality, it is little more than socialising with the same people over and over again," Helena admitted. "It is fine, if within that group, is the person you wish to share your life with, but… "

"So, you have not met anyone to fall in love with?" Heather asked, grinning at her new friend.

"No. Not even close," Helena admitted with a sigh.

"Good morning, Lady Helena!" Henry said, riding up to the small group.

Helena curtsied and smiled warily at Henry. "Lady Marianne, Lady Heather, might I introduce the Earl of Ince, Lord Henry Roby. My Lord, please let me introduce Lady Marianne and Lady Heather, lately of Glenloch Manor." Helena made the introductions with defiance in her tone. She was challenging Henry to be anything other than gentlemanly.

Henry jumped off his horse and made his bow. "Ladies, a pleasure to meet you. I've already met your sister."

"Have you?" Marianne asked in surprise.

"Yes. She made a unique entrance when I first met her," Henry said smoothly, enjoying Helena's discomfort.

"That's Lou for you. Never one to be forgotten," Heather said with a grimace.

"No. Not at all," Henry said with a raised eyebrow. "Shall you be attending the Burford's ball?" Henry asked Helena.

"I'm not sure," Helena admitted.

"Oh. I was hoping to secure dances with all you lovely ladies," Henry said.

"We will not be attending, My Lord," Marianne said quickly, flushing red.

"That's a great pity," Henry responded. "Perhaps I would be allowed to call on you on the morrow?"

"That would be lovely," Helena said, making it sound anything but. She wondered what games Henry was up to. He could only be up to mischief. He had made it quite clear he wasn't happy with socialising with the family. Helena was convinced he wasn't to be trusted.

Henry left soon after talk of the weather had been exchanged. Heather looked at Marianne with a laugh in her eyes when Henry was out of earshot. "I think my sister is wishing she could attend tonight's ball, from the dreamy look on her face!"

"I was only admiring a handsome face!" Marianne flushed as both Helena and Heather looked at her.

"Take my advice," Helena said, seriously. "Lord Roby isn't the nicest of characters. He is handsome to be sure, but there is a cold heart underneath that pretty face."

"Never mind, Marianne. I am sure there'll be lots of other handsome men, who are decent and handsome," Heather said, linking her arm through her sister's. "Lady Helena has obviously been spoiled if she can reject Lord Roby so easily. We will be far easier to please than she is!"

The three laughed and continued to walk.

Heather suddenly stopped and squeezed Marianne's arm. "Look! Marianne! Can it be?"

Helena and Marianne looked in the direction Heather was pointing to see a tall, broad-shouldered cavalry officer walking through the park in full uniform.

"Cameron!" Marianne almost whispered.

Heather let go of Marianne and sped across the grassed area that separated her from her beloved brother.

Marianne tried to restrain herself and walk across in a more dignified way, but she couldn't stop herself from picking up speed to catch-up with her sister.

"Cameron!" Heather said, before hurling herself at him and sobbing. "Oh, you're safe! And here!" she sobbed.

Marianne wrapped herself around both brother and sister and tearfully kissed her brother.

Cameron had been completely taken by surprise by the sudden assault but had very quickly realised who was clinging to him as if they were drowning. He looked over their heads to Helena, who'd approached at a more ladylike pace.

He exchanged an amused look with Helena, before separating himself slightly from his sisters. "Ock, now, now! Anyone would think I had not seen you for a year or more!"

Marianne separated herself a little. "Thirteen months and three days," she said, seriously.

Cameron smiled softly at his younger sister. "And I've counted every one," he said quietly.

Heather managed to gather herself and turned to Helena. "How did your brother do it, Lady Helena?"

Helena smiled. "I think my brother is perfect, but even I know he could not produce your brother from Portugal in two days!"

"I think you'd best introduce me to your new friend," Cameron said with curiosity at the blond-haired beauty with his sisters.

Marianne quickly performed the introductions. "We are staying with Lady Helena. Lou's been ill, but she is getting better now. I am so relieved you are here, Cameron!"

"Why are you in London?" Cameron asked.

"It's that brute Duncan's fault!" Heather hissed.

"Perhaps we should return to Half Moon Street, and you can spend some time together and see your sister?" Helena suggested. They had already caused a bit of a stir with the overt welcome Heather and Marianne had given their brother. She didn't think it was a good idea for Heather to get even further animated when talking about her eldest brother.

"Thank you. That's very kind of you," Cameron said with a smile. He was very like his siblings. Each had a full head of red hair and dazzling green eyes. Only Marianne had a deeper auburn hair than the others. Cameron had confident laughing eyes Helena thought when walking along with the group. Lou was prone to glare out of hers. Heather wasn't too dissimilar from Lou; Marianne was reserved, but Cameron's expression made Helena inclined to like him immediately.

She wondered what this new family member would add to the mix.

Chapter 6

Entering the hallway at Half Moon Street, Helena immediately ordered refreshments to be served in the drawing room.

"Your sister hasn't been below stairs as yet, but I am sure she would like to see you once you've had some tea," Helena said, leading the way into the bright, welcoming room.

"Lou would scold us something rotten if we did not tell her immediately that Cameron was here," Heather said, already stepping on the stairs. "I will tell her and join you in a moment."

"How did your acquaintance with my family start? Lou's never mentioned you in any of her letters," Cameron asked Helena, as he made himself comfortable on one of the larger chairs.

Helena noticed how he filled the space with muscle rather than bulk. She paused at his question. "We met Lady Lou initially and went to collect Lady Marianne and Lady Heather when Lady Lou had recovered a little from her fever." It was a purposely vague response, and Helena hated appearing so dim-witted in front of the handsome captain, but she couldn't tell him the reality.

Cameron frowned in puzzlement. There was so much that Helena hadn't said that stirred his interest.

"Lady Helena and Lord Ashton have been so welcoming," Marianne interjected before Cameron could ask further questions.

"My brother is not at home this morning, but I'm sure he would like to make your acquaintance," Helena said, knowing it would be the case. Simon would be as curious as she was about the brother.

Heather walked into the room, closely followed by Lou. Heather shrugged her shoulders at her brother, expressing without words that Lou would never have been stopped once she knew he had returned.

Lou looked pale, but her eyes sparkled. She wore a cream lace dressing gown over her nightgown, which belonged to Helena. It draped behind her being too long for her slight frame. She had not had the energy to go through the few clothes that had been brought with Heather and Marianne, so she appeared downstairs in an undressed state.

"Cameron! How on earth did you get here so quickly?" Lou asked, moving to her brother. She flung one arm around him and squeezed him tight.

"I'd like to know why you are in London and what has happened to your arm?" Cameron responded, but held his sister close.

"I shall leave you to catch-up," Helena stood.

"No!" Cameron said without hesitation. "You clearly know some of my family business; there should be no secrets between friends. You can help tell the story." He wanted the opportunity to find out what was going on. His instinct suggested something wasn't quite right, and he was going to keep everyone around him until he knew the full story.

Lou and Helena exchanged an uncomfortable look, which Cameron noticed but did not comment on for the moment. The group sat, with the three sisters all positioned as close to their brother as they could be.

"Tell us how you reached us so speedily?" Lou insisted, wishing the conversation to remain focused on anything but herself.

"I don't really understand how you mean? I have been travelling for more than a sennight," Cameron said in confusion.

"Oh! Why? You are not injured, are you?" Heather asked quickly.

"My brother sent an express to you, advising you of your family's new address. It was only a day ago," Helena explained.

"I did not receive it. It's probably still on its way," Cameron said with a smile. "But I am not injured. Not at all. I suppose I had better start from the beginning, and then I want to hear your story." He noticed Lou's expression change but continued. "I received a letter some weeks ago from Mr Argyle, our steward," he supplied the job title for Helena.

"I didn't know he had sent you anything," Lou said, her shoulders sagging.

"I'm glad he did," Cameron said grimly. "He explained what Duncan was doing with our estate. He had tried to stop him but didn't see any way of being effective without me in the country."

"But you were at war! How could he trouble you?" Lou asked with censure.

"Sometimes officers are called back home. I actually returned with a friend of mine, Captain Philips, as his father has just died. Wellesley says that he wants his men fully focused on the battle; there is no point going into a skirmish when our minds are on something else," Cameron said with a smile. "He knows we'll return as soon as we can and be attentive and efficient once more."

"Oh. I did not realise," Lou said. "I wish I had."

Cameron once more suspected there was a lot more behind the words of his sister but didn't question her further. Yet. "There was no point in travelling all the way to Scotland when Duncan was in London, so I came straight here."

"I'll bet the Friday-faced clunch panicked when he saw you!" Lou said, relishing the discomfort her half-brother would have felt.

"Lou!" Marianne scolded, ever the one to try to keep either of her sisters respectable.

Cameron laughed at Lou's description of their half-brother. "He did, rather. But he was also still very angry about a certain punch landed by a hot-tempered sister!"

Marianne gasped, but Heather laughed. "Oh, Lou! You didn't?" Heather asked with admiration.

"He deserved it, but it is not ladylike behaviour, and I do not expect either of you two to act in a similar fashion!" Lou said with a twinkle in her eye. "The action gave me a lot of satisfaction. What else did the addlepate have to say for himself?"

"Your language has gone downhill since I was last home!" Cameron scolded. "I knew I should have arranged a companion who could keep you on the straight and narrow!"

"There isn't a person alive who would have the backbone to take on that task," Lou said. She flushed slightly. There was one person who'd stood up to her, who'd laughed at her surliness. A pity she wanted nothing more than to argue with him.

"Anyway, to forget my sister's gutter-mouth for a moment. Yes, Duncan was surprised to see me, especially as I had my own copy of father's will. He thought there was only the one copy, but I think father suspected he might do something underhanded and gave me an identical copy of his will long before he died. I'd already had it checked by a solicitor, one our own man had recommended, and all was in order. Duncan was especially unhappy to learn that I had already been to see the person who was supposed to be buying the property, and we are both going to be seeking some form of recompense for what he tried to do."

"Will he pay?" Marianne asked in shock.

"From what Mr Oswald, the supposed buyer, promised to do to him if he didn't, I do not think he will be as resistant as he would have been if it was only me in the fight," Cameron admitted. "He might be slightly afraid of me, but he likes his money more! But when someone else is involved, his reputation is also called into question. He will not want to risk that so easily as he prefers to live in London and move in the highest of circles."

"I am so glad you are here, Cameron. It's been a scary time," Heather said quietly, for once looking more like her twin than like the fiery Lou.

"You can return home anytime you wish. Everything is back in order."

"When do you go back to Portugal?" Marianne asked.

"I'm to travel back with Captain Philips, so I expect it will be in a week or two. Philips' brother is to inherit, so he said he is determined to return to Wellesley," Cameron said. "Whether that changes once he is in the company of his mother and sister, who knows?"

"I would like to stay in London until you leave. Would that be acceptable, Lou?" Marianne asked.

"I am not sure," Lou said, doubtfully.

"You could stay here," Helena offered, not sure what Simon would think of her scheme.

Lou looked at Helena with a slight frown. "We have already imposed on you too much. Far too much," she said quietly.

Helena smiled at Lou. "Yet, from my perspective, the season has become more interesting since you burst into our lives!"

"Let me take you back to your chamber, Lou. You're looking a little wan," Cameron said. "We can discuss your stay while you return to bed. I do not want you ill when I leave the country."

Lou flashed a look of alarm at her brother, knowing without doubt theirs was about to be a difficult conversation. Cameron was indulgent of his younger sisters, but even he was going to be upset at what she had to tell.

*

Lou lay on the bed. It was a surprise to the normally vibrant woman to feel so drained. The fever had taken her strength, and it was being frustratingly slow in returning.

"So, are you going to tell me what has really been happening?" Cameron asked, making himself comfortable in the chair placed at the bedside.

"Is there any point in trying to delay?" Lou asked.

"No. I have got all day if I need it."

"Has anyone ever told you, you can be stubborn sometimes?"

"My equally stubborn sister, usually," Cameron said with a smile.

"Oh, Cameron, I don't know what I was thinking!" Lou admitted for the first time. She started telling her brother the whole story, from her receiving notification they had to leave their home, to waking after her fever.

"Lou!" Cameron groaned, his head in his hands at the end of the story.

"I know! I didn't think things through properly until we were stuck in London, almost penniless and with not a friend in sight!" Lou said, the worry finally being voiced. "I was terrified, Cameron. I never expected London to be so soulless. There was no one we could turn to and no way of getting home! I had thought Duncan would have been more accommodating. I misjudged everything!"

"But a highwayman, Lou! I don't think I will ever trust you again! What were you thinking?" Cameron asked, his face filled with worry.

"It was just a reaction to circumstances. I thought if it was the aristocracy taking our home, I would punish them in return," Lou explained.

"Please tell me you see the flaw in your plan?" Cameron almost pleaded.

"I think I was lucky the first couple of times I did it," Lou admitted. "But then I tackled Lord Garswood's carriage and found out not everyone in the *ton* is as spineless as Duncan!"

"He could have killed you outright!" Cameron said almost shouting with frustration. "What would the girls have done then?"

"I know! I know!" Lou said, blinking rapidly. She couldn't break down in front of Cameron. She would not stir his sympathy in such a contrived way, but she knew when he'd gone, her tears would flow. "I owe this family so much. They have decided not to call the magistrate. There's only the four of us who knows the truth of the matter." Lou had no idea of Henry's presence on that fateful night.

Cameron rubbed his hand over his face. "Lord Garswood must be a decent sort."

"He would be if he was not so annoyingly interfering," Lou said mulishly.

"Thank God he is, or Marianne and Heather would be goodness knows where now!" Cameron said.

"Don't," Lou said quietly.

"One express to me at the first sign of problems and I would have returned home. I'm really disappointed, Lou. I trusted you to care for them," Cameron said, seriously.

"I didn't want to worry you!" Lou said in defence of her actions.

"Yes, finding out you'd been hanged would not have bothered me at all!" Cameron snapped. "How the hell am I going to repay the service that man has done for this family?"

"I'm sorry," Lou responded. Cameron had always been the one to rein her in on her more foolish escapades.

"Your lack of thinking the scheme through has shocked me; at the moment, it is beyond comprehension. I need to find Lord Garswood," Cameron said. He stood to leave the room. His hand on the door handle, he turned back to his sister. "I'd have been devastated if anything had happened to you, Lou. You need to learn to ask for help. You are not invincible."

Lou nodded, afraid the tears would fall before Cameron left the room. Her brother knew that Lou would hate for him to see her cry, so he left her alone.

Walking down the stairs, he saw Helena coming out of one of the many ground floor rooms. She smiled up at the captain but faltered a little at seeing the expression on his face. She indicated that a footman should take the book she held to Marianne before turning to Cameron.

"Captain Drummond, would you like to join me for a moment in the library?" Helena asked.

"Of course," Cameron answered, following the young woman into the room she had just vacated. It was covered along three sides with bookshelves, the fourth side having two large windows, letting light into the room. Two chairs with a side table between were the only furnishings. It was a restful room used by the family when needing respite.

Helena did not close the door but pulled it as close as she could without actually breaching propriety. She didn't want the staff or

Marianne and Heather to overhear what she said. She walked over to the side table and poured Cameron a large brandy.

"My brother always keeps a decanter here for his late night reading sessions. He sometimes forgets to go to bed," Helena said with a smile, handing over the glass.

"Thank you," Cameron said, taking a long drink. The liquid flowed through him, warming his body, which had been unnaturally chilled since he'd found out how his family had been living.

"Your sister has told you the full story?" Helena asked quietly.

"Yes. I didn't think I shocked easily, but it always seems that Lou is the one to push the boundaries," Cameron admitted.

"She certainly is a character!" Helena said. "I am quite in awe of her. We have only a few years difference in age, but I feel she is far more worldly-wise than I."

"I dispute that after the foolhardy scheme she embarked upon recently. We owe you and your brother a great debt."

"For shooting your sister?" Helena asked with a smile.

Cameron laughed for the first time since he'd arrived in London. "Yes! A pity it wasn't done years ago. It might have taught her a thing or two then."

"It was a strange way to go about things, but she meant well," Helena said.

"Pfftt! She meant to punish everyone because of one clot. Why didn't your brother call the magistrate? I would have done," Cameron admitted.

"I think we both came to the conclusion that we hadn't the right to destroy the family. We had come to no harm. She has been punished and will suffer with her shoulder for some time to come. There really was nothing to be achieved," Helena said.

They were disturbed by Simon walking into the room. "Mrs Cox said you wanted to see me?" he asked as soon as he entered.

"Oh, yes," Helena said. She introduced her brother to Cameron.

"Shall we retire to my study?" Simon asked.

Cameron agreed, but as he stood, he reached for Helena's hand, lifting the hand to his lips. "Lady Helena, I owe you a huge debt of gratitude. Thank you," he said before following Simon out of the room.

Helena sank back into the seat she had recently vacated. She wondered if it were possible to fall in love within an hour of meeting someone.

Chapter 7

Simon indicated that Cameron should sit. He offered him a drink, which Cameron accepted.

"Ah, whisky," Cameron said with appreciation after taking a drink. "I do miss a good Scottish whisky when I'm away from home."

"This is Bowmore's finest. My father loved it, and I always have a ready supply on hand," Simon said with admiration at Cameron's ability to pin-point that his whisky was from Scotland.

"In Portugal, it is all port, madeira and brandy. It's passable, but it doesn't warm the insides quite like a good whisky," Cameron said.

"You're back in England a lot earlier than I expected," Simon admitted. "The postal service is good, but even I know it isn't that good."

"Ah, yes. It seems I have passed your letter at some point," Cameron stated. He told Simon of the reason he had returned and admitted all that Lou had confessed.

"I was not sure whether you'd want to call me out when you heard what had happened," Simon admitted.

"I think I should be on my hands and knees begging you to forgive my foolish sister," Cameron said with a grimace. "I would like to say it is unlike her, but she's a force unto herself sometimes."

Simon smiled, picturing flashing green eyes. "She has already threatened to run me through with a broadsword when she's well enough!"

"Good God! This is what happens when a young woman is left to roam free," Cameron ground out. "Our father gave us all too much freedom; it enabled us to develop parts of our character that would have been more subdued if we had been punished more."

"I wasn't best pleased at the beginning," Simon admitted. "The only reason I did not shoot to kill was because I wanted to see the blackguard hang for putting my sister in danger, but Helena soon convinced me what I was already coming around to: We could not inform on her. It was a foolish scheme she embarked on, but then again, there would not be highwaymen if fools like me didn't travel in the dead of night," Simon admitted.

"But to then protect all my sisters. I thank you," Cameron said.

"You are protecting our country from the scourge of the Bonepartes. You could say I am repaying you in kind," Simon said fairly.

"I am glad Philips will not be ready to leave for a few weeks. It would grieve me to leave immediately after what has happened. I will arrange accommodation, and we shall leave you in peace. Once I'm satisfied Lou is fit to travel, I will send her back to Scotland and make sure she never leaves the area again!"

Simon felt a lump in his stomach at the thought of Lou being confined to a remote Scottish manor house. Someone with so much spirit should be in the centre of Society, making all their lives more interesting.

"You can stay here," Simon said, without letting the thought register fully, so he couldn't talk himself out of it.

"No! You've done too much already," Cameron said quickly.

"I insist," Simon responded. "Think of it as doing me a favour. Helena has not taken to Society as much as I had thought she would. Your sisters will be good company for her, and if they can go to small entertainments together, she might not be so eager to leave London."

"I thought all young women enjoyed the season," Cameron echoed Simon's earlier words to his sister.

"So did I. Apparently, there are the same dull people attending all the events. I don't think she sees the admiration she attracts. She is not vain, so she does not really see herself as one of the debutantes who are certain of marriage proposals," Simon admitted.

"She's a beautiful young woman," Cameron admitted about Helena, who was clearly someone who had a kind and generous spirit to add to her charms. "But a lack of vanity is to her credit."

"It is. She is naïve. I just hope her impact on the beaux of the season remains unnoticed by her. It makes my life easier," Simon said through gritted teeth. "I didn't realise that the responsibility of ensuring that a younger sister makes a good match would weigh so heavy!"

Cameron smiled in sympathy. "How do you think I feel, having three to match? Especially when one is Lou! Can you understand why I ran off to Portugal?"

Simon chuckled. "I can indeed! I mean what I say though: Stay here. I would be glad of your company."

"Thank you," Cameron said.

*

Helena willingly cancelled her evening's entertainment. She would much rather remain home with a handsome captain and his sisters than go out to a ball. Simon had raised his eyebrows when she'd informed him of her decision, but he hadn't tried to persuade her otherwise. He was obliged to go out, but unusual for him, seemed as reluctant as Helena had been.

The sisters and brother, along with Helena, at their insistence, gathered in Lou's chamber. The room was large enough to seat the five visitors, all gathered around the bed. A wooden board had been placed across the bedcovers and a card game was being played on it.

Helena watched the interaction between the siblings with interest. There was a far more fluid relationship between the group than was the case between herself and Simon. She wondered if it was because her father had died a number of years ago, and Simon had taken on the role of father and brother. Having no memory of her mother being anything other than a meek character, her life had always been male dominated, so the interaction between the sisters was especially fascinating.

Lou and Heather were obviously of similar character. They voiced their opinions and challenged whenever they wished, never holding back in respect for their opponent. Marianne was more restrained, more demur, but she could give a good set-down if required. In the midst of the chaos, Cameron laughed, teased, and took them all to task in a way Helena had never seen before. Simon was loving towards his sister, but it was in a more formal way, whereas Cameron was relaxed and openly tactile. It was appealing to watch.

  The visitors knew Helena was their saviour, two of them not realising quite how much, but they respected that, although young, she had been their supporter. They treated her gentler than they treated each other, but Lou couldn't stop herself exclaiming when Helena gave away a card to her opponent.

  "For goodness sake, Lady Helena! I thought you knew how to play this game," Lou groaned, when Heather crowed with glee.

  "I do!" Helena defended herself with a blush. "I have just never played with such mercenary people," she said with a huff.

  "We take no prisoners," Lou said with a non-apologetic shrug.

  "I wish I'd been informed of that small fact before I agreed to play," Helena said.

  "They are a bunch of termagants," Cameron said affectionately.

  "You should be grateful for our existence. Just imagine if you'd had only Duncan as a brother!" Lou taunted.

  "Don't!" Cameron groaned. "Speaking of whom... "

  "Do we have to spoil this evening?" Lou interrupted.

  Cameron grinned at his sister. "I think you will be in favour of what I have to say."

  "Go on, Cameron," Marianne encouraged.

  "I checked something else with my solicitor while I was with him," Cameron started. "If Duncan was prepared to sell our home, I don't trust him with your inheritance. I am going to apply to become your guardian in his place. The solicitor assured me the evidence against Duncan with regards to our home, would support my claim," he finished.

"Have you told him?" Lou asked.

"Not yet," Cameron admitted.

"Please let me be there when you do," Lou grinned.

Cameron smiled. "Only if you promise not to punch him."

"If he agrees, there won't be any need!" Lou responded tartly.

"You will have to start controlling yourself, Lou. You are one and twenty and old enough to act like a lady," Cameron chastised gently. "I cannot return to Portugal wondering what scrape you will get into next."

Lou looked uncomfortable. "You don't need to worry. I promise."

"Please stay for as long as you can," Heather pleaded. "We could have a late come-out if you are here!"

"I had every intention of sending you back to Scotland. I thought you'd want to return home?" Cameron asked in surprise.

"We do, but it would be nice to attend some balls," Marianne said quietly.

"I can't delay my return because of that," Cameron said gently. "But I can appoint a chaperone who can do the job of ferrying you around town. Just think, you could all be married when I return!"

"Pfft!" Lou muttered.

"Excellent!" Heather said.

"We are not ready to come out," Marianne said, looking down at her hands and flushing slightly.

Lou also flushed and shot a look towards Helena. It was clear she wasn't comfortable having their family difficulties aired.

"I have some gowns that are too tight for me," Helena stated, hoping she wasn't about to offend. "I'm sure they would be perfect for you. You are both so much slimmer than I."

Realisation dawned on Cameron. "Ah! I see! Lady Helena, that's a generous offer, and my sisters thank you, but if you could advise me of your preferred modiste, we will have new wardrobes sorted at the earliest opportunity."

"Of course," Helena said.

"But in the meantime, we could use Lady Helena's dresses," Heather said, wishing to get out of what were rapidly turning into rags.

"Heather—" Cameron started.

"It's absolutely fine!" Helena interjected. "I would not have offered if I hadn't meant it. Truly. I am keeping them because I cannot bear to get rid of them for no reason other than not wishing to waste the fabric."

"Thank you," Cameron said humbly.

"I will send a message round to Madame Francois, but there might be a delay in making anything new with this being the height of the season," Helena explained.

The party broke up when Lou started to look pale and drawn. She was recovering quickly, but activity still took its toll on her. The twins left along with Helena. Cameron was left with Lou.

"Why are they being so damned nice, Cameron?" Lou asked when the door had closed behind the others.

"I don't know. I'm not sure I could be so forgiving or welcoming in the circumstances," Cameron admitted.

"I certainly could not! I half expect them to turn on us, but they never do. I have never known anyone so willing to help people so unrelated to them," Lou admitted.

"Which makes their acceptance and generosity even more special," Cameron admitted. "Sleep now, Lou. You need to recover fully. We cannot impose on this family forever."

Cameron walked to the door after lifting the wooden board off the bed. He looked back at his sister who was already lying down with her eyes closed, looking drained. He frowned slightly, hoping what he had to do would prove as easy as he hoped. At four and twenty he had shouldered a lot of responsibility, and sometimes, it weighed a little heavy.

Chapter 8

Entering the hallway, Cameron didn't quite know where to go. He was very much a visitor in this house, and because of the beginnings of the acquaintance, didn't feel comfortable enough to wander around. He faltered slightly just as Lady Helena started down the stairs behind him.

"Captain Drummond, I've left Lady Heather and Lady Marianne fighting over a number of dresses," Helena said with a smile. "Would you like me to bring them down to you, or would you like to go to them?"

"No!" Cameron said quickly. "I would hate to be put in a position in which I'd have to choose sides."

"That is the reason I left them to their own devices," Helena laughed. "My brother said you are a connoisseur of Scottish whisky. He had some put in the library for you to enjoy, if you'd like some?" Helena asked.

"That's very kind of him. It is in my blood to enjoy a tipple," Cameron smiled.

"In that case, if you'd like to join me?" Helena said. She could leave him to his own devices, but there was more than being a good hostess that was making her wish to spend time in the company of such a handsome, considerate man. Added to the fact that he clearly loved his sisters, it was difficult for Helena to find any fault with him at all.

"Lead on, My Lady," Cameron said gallantly with a smile that did nothing for Helena's fluttering stomach.

Helena ensured a large whisky was poured for the captain, before sitting opposite him with a small glass of wine. She hoped it would give her courage to appear to be a lady of the world instead of a debutante in her first season.

"Do you not take any whisky?" Cameron asked, watching the pretty Lady Helena sip daintily on her wine.

"No. I'm afraid it is too strong for my taste," Helena admitted.

"In Scotland we bring our bairns up on the stuff."

"Really?" Helena gasped.

Cameron laughed. "Not really. We would be fit for naught if that were the case. Lou likes a dram now and again, but she is not your average lady."

"No. I feel quite young when I'm in her company," Helena admitted.

Cameron smiled gently. "You are quite young, Lady Helena, as is Lou."

"Yet, I could feasibly have come out last year and been married by now."

"Why didn't you?" Cameron asked, curious. "You are a titled lady, beautiful, and I am guessing, have a reasonable dowry. What was to stop you from securing an early marriage?"

Helena had flushed at the compliment. "My brother said he wanted me to enjoy a little freedom after leaving the schoolroom before I became a wife and mother. My friends are envious of the fact," Helena admitted.

"I can believe so," Cameron said. She was even prettier when she flushed, the heightened colour having the effect of making her blue eyes sparkle. Her golden locks also made her look younger. He imagined she'd not seen anything to upset her equilibrium before Lou burst into her life. He was only six years older than she, but at that moment, felt far more.

"So, you're being chased by every dandy around the balls of London at the grand old age of eighteen?" Cameron asked, openly flirting.

"No!" Helena said, blushing deep red. "My brother would soon see them off!"

"Yes. That's the issue I have with leaving my sisters in the sole care of a chaperone," Cameron admitted.

"Could you not stay?" Helena asked quickly. Her motivation was not purely for her new friend's benefit.

"No. I could perhaps make a case to, but it would not be fair. Sir Arthur needs every man. I said I would do my duty, and I will," Cameron said.

"Your sisters worry about you," Helena said, knowing that in future she would worry as much as they did.

"A military life is precarious. It is hard enough for one's family," Cameron said. "At least I have no wife or children to worry about."

His words made Helena ache as she'd never ached before, and it took her a moment to respond. "Wives follow the drum, do they not?"

"Some do," Cameron admitted. "I'm not sure I would want my wife to live in such conditions."

"If she loved you, it would hardly be of concern to her. It is not a hardship I would shy away from!" Helena said heatedly.

Cameron sighed. "I'm not the marrying kind, so it is not a concern," he said firmly. He'd been teasing her, but he wasn't going to lead her on in any respect. This was the danger when speaking to debutantes. The most innocuous of comments could be misconstrued.

Helena blinked at the change in the tone of voice and coloured deeply. "I did not think I was talking of particulars. I was talking in the hypothetical," she said with enough haughtiness that Simon would've been proud. She'd seen him give enough put-downs in his time, so she had learned from an expert.

"I apologise. My mistake," Cameron said quickly. He stood. "Lady Helena, please forgive me. I think I'll retire to my chamber, if you would excuse me?"

"Of course." Lady Helena stood and watched the captain leave her alone. She sighed. "That went well," she muttered.

*

Simon entered quietly through the large wooden door that opened into the hallway. He'd left instructions that no one was to wait up for him. When Henry was in a mood to socialise, it always proved to be a late night. Leaving his hat, gloves, and cane on a side table he made to walk up the stairs but was distracted by a noise coming from the library.

Walking towards the slightly opened door, he pushed it open more fully to reveal the sight of Lady Lou, dressed in her nightwear, hair cascading down her back, climbing down from the library steps, holding a large tome.

Simon moved quickly across the room. "Here, let me," he said.

"What?" Lou exclaimed in surprise, letting go of the book.

Simon lurched forwards, just managing to catch the heavy object, but it was done in an ungainly fashion.

"Were you trying to give me heart failure?" Lou asked heatedly as she climbed down the remaining steps. "It would seem my life is still in danger!"

"My precious books are in danger if you insist on climbing to reach heavy objects with an injured shoulder!" Simon snapped back.

"I could not sleep!" Lou responded, snatching the book out of Simon's grasp even though it wasn't her property.

Simon smiled despite his previous sharp tone. "Are you ever apologetic?" The sight of her standing in her dressing gown in the flickering candlelight of one candelabra was very appealing, even though her eyes were flashing daggers at him.

Lou's mouth quirked slightly. "As little as possible," she admitted.

"That's what I supposed," Simon said. "Is my library so lacking that this was the only book that appealed to you out of the two thousand pieces in it?"

Lou reddened a little. "I wanted this particular book," she said, not wishing to carry on the conversation. "Now, please excuse me. I will return to my bedchamber."

"Of course, if you wish. But then again, you could stay, have a drink, and explain why you need to read a book on the law at four of the clock. What is it that it couldn't wait until morning and be solved by seeking the counsel of your brother?" Simon asked pleasantly, moving over to the decanters of brandy, whisky, and cognac.

"Why would I explain to you?" Lou asked roughly, but she didn't leave the room.

Simon noticed her hesitation. "Whisky?" he asked glancing at her.

Lou nodded and sank into one of the chairs near the fire. She curled her feet underneath her, a position most women would be mortified to do in company, but although Simon noticed the way she sat, he made no comment. She accepted the glass and took a large swig from it.

Glaring at Simon for his amused look, she said, "I am not some Society miss who has to drink negus or become inebriated! I can drink a glass of whisky without effect."

"You are as far from those kinds of women as you could possibly be," Simon admitted.

Lou looked quickly away. He had agreed with her, so why did she feel bereft at his words? She had never longed to be something she wasn't and yet…

She sighed. "It's a good whisky," she admitted.

"Your brother approved," Simon said with a smile. "Now, what has taken you from your sick bed? Or am I to be abused until daylight?"

Lou smiled widely at the remark. "It is so tempting. I find it's an enjoyable pastime, but I am not quite up to snuff at the moment, so I probably wouldn't last 'til dawn."

Simon paused with the effects of Lou's smile. It lit her face, and he felt a rush of deep pleasure that his words had caused it. He faltered before responding; he wasn't quite comfortable with the effect she had on him. It was ludicrous, but he couldn't deny that she stirred him.

"I'm not your brother, but can I help? You are obviously concerned about something," he said gently as if he were talking to Helena.

Worry clouded Lou's eyes. "I cannot say this to Cameron. He has said he's going to apply to take over as our guardians because he no longer trusts Duncan with our funds. That is fine. I completely understand, but I wanted to know if anything — if he should be — if the worst should happen, would the guardianship revert back to Duncan?"

"Ah, I see," Simon said with sympathy. "Your brother would need to update his will and appoint someone to act in his absence. He should do it anyway. Who is to say you would not attract someone unsuitable while he's away in Portugal and Spain? Someone needs to stop a fortune hunter from convincing you to marry him!"

Lou laughed. It was a loud, raucous, infectious laugh. "I have no fear of that! I haven't got a huge fortune, and I am quite capable of persuading anyone foolish enough to think I have that I am not the woman for them!"

"How half-witted of me to think otherwise!" Simon said with a smirk. "But you have sisters."

"And I can look after them equally as well!"

"Sometimes we all need counsel and guidance. None of us is infallible," Simon pointed out, not willing to say she had made an error of judgement already.

Lou narrowed her eyes at Simon, as if reading his thoughts. "I hate to bow to anyone else's superior knowledge."

"If you do not, you're destined to make mistakes. We all are. I thought Helena would enjoy the season, yet she has come to life only since your family entered our acquaintance... apart from the first evening, of course," Simon said, unable to resist taunting her.

Lou smiled, despite the urge to glare. "If you will travel across dark heathland in the dead of night... "

"Yes. You taught me a hard lesson that night!" Simon said grimly.

"The lesson was mutual," Lou admitted.

Simon smiled at her words. The anger and upset of that night had disappeared. "Do you have any family who could step in if anything were to happen to your brother?"

"Only an aunt who lives in Fort William," Lou admitted. "She wouldn't be any use against Duncan. He can be as charming as a snake when he wants to be!"

"I am glad I don't really know him," Simon responded. "Captain Philips is a good man. I know his family. If I were appointing anyone, he would be a good choice. He would step in if needed."

"Yes. Cameron speaks highly of him. I suppose he would be the sensible alternative. It's just difficult when I do not know the individual personally. Having someone else in charge of your destiny is not easy," Lou admitted.

Simon shook off the urge to offer to be her protector. It would be wrong and probably unwelcome, but for some reason he didn't like the thought of her being reliant on someone else. He groaned silently. This involvement was proving more complex than he could have ever imagined.

"To change the subject slightly. How many robberies did you carry out?" he asked, bringing the conversation back onto a topic that would restore the glares aimed in his direction rather than the too appealing smiles.

True to form, Lou glared. "Four, before you," she admitted.

"It would be a good gesture to send whatever you gained back to the people involved," Simon suggested.

Lou looked uncomfortable. "It would. I had already thought of that the moment Cameron returned. Unfortunately, I've no idea who I robbed, and I sold the jewels for blunt. It was money not trinkets we needed."

"That is a pity," Simon responded.

"I have given it to a charitable cause," Lou said. She didn't like to see the disappointment in Simon's eyes. "Cameron took it after our first conversation. Marianne had given it to me as soon as she arrived here. The people I robbed won't miss what they lost, but the money will benefit those it is now helping. I know it is not a perfect solution."

"No. But it is better than nothing," Simon acknowledged.

Lou sighed. "Life is too complicated sometimes."

"It feels worse in the dead of night. In the morning it never seems so bad."

"And on that note, I'll return to my chamber," Lou said standing. "Thank you for your company. After the initial fright, you are not too bad as a companion!"

Simon laughed as Lou left the room. Finishing his whisky, he stretched his legs. Tonight he would fall asleep with a smile on his face.

Chapter 9

Captain Philips called on Cameron the following morning. The captain was reacquainted with Simon, after which Cameron took him to be introduced to his sisters.

Lou was dressed in a borrowed day gown and was sitting downstairs in the drawing room along with Helena, Heather, and Marianne.

Captain Philips greeted the ladies warmly, his dark good looks, tall figure, and fine military uniform a guarantee to be a hit with the ladies wherever he went. His black armband was the signal to everyone why he was home.

After being served refreshments, the group were keen to speak to the newcomer.

"We were sorry to hear of your loss," Lou said, handing Captain Philips a cup of green tea.

"Thank you. Father suffered from ill-health for a while, but it was still a shock," Captain Philips admitted.

"You are returning to Portugal?" Helena asked. "Are you not forced to stay home?"

"I was hoping to return as soon as possible, but it seems my brother needs a little support in being the head of the household," Captain Philips admitted.

"So, I'm to travel without your company?" Cameron asked. "You will be missed by us all, especially your men."

"Thank you. I am hoping to still join the company. I can only stay away for a little while longer. My brother, James is perfectly capable of learning as he goes along," Captain Philips admitted. "He's expressed the opinion that, as his heir, I should not be returning at all. He hasn't any children as yet, so I am the next in line. I think mother is behind the words rather than my brother. I was quick to point out that, if every heir refused to fight, there would be no one on the battlefields!"

"Ah, so you consider yourself as invincible as my brother seems to think he is!" Lou said.

Captain Philips laughed. "Not at all! I have not had the chance to forget about my mortality, thanks to my mother and sister, but I am struggling in that all I've ever wanted to do was be a military man. Father understood that, but now the reality of responsibility is a little closer than it was. It was inevitable the objections would increase as a result, I suppose."

"It's a shame we cannot do as we wish," Heather said with a sigh.

"What escapades would you get up to, Lady Heather?" Captain Philips asked with a smile.

"I want to do something that would make a difference," Heather responded with conviction.

"That is a commendable wish for a young lady to have," Captain Philips acknowledged.

"And you sound as patronising as everyone else does when I voice my opinions," Heather said defiantly.

"Heather!" Lou chastised, shocked at her sister, even though she wouldn't have faltered at uttering the same scolding if she'd been in a similar position.

Heather flushed but responded. "It is! No one believes I am capable of doing anything other than sewing poorly and playing the pianoforte well!"

"And what would you like to do instead? And I ask this with genuine curiosity and nothing more," Captain Philips said.

"Cameron has been tested. I'd like to be pushed to the limits in a similar fashion to see if I had the ability to be the best I could possibly be," Heather said.

"I'm glad you cannot be involved in any aspect of this campaign!" Cameron said roughly. "The way the French are, there is no guarantee we will win overall."

"And that's the reason why whoever can help, should help!" Heather said heatedly.

"One woman in the family with too much spirit is quite enough, my dear Heather," Cameron smiled at his sister. "Perhaps we should separate you from Lou, so she can't corrupt you further!"

"My brother complains too much!" Lou said, chipping in. "I would think it is the brother's fault if he let his sisters run wild. Wouldn't you say so, Captain Philips?"

"I would indeed!" Captain Philips said with a laugh at his friend.

"On that note, I think it is time we made our excuses, Michael," Cameron said, rising.

"Ah, always the one to keep me in line!" Captain Philips said with a smile but rising also. "Good afternoon ladies. I do hope to see you again soon."

When the four were seated again after the gentlemen had bowed and left the room, Heather turned to her sister. "Do you have to monopolise every man we meet, Lou?"

"Whatever do you mean?" Lou asked in surprise. "I was just talking to him!"

"You flirt all the time, and there's no opportunity for any of the rest of us to make a favourable impression!" Heather scolded her sister.

"Lou is the eldest," Marianne soothed. "She should be married first."

"Married? It's a huge jump from being polite to someone to wedding them!" Lou said, trying not to laugh. "Goodness, I cannot win! You scold me when I glower and snarl at people, and now I am being taken to task because I was pleasant!"

"You know what I mean!" Heather snapped.

"Did you like Captain Philips?" Helena asked Heather.

Heather blushed. "Yes. For what good it'll do me!"

"The cavalry are very striking in their uniforms," Helena admitted.

"Do you like Captain Philips too?" Heather asked, looking downcast.

"No! Not at all!" Helena said quickly. "Although, he seems very nice. But nothing else. I don't have any designs on him!"

"And neither do I!" Lou exclaimed. "Now, I am going to return to my bed. My shoulder is aching."

"I am sorry, Lou," Heather said.

"Don't worry about it. If I thought you were chasing someone I'd set my cap at, I would take you to task just as quickly!"

Heather smiled with relief; Lou was very much an idol of Heather's.

As Lou left the room, Helena couldn't resist her next question. "Does your brother have a sweetheart?"

Both Marianne and Heather turned to the red-faced Helena. "No, not that we know of," Marianne said.

"Oh."

"I wouldn't mind if he had one… " Marianne started with a smile.

"Especially someone we like… " Heather continued.

"Oh, stop!" Helena laughed. "Please do not tell your sister! I think she would ridicule me, but he is very handsome!"

"Do you think so? I've always thought he's very ordinary," Heather admitted.

"Heather! That is no way to speak of your brother!" Marianne scolded. "We should be extolling his virtues to Lady Helena, not dissuading her affection."

"He has mentioned that he doesn't wish to marry," Helena admitted, her cheeks stinging at mortification of the conversation she'd had with Cameron.

"We'll have to persuade him that he does!" Heather said, rubbing her hands together. "We need to put you in his company as much as possible before he goes away once more."

"Would he not guess what we're doing?" Marianne asked, having more faith in her brother's abilities to foil a silly scheme.

"We will be subtle!" Heather said. "Now we need to plan flirting techniques. You have only a limited time with him."

"Oh, dear me," Helena moaned.

*

Helena was to have unexpected aid from events that transpired later that evening. She was at a ball at the Duchess of Oxford's grand London home. Many from the *ton* were in attendance, and although she'd been looking forward to the event, Helena had been reluctant to leave her new friends behind.

Simon had promised Helena they would hold a small entertainment at home to enable the younger ladies to enjoy some of the Society in London, which had pacified his sister.

Walking down the stairs at Half Moon Street, Helena felt her heart race a little faster when she saw Cameron at the bottom of the stairs with her brother. She was glad of her white gown edged in pale blue flowers and delicate lace. She was astute enough to realise she looked handsome with her curls tumbling around her face and a little colouring added to her lips.

Both gentlemen looked up as she walked downstairs. Simon smiled, but Cameron's eyes betrayed no emotion.

"My dear, you look lovely. You'll be fighting off partners tonight! Will you save me a quadrille?"

"Of course," Helena said with a flush and a quick glance at Cameron.

"Would I be too presumptuous to ask for the first two with you, Lady Helena?" Cameron asked politely.

"No. That would be lovely. Thank you, Captain Drummond," Helena responded.

They travelled in Simon's carriage and soon joined the throng converging onto one of the events of the season.

The three made slow progress through the crowd of people, all seeming intent on calling to everyone of their acquaintance, pushing by people to reach others farther away.

"I feel this skirmish isn't too different from a battle, without the guns and blood of course," Helena said to Cameron.

Cameron chuckled. "You are not far wrong, Lady Helena! I had forgotten what a crush entertainments are."

"Yes, one sometimes feels there isn't enough air to breathe," Helena said. "Very often, I long for wide open spaces, even though I have never experienced such. The lanes around our country home are the remotest I have ever been!"

"Ah, you need a trip to Scotland," Cameron said smiling. "The space there cannot be expressed eloquently enough in an environment as crowded as this. Fields and hills as far as the eye can see. A walk through forests where you don't see another human being."

"Don't!" Helena said with a groan. "You make me long to escape, and I must be polite and pretend I am enjoying fighting for an inch of space."

Cameron grinned. "Let's hope there is more room to dance."

"I think you'll be disappointed, Captain Drummond!"

They were interrupted by the arrival of Henry, who bowed after Simon made the introductions.

"Lady Helena, I hope you have kept the first two dances for me?" Henry asked.

"I'm afraid not," Helena responded, her tone a little cool. "I am already promised to Captain Drummond."

"Ah, I see." Henry shot Cameron a look that was anything but friendly. "In that case, might I request the following two?"

Helena looked as if she would rather not but nodded her head in agreement.

"I shall look forward to our time together, Lady Helena," Henry said with a short bow before turning on his heel and walking away.

"Charming man," Cameron said quietly to Helena. "I think you've made him jealous."

"Lord Ince! Heavens no!" Helena laughed. "He delights in discomfiting me. Having to wait longer to dance than usual will have vexed him, that's all! He is an old friend of Simon's and likes to torment me. I can assure you he has no other thought than to ridicule my opinions for an hour."

Cameron frowned. He was enough of a man of the world to have detected that Helena had some attraction to himself. It was not arrogance on his part. Very often it was the coat that appealed to the ladies in Society rather than the man wearing it. To some extent he'd dismissed Helena as the same, but this evening was proving more difficult to maintain that opinion.

When she'd walked down the stairs in Half Moon Street, he'd swallowed and struggled to school his features into a bland expression. She'd looked stunning. She was beautiful, and he'd realised almost with a physical thud in his chest that his first assessment of her had been too hasty. She was well on the way to becoming an alluring woman of Society.

He'd felt privileged when she'd shot him a shy look when Simon had asked her to dance, and it was no hardship on his part to ask for two dances. Suddenly the chance to spend an uninterrupted hour or more with her was extremely appealing.

Seeing her with Henry had brought a frown to his face. She was clearly uncomfortable with the gentleman, yet her brother seemed happy for her to be dancing with him. Cameron was used to feeling protective towards his sisters, but what he'd felt at Helena's discomfort had gone beyond the natural feelings of a bother shielding his siblings. He'd wanted to punch the lord's nose and threaten him to never approach Helena's company again. The feeling disturbed him enough to move closer to Simon.

"Your friend is easily upset, I fear," he said, his voice quiet.

"Henry? He's used to dancing with Helena first. They have a lively relationship," Simon said easily.

"She seemed uncomfortable to me," Cameron admitted.

"I don't think it is anything serious!" Simon smiled dismissively. "Theirs is the type of friendship that thrives on conflict. She's admitted she cannot banter with him as she'd want, but that is due to an age difference. I am confident there is no harm in their sparring."

"If we were talking about Lou, I would agree, but it surprises me to hear that of Lady Helena," Cameron admitted.

They reached the ballroom just as the music began. Cameron offered his arm, and with a grimace at the number of people moving towards the dance area, Helena and he moved as one.

Helena was to have the pleasure of being in close quarters with Cameron as a result of the crowd, which was a mixed blessing. She hoped her flushed cheeks would be mistaken as caused by the heat in the room rather than as the result of being so near the gentleman she was very attracted to.

"I know very little of the life you lead when abroad," Helena admitted as they danced. "Do you enjoy entertainments while you're away?"

"We certainly enjoy some," Cameron admitted. "But nothing as grand as this."

Helena felt jealous at the unknown women who were lucky enough to spend time with Cameron.

As if Cameron suspected what she was thinking, he smiled at Helena. "Any women who follow the camp are never short of partners, although they very often have their husbands watching from the side-lines."

"Oh! So there aren't many single ladies?"

Cameron smiled. "There are sisters and daughters, but they are not necessarily there to look for husbands. Admittedly though, they very often find them." Despite his early keenness on putting her straight on the fact that he wasn't looking to marry, he couldn't resist teasing her a little.

"I see," Helena said a little stiffly. She was inwardly cursing herself. Heather particularly had tried to convince her to be coy and flirting, but instead she was being far too open and transparent.

"No one in the camp could match my current partner for beauty or dancing ability," Cameron gently smiled at her.

"Please do not tease me, Captain Drummond," Helena responded with a flush. "I'm no woman of the world; I cannot pretend to be. If I did try to be someone I'm not, I would be found out by cads like Lord Ince and ridiculed in every ballroom in London."

Cameron frowned as they passed in the set. He waited until they could speak for more than a few seconds. "I speak the truth. I haven't looked at anyone else since you floated down the stairs at home. And for the record, I am happy you are who you are. It is very appealing to be with someone untouched by cynicism or who does not have a bleak outlook on life. I'm a hardened cavalry man, and I have seen too much death to be as carefree as I was. To spend time with someone who is untouched by horror helps to restore my soul, Lady Helena."

Helena smiled, unable to stop herself. "I should be reticent and refute the compliment you have given, but I'm vain enough to enjoy such praise. It is rarely given!"

"In that case, we are surrounded by fools!" Cameron said sincerely.

*

Across the ballroom, Henry stood with Simon, watching Helena and Cameron.

"I think you must be going mad, my friend," Henry said.

"Why is that?"

"Not only have you chosen to forget a heinous crime, you have welcomed the whole of the family into your home!"

"The situation was a reaction to unusual circumstances," Simon defended. "They're members of the aristocracy in their own right."

"In Scotland, certainly," Henry said with derision.

Simon laughed. "It is still nobility! They are not savages. The brother is an honourable man."

"Who has designs on your sister by the look of things," Henry spat.

"Hardly! 'Tis the first time they've danced. I am not expecting either of them to be speaking of matrimony in the morning!" Simon grinned.

"I know the signs," Henry insisted.

"Why would you be concerned? You and Helena are constantly chaffing against each other! Don't tell me you had designs on her?" Simon asked, suddenly realising his friend might have more serious intentions than he'd imagined.

"Of course, I intend marrying her!" Henry snapped. "Just didn't want to reveal my intentions too early in the season."

Simon became serious. "Henry, don't bam me by trying to convince me that you are in love with my sister. That would be too much of a Banbury Tale!"

"Love is for fools! We would make a good match," Henry said, sounding as far from being in love as a man could possibly be. "She is pretty enough, and with a bit of work, could be forced into being a wife who lets me carry on with how I want to live my life. I would hardly pick someone who had a difficult character. It would be far too exhausting. Although sometimes she scolds like a fish wife, your sister is usually amenable and malleable where family is concerned; I'd say she is a perfect choice."

Simon's glower would have frightened many in the ballroom, but Henry seemed oblivious. "That's my sister you are talking about. My only sister. If you think I am about to let you offer for her under those terms, you have sadly mistaken me," he snapped.

"I see. So, you'd be happy to see her married to a fop like him?"

"I am not intending her marrying anyone just yet," Simon bit back. "Nor will I look favourably on anyone who is only prepared to offer her a life of coldness and drudgery while he roams around town as if he isn't married! What kind of life would that be for her? I like to play the fool and the rascal Henry, but I think ultimately you have misunderstood me." This was the type of marriage Simon had dreaded for his sister. It would be reliving his mother's life all over again. He couldn't have influenced his parent's life, but he certainly wasn't about to abandon Helena to that fate.

"You are nothing more than a fool and a sap!" Henry growled. "I will take my leave of you, Garswood. I hope you come to your senses soon enough. Send my apologies to your sister. I'm suddenly desirous of more welcoming company!"

Chapter 10

The party returned earlier than they'd anticipated. Simon had been discomfited by Henry's words and had claimed a sore head. As Helena had already danced with Cameron, and there was no sign of Henry to claim his dances, she was happy to leave.

Entering the house at Half Moon Street, Helena kissed her brother and curtseyed to Cameron before seeking out Heather and Marianne.

Simon looked at Cameron. "Could you excuse me? I have a few things I want to mull over. I'm afraid I am not the best of company at the moment."

"Of course. I wanted to speak to Lou before she retires as I wish to visit Duncan tomorrow and best inform her," Cameron responded easily.

"I'll bid you goodnight then," Simon said, heading towards his study.

Cameron walked quickly up the stairs to Lou's bedchamber. A quick knock on the door was answered with a welcoming shout from inside the room. Cameron popped his head around the door with a grin.

"Still awake?" he asked entering the room and sitting on the edge of Lou's bed.

Lou was reclining on her large bed, reading a book she'd obtained when she'd returned the large volume about law to the library. "Of course. I find the ache is less when I lie-down, which makes me hope for a life of luxury in the future, as one can quickly become used to being indolent!" Lou responded with an answering grin. "You are back early. Was London's finest not tempting enough for you?"

Cameron smiled at the memory of dancing with Helena but focused on Lou. "Not at all. Lord Ashton seemed a little out of sorts after what must have been a run-in with one of his friends. An unpleasant fellow in my opinion. He wanted to return early and has holed himself up in his study."

"Oh," Lou responded with a frown.

"I thought it a good idea to have an early night anyway. I am going to visit Duncan tomorrow. Do you still wish to accompany me?"

"Yes! It is our future you'll be discussing. I definitely want to be there!" Lou said through gritted teeth.

"Are you sure you are up to snuff? I don't want you catching a chill on your first trip outside," Cameron cautioned.

"I am perfectly well. Just a little tender at the end of the day, that's all. I didn't realise how often one uses an arm until I injured mine!" Lou said, rubbing her shoulder with a grimace.

"We will leave around eleven. I have not let Duncan know we are to visit."

"Good idea. The gutter rat would run and hide if he knew we were coming!" Lou responded fiercely.

Cameron smiled but said nothing. He agreed with most of the criticism Lou aimed at Duncan; she wasn't far off the mark. Standing, he reached over and kissed Lou's cheek.

"He's not going to be happy to see us. He never liked his authority being questioned," Cameron said, moving to the door. "Goodnight, Lou."

"Goodnight," Lou responded.

She remained looking at the door after Cameron had closed it. They'd returned early from one of the highlights of the season. It must have been serious to so upset their host. She sighed. It was none of her business, but she felt a pull to be near him and stood to get dressed. For some reason, she didn't want him left alone with his struggles.

*

Walking quietly downstairs, Lou wasn't filled with self-doubt as other women might have been in a similar situation. She'd made a decision and was confident that it was the correct thing to do. Ignoring the motivation beneath her decision, she knocked quietly at the study door.

Losing a bit of confidence at the lack of sound from within the room, Lou turned the handle slowly and pushed open the door.

The room was smaller than the others on the ground floor. A large desk, placed near the shuttered windows dominated the room. One bookshelf filled a corner, but was not packed with books the way the library shelves were. Two leather chairs were placed in front of the fireplace rather than at each side of the fire, as was more common in such rooms. A small table, on which a decanter of brandy stood, separated the chairs. A hand held onto a glass, using the chair arm as support.

Lou hesitated. He obviously didn't want to be disturbed. She faltered slightly until she heard a heartfelt sigh, and that gave her the impetus she needed.

Closing the door and walking over to the empty chair, Lou sat down without looking at Simon.

"So away from our prying eyes, you revert to being a brandy drinker? The next thing you'll be telling me is that you don't actually like whisky!" she said, watching the fire.

Simon had purposely ignored the knock on the door, presuming it to be one of the servants. He was startled when Lou started to speak and had flashed her a look, unable to stop the smile at her words.

"I wouldn't dare face your disapprobation!" he responded.

"Good. I would hate to be disappointed," Lou beamed. "Now, what is this about your coming home early?"

Simon sighed again. "I didn't realise Henry had designs on Helena," he said rubbing a hand across his frown. He didn't falter in telling Lou his concerns as he had with her brother. She could annoy him and make him laugh, but he'd felt drawn to her from the start, and he wanted to speak to someone about his inner turmoil. Now that she was here, he could think of no one better than she.

Lou had the overwhelming urge to reach out and touch him. He seemed so alone, and she knew how a feeling of not being in control could unsettle one, but she restrained herself from moving.

"Does she have affection for him?" she asked.

"I'm fairly sure in thinking Henry would be the last person she would chose. And after this evening I can hardly blame her. I did not like the way he thought it was acceptable to speak to me about her as if she were a possession to own," Simon said through gritted teeth.

"Do you want a love match for your sister?" Lou asked gently.

"Isn't that what everyone wishes to have these days? My parents had a cold marriage, and I realise there are still marriages to obtain titles, land, or money, but deep down, I think most people would prefer a love match, wouldn't you say?"

Lou paused. "Yes. But sometimes the probability of that happening is remote."

"This is her first season. I refuse to contemplate such a cold marriage as Henry offers at this early stage! What am I saying? She is beautiful, considerate, and loving. There is someone out there who's worthy of her. Certainly not someone who wants to carry on with his single life after he is married!" Simon responded, angry at his friend.

"You're a good brother."

"I have mentioned to Helena that I think we should employ a chaperone. I need to get to it as soon as is feasible. I'm not cut-out for this," Simon groaned.

Lou boldly reached out and placed her hand over his. "Do not underestimate the support you give your sister. I'm speaking from experience. Having Cameron nearby is like having a weight lifted off my shoulders. I am sure Lady Helena feels the same. She is a confident young woman because she has your support."

Simon turned his hand so he could grasp Lou's. He squeezed her fingers gently. "Thank you. Although, don't underestimate yourself. Your sisters look to you as the person who can deal with anything."

"I thought I could," Lou admitted with a wry smile. "Look what a mess I made of things!"

"I am glad I didn't shoot to kill," Simon said quietly.

"As am I," Lou responded. "Although you are still marked for a beating of some form when I'm completely recovered."

Simon laughed, pulled Lou's hand to his mouth, and kissed her fingers. "I shall await with anticipation!"

Lou stood quickly. "I will win," she muttered, her cheeks flushed.

Simon smiled at her as she walked away. When she opened the door, he spoke. "Lady Lou."

"Yes?"

"Thank you for coming in here tonight. Things don't seem quite as weighty as they did."

"Good," Lou said with an answering smile before disappearing out of the room.

*

Lou was ready to go out and face her eldest brother. Duncan had never seemed to be linked to his younger siblings even though they shared the same father. He was only a few years older than Cameron, but in nature, outlook, and experience, they had nothing in common. He'd been indulged when his mother died, and the habit, once started, was hard to break. His step-mother had tried her best, but his self-absorption had alienated even her loving nature.

Cameron entered the morning room and smiled at Lou, who was already dressed in spencer and bonnet.

"Keen to get going?" he teased.

"Keen to give him a piece of my mind when he no longer has any control over us!" Lou responded.

"That will not be today, dear sister, so I expect ladylike behaviour," Cameron warned.

"Hmm," came the worrying response.

They walked to Duncan's abode, even though it was a number of streets away in Portman Square. Lou was keen to be outside after so many days of forced recuperation.

"I don't know why people like London so much," Lou said, as they crossed the road behind the road-sweeper, who cleared a path for them amid the detritus that filled the streets.

"It is the place to see and be seen," Cameron said. "It has its purpose, but I do miss home."

"As do I. I'll be glad when it is time to go," Lou responded, but for the first time, the highlands of Scotland weren't calling her back as much as they normally did. She would have to return home; she knew that, but there would be some sadness at leaving London. There would be no opportunity for her path to cross with the one who kept her mind in turmoil long into the night and was the first person she thought about on waking, something she wasn't about to admit to anyone quite yet.

"Once we have sorted this out, there is nothing keeping you here," Cameron said. "I think it would be good for the girls to have another year before they come out."

"I'm not sure they would agree with you!" Lou laughed.

On presenting his card, Cameron and Lou were shown into a small waiting area of the five-storey townhouse. A marble floor in the entrance gave a hint to the wealth of the leaseholder. Lou sat stiffly on a chair whilst Cameron stood impatiently.

A stern-faced butler returned to them and indicated they should follow him. Leading them into a drawing room, he announced them to Duncan and his wife.

Duncan was seated on the chair facing the door, his banyan flowing over the arms of the chair. He wore neither cravat nor waistcoat. He looked like his siblings with red hair and green eyes, but anyone looking closely would see a familial difference. His mouth was pinched, frown deeply engrained. He looked as if he enjoyed the finer things in life more, perhaps, than one should. A wide girth and bulbous nose gave hint to some of the excesses he enjoyed.

His wife was fully dressed in an outfit that was excessive for a day gown, being made of the finest silk. The jewels around her neck would never be considered subtle and would've usually been only retrieved from a safe for special occasions.

Lou bridled at the sight. She had been living in almost abject poverty when they arrived in London while her family displayed their wealth in such a gauche way. Her mouth set in a grim line.

"Not returned to Portugal yet, brother?" Duncan asked, without offering a seat.

"Not quite. I've some business to sort out," Cameron stated. "I am applying to take over guardianship of the girls."

Duncan immediately sat straighter. "What? I'm the head of the household! It is my responsibility!"

"You are never in Scotland. You do not spend any time with any of us, therefore you don't know the needs of the family," Cameron reasoned, not wishing to get into an argument quite so soon.

"Trifles!" Duncan dismissed with a wave of his hand. "If needs be, I can be contacted."

"I'm applying to the court. I have sought legal advice, and because of Glenloch Manor, I have a strong case that you are unsuitable," Cameron said roughly.

"How dare you!" Duncan spat, standing up and glaring at Cameron. "You cannot do that!"

"I can and I will," Cameron said, calmer than his brother. "You've already let us down, Duncan. I cannot return to Portugal and leave my sisters in your care. Goodness knows what I'd find on my return."

"How dare you speak to the head of your family in such a disrespectful way!" Lady Glenmire finally spoke. "Your brother has looked after everyone's interests in the years since your father died, and this is all the thanks you give!"

"He almost sold our home out from under us, you stupid woman!" Lou snapped at her sister-in-law.

"Don't speak to Fanny like that!" Duncan snapped, scowling at his sister. "This is exactly why I need to be in charge. Cameron lets you run wild!"

"As you are our guardian at present, there are flaws in your argument, brother dear!" Lou responded tartly.

"There's no point arguing about this, Duncan," Cameron interjected before a full-blown disagreement could develop. "I have taken legal advice. I was giving you the courtesy of warning you — something you overlooked when you tried to sell my property. You will be sent a court date within a week."

Duncan flashed a concerned look at his wife, but she subtly shook her head. The exchange was noticed by both Lou and Cameron, who were fully aware of the underhandedness of their relative.

"What is it?" Cameron demanded.

"Nothing!" Duncan responded quickly. Too quickly.

Cameron sighed. "What have you done?"

"Why do you always think the worst of me?" Duncan asked petulantly.

"We expect very little of you, and yet at every opportunity you still let us down," Lou said.

"Duncan, I haven't got the time or inclination for devious games. What aren't you telling me? It will come out in court, if not here," Cameron said, sick of the sight of his brother.

Duncan shifted, almost as if he wished to make his escape, but said nothing.

Lou narrowed her eyes. "How much is in each trust fund, Duncan?"

Duncan's immediate look of panic confirmed Lou had guessed right.

"What have you done, Duncan?" Cameron said, anger bubbling to the surface.

"It is all under control!" Duncan said defensively. "Lou only comes into her fund when she's five and twenty. There are years before then. Heather and Marianne have even longer until they come into their inheritance."

"How much is in each fund, Duncan?" Lou repeated quietly.

"By the time you reach your majority, there will be the amount you're expecting! There or there about!" Duncan snapped.

Cameron stepped forward. He might be younger than his brother by six years, but he was a cavalry man whose physique was in prime condition. "I want to see what is in the trusts. Now. Show me the paperwork."

"There is nothing to show," Duncan responded paling at the expression on Cameron's face.

"What? It's all gone?" Lou gasped, sinking into the nearest chair.

"Answer our sister, Duncan," Cameron said, his tone low.

"I invested the money," Duncan said quickly. "I wanted to make more for our sisters, but the investments failed. I'll be able to replace the money by the time Lou needs hers. Hopefully."

"What investments?" Cameron asked, his blood was at boiling point, but he was trying to remain calm whilst he found out exactly what was going on.

"Some shipping scheme or other, but the ship sank without insurance. Damned unfortunate, but I will rally!"

"Just use some of your own inheritance to replace it," Cameron said, half-expecting what the reply was going to be.

"Ah, well, you see. About that. There isn't anything left as such. Keeping three establishments going costs quite a bit. We are not all fortunate enough to live in tents!" Duncan said.

"That is why you tried to sell the manor, isn't it?" Cameron asked. "You have run out of money."

"I would like to see you fare any better!" Lady Glenmire snapped.

"We have nothing," Lou said with a sob. She would hate herself later that she'd shown any weakness to Duncan, but the emotion her brother's words had caused was too overwhelming to contain.

"You will just have to marry a rich man!" Duncan said cheerfully.

"Who would take us without any dowry at all?" Lou snapped. "You destroyed our chances before we even ventured out into the world."

"Oh, stop being dramatic!" Duncan snapped. "You always were prone to overstating the matter."

Lou shot out of her seat so fast Duncan sat back in his chair as if wanting to blend into the actual material, but Cameron moved and caught hold of Lou.

"No, Lou. You've been hurt. I do not want to see you injuring yourself further on this wastrel," Cameron said.

"Wastrel! I am a well-respected member of Society!" Duncan snapped.

"We will see how long that lasts when it's made common knowledge what you have done and who you have injured," Cameron bit back. "You are not the only one to have well connected friends."

"You won't publicly shame me. It would affect us all," Duncan said smugly.

"I can and I will," Cameron responded. "But first I have something else I need to do." He pulled Duncan out of his seat by the lapels of his banyan.

"What are you doing?" Duncan asked, before receiving a punch that was so swift in reaching its target, he didn't have time to blink, let alone avoid the impact.

Duncan fell back into the seat he'd vacated, but Cameron dragged him back out. "Oh, no! You're not cowering for this Duncan. This has been a long time coming."

With his words, Cameron let fly his fists and rammed one firm fist after another into his brother. It didn't seem to matter where the punches landed as long as they found their target. Lady

Glenmire screamed, which brought the servants running into the room, but Lou put up her fists in readiness.

"I'm presuming none of you are being paid enough by this damned cur to put yourself in a fight with a woman who is prepared to fight dirty," Lou said.

As Duncan and Fanny had never treated any staff with consideration or kindness, none were willing to risk even minor injury for their employer, so instead of helping, they stood watching the spectacle.

When Duncan lay crumpled on the floor, Cameron stopped his bombardment. Apart from his hands there was no injury on any part of him. He was breathless but stood over his brother.

"If I ever see you again, I shall inflict the same on you, no matter where you are or who you are with. I will make my solicitor aware of what has happened, and we shall sue for recompense. I'm sure you can sell a household or two," Cameron said with a growl. He turned to the servants. "If this man casts you off without a reference, write to me, and I shall provide a glowing one for every member of staff, if needs be, but I suggest you start to look for other employment. The fortunes of Lord and Lady Glenmire are in a bad state."

"You can't do this! How can you treat your family so poorly?" Fanny cried.

"How dare you utter such words after what you have done?" Cameron asked incredulously. "I will be telling everyone in my acquaintance of how you've injured your sisters — both of you."

"We'll be ostracised! We won't be able to stay in London!"

"Perfect retribution then! Come, Lou. I need to find something cool before my knuckles seize," Cameron said.

The butler rushed out of the door before Cameron, uttering, "If you'd kindly wait, sir."

Cameron waited in the hallway and smiled when the butler returned moments later. "That is decent of you, thank you," he said, accepting the towel that had ice wrapped in its middle.

"It is the least I could do after your kind offer, Captain," the butler said seriously. "Most of us have stayed in our employ purely in fear of receiving a poor reference."

Cameron shook his head, only imagining how poorly they must have been treated. "If you want to leave immediately, I will write references. Send the requests to number ten Half Moon Street if it's in the next week."

"I think it will be within the next few days, Captain," the butler said, as servants started to climb the stairs as the news travelled. They used the main staircase in their hurry to reach their personal belongings and leave.

Cameron smiled. "I shall await the correspondence. Good day to you and good luck."

"Thank you, Captain," the butler responded, before closing the door and starting up the stairs himself.

Chapter 11

Cameron hailed a hackney as soon as they were outside. The brother and sister didn't say a word as they clambered into the vehicle.

As they seated themselves, Cameron took hold of Lou's hand. "I'll sort this out, Lou," he said gently. He had never seen Lou wear such an expression of abject sadness.

Lou was quiet for a few moments. Cameron wondered if she hadn't heard him. Eventually meeting Cameron's worried gaze, Lou tried to smile. "You cannot. Not this time. No matter what you do, you cannot create money enough for three sisters. He has all but ruined us."

"I will do as I threatened. He must have things to sell," Cameron insisted.

"It could take years," Lou said, looking out of the hackney window. She couldn't face the pity in Cameron's eyes. "Don't waste your time and your own money Cameron. It is not worth losing what little is left of father's legacy to us all. We're already going to be burden enough on you."

"You would never be that," Cameron said gently.

Lou couldn't answer, so she remained quiet. Her throat burned with the need to scream, shout, and cry out in frustration and anger. What frightened her the most was a sadness that snaked its tentacles around her heart and squeezed. Her life no longer had options. She had a title but no funds and few friends. What made her saddest of all was the realisation that she could no longer have a season and be in Simon's company. She hated to admit it, but that was the hardest thing to accept. She might have talked about returning to Scotland, but inside, deep inside, she'd hoped for more time with him. She would have to push that longing firmly away. It was lost. Very few would want a penniless spinster of one and twenty. For the first time, her age would work against her. A young lady with a fortune wasn't given the label of old maid quite as quickly as a poor one.

The pair remained silent until they arrived at Half Moon Street. Entering the hallway, they met Simon and Helena coming out of the study. The siblings had been laughing over something but immediately sobered when they saw the serious faces of their two visitors.

"What is it?" Helena asked in concern.

Lou shook her head sadly. Their new friends would have to be told, but she couldn't face their commiseration at the moment. "I'll tell Heather and Marianne," she said quietly to Cameron before, with a regretful glance at Simon, she went slowly upstairs. Tears stung her eyes, making her blink, but she could not give in to the desolation she felt. She needed to be strong for her sisters.

"Drummond, you look fit to drop. Come into the study," Simon said firmly.

"Only if whisky is on offer. Lots of it," Cameron said with a small smile, but for once, the smile didn't reach his eyes.

"As much as you can stomach," Simon responded, leading the way. Helena followed the pair into the recently vacated room and pulled a footstool up to her brother's chair and perched herself on it.

Cameron sat down and accepted the large glass of whisky. Taking a gulp, he let the liquid soothe him. "It's such a damned mess!" he said quietly. "Lady Helena, I beg your pardon for my base language."

Helena inclined her head slightly, acknowledging the apology, but not speaking. She wanted Cameron to be able to speak without restriction.

Then Cameron started to speak, explaining in a dull voice what had happened, while Simon and Helena both listened in shock.

"That's a low thing to do!" Simon said at the end. "I agree with you; they should be made to pay, but cases such as these can take decades in the courts. It could cost a fortune to pursue a claim. Your brother would be motivated to cause as much delay as possible."

"Yes. And a captain's pay, even with my inheritance supplementing it, which thankfully I have already received, wouldn't stand years of legal fees if I did decide to take him through the courts. I suppose the reality is, the best I can do for my sisters is offer them a home and hope that they can make some sort of marriage without a dowry," Cameron said.

Simon pushed aside his inner feelings. This was not a time for selfish longings. Even though he could offer much, he would not be accepted if he offered out of pity. He had never considered offering for Lou until that moment, but the feeling of protectiveness at Cameron's news threatened to make him rush upstairs and declare that she, at least, would be secure.

Simon focused on Cameron. "You have a place here for as long as you need it."

"Thank you. Again," Cameron said.

"Could I not share my dowry?" Helena asked quietly. "It seems unfair for me to have such a large advantage over my friends. I wouldn't mind having a smaller settlement."

Cameron smiled at Helena. "That is an offer of assistance I couldn't accept," he said gently. "But the offer does you credit, Lady Helena."

"It's just so wrong!" Helena said, clearly upset. "We had so many plans!"

"I'm sorry. The reality is, we had best start making arrangements to head home. I will remain with the girls until they are settled back in, and then I will return to Portugal. The sooner they become accustomed to a quiet life the better."

Simon knew without doubt that such a life would stifle Lou. He couldn't bear the thought of her being hundreds of miles away from him, but he could not act rashly. She was a proud woman, and he couldn't respond to their new circumstances in a way that would risk losing her. If she thought he made any offer out of sympathy for her situation, she would reject him without hesitation.

"Oh no! Please let's have the dinner party we have been planning!" Helena appealed. "We are all so looking forward to it."

"I don't think it's a good idea," Cameron said gently.

"They have been planning it for days," Simon reasoned. "Perhaps it is the thing to lift their spirits?" He wanted to delay their return as much as possible. For different reasons than Helena did, or so he presumed.

"Maybe. I'll speak to Lou about it," Cameron acceded.

"Thank you," Helena said. "We have planned to invite guests who will dance; Lady Heather and Marianne are keen to dance."

A flash of pain crossed Cameron's face, but it was soon disguised. Simon looked at his hand, still wrapped in a towel.

"You're dripping on the floor, Drummond. Are your knuckles very sore?"

"Worth every moment of stiffness," Cameron growled. "I should get rid of this."

"Let me," Helena said, jumping up immediately. "Would you like something cool?"

"A fresh towel and some more ice would be appreciated," Cameron admitted.

"I will get it immediately."

Helena left the room, and Simon looked at Cameron. "I am sorry it has come to this."

"As am I, but I should've expected as much. Duncan has always been self-centred and concerned only with his own needs. He will have justified to himself why he was more deserving than our sisters for the money. He's a disgrace. The only small comfort in all of this is that he isn't a full blood relation," Cameron said angrily.

"Does he take after his mother?" Simon asked.

"Not really from what I've been told. I think it's from too much indulgence when she died and then even more so when we came along," Cameron admitted. "I could kick myself for being so naïve! I should have argued to be joint guardian!"

"It isn't your fault," Simon reasoned. "Expecting money to remain in a trust fund is a reasonable assumption to make."

"Not in Duncan's case, obviously."

"Well, if he was willing to sell property that didn't belong to him, joint guardianship wouldn't even have slowed him down. There was nothing you could have done."

They were interrupted by the butler who announced that Lord Ince had come to pay a visit to Simon. Cameron moved to stand-up. "I will leave you to your guest," he said, not wishing to see the man he had disliked on sight. He wasn't in the mood for polite conversation and didn't think his fists would stand inflicting another beating if the dandy was disparaging towards Lady Helena.

"No! Stay where you are," Simon insisted. "I will see him in the library. Drink as much as you wish. You will not be disturbed."

"Don't tempt me! You could return to find a roaring drunk and your stocks depleted," Cameron said with a pained smile as Simon left the room.

Helena returned shortly after her brother had left. She looked in surprise at Cameron. "Has Simon abandoned you?"

Cameron smiled. "No. Lord Ince has arrived for a visit. He is with him in the library."

"Oh. I see. Good," Helena responded before indicating Cameron should hold out his hand to her. She moved the footstool across to Cameron and used a bandage to secure a cloth containing ice onto his knuckles. "That should help."

"Thank you," Cameron said.

"I'm glad my brother has gone," Helena started, flushing a deep red. "I would like to talk to you privately, if I might?"

"Yes, of course," Cameron said, curious as to what she was going to say.

"I understand, why my dowry could not be split between your sisters and myself," Helena started. "But I have been thinking… "

"Please don't fret," Cameron soothed. "We aren't destitute!"

"Oh! I know! I do not wish to cause offence. But I was thinking. It would solve quite a few things if... " Helena faltered.

Cameron frowned. "What are you proposing, Lady Helena?" he asked.

"W-well, you need to marry, and I have a large dowry... " Helena said in a rush.

Cameron faltered. He didn't want to cause offence, but he couldn't let such a foolish scheme continue, and there was something else he felt: disappointment that she would sacrifice herself so easily. "Lady Helena," he said gently.

"Oh, I know you don't love me! But you like me, do you not? I think we would rub along together well enough. And I don't mind following the camp. I truly don't!" Helena babbled, her cheeks crimson.

Cameron reached over and took her hands in his. "Thank you," he said quietly.

"Then you will agree to marry me?" Helena asked hopefully.

"No. I cannot. You are worth more than a marriage of convenience."

"But I like you," Helena said quickly.

"I know. And I like you. But it wouldn't do, Lady Helena. I want you to enjoy flirting with many men before you settle down. When that happens, you deserve a husband who would dote on you the way any new wife should be doted on," Cameron said, his tone gentle, his eyes looking into hers while he kept hold of her hands. What she'd offered touched him deeply.

"I've made a fool of myself!" Helena moaned.

"No! Not at all! You are one of the most beautiful women of my acquaintance and have the best of hearts to match. You are truly special, and I thank you for your offer, but I would hate to see you unhappy in a marriage you had offered because you are good and not because you're in love," Cameron assured her. "And let us be honest. If I don't survive the battlefield, my sisters will have my funds to share among them!"

"Don't say that!" Helena exclaimed, mortified.

"You are a wonderful young woman." Cameron smiled at the force of Helena's words.

"All this praise, and yet you still say no," Helena responded, a little confused.

"Because it's a marriage for the wrong reasons. We each need to choose a partner whom we love deeply."

"And you could not do that with me?" Helena asked, unable to stop the desperation sounding in her voice.

Cameron knew he had to be cruel to be kind. She was young, naïve, and lovely. He couldn't let her waste herself on him. Not when he was going back to war. "No. I'm sorry."

Helena rose, and Cameron mirrored the action. He could see the mortification on her face and had to make things easy between them. "I would like something from you. Well two things, actually," he said with a smile.

"Anything," Helena said.

"I need a friend. My sisters need a friend. You have been steadfast in your support, and I'd like to know that when I am away, they have your friendship to rely on."

"Of course!" Helena answered quickly.

"The next thing is a little more difficult to ask for, so perhaps I will just do it," Cameron said before putting his hands gently on her waist and leaning in to kiss her on the lips. It wasn't a passionate kiss, but it wasn't chaste either. It was one that left each of them longing for more.

When Cameron ended the embrace, he kissed Helena's nose gently. "You are a beautiful woman, Lady Helena. Don't ever forget that. I could easily have agreed to marry you and been perfectly happy, but you deserve better than me. Be my friend, please?"

He didn't know why he'd needed to kiss her, but he had. It could be considered cruel, but although he said he didn't wish to marry her, he hoped the kiss would reassure her she was desirable. She was everything he wanted in a wife, but he couldn't ask her to follow the drum or wait for him. If she was still unmarried, and if he managed to survive whatever he was going to face, he would offer for her then. But he wouldn't ask for her to waste years of her life because of her affection for him. He wasn't sure how he'd be able to face a life without her, she'd so quickly affected him, but his sense of what was right was strong enough for him to act unaffected by her.

Helena forced herself to open her eyes. The kiss had been everything she'd dreamed of since meeting the magnificent captain. The words took a moment to register, and although they could have been crushing, they offered her a little hope.

She smiled at Cameron and reached up on her tip-toes, kissing him gently on the lips in an act of brazenness she'd never experienced before. "I will always be your friend," she whispered before turning away from him and leaving the room.

Leaving the study she smiled to herself. He had feelings for her. She was sure of it, and if she could, she was going to help him see the error of his ways. He was the only man she wanted and would ever want.

Chapter 12

Simon had gone into the library with some reservations. Henry and he hadn't left each other on the best of terms, and he wondered what Henry wanted with him.

Henry stood as Simon came into the room, a smile on his face. "Garswood! I'm glad you agreed to see me. I have an apology to make!"

"Oh?" Simon asked, offering a drink that was given a nod of acceptance.

"I don't know what got into me. Some of the blue devils, I think!" Henry said cheerfully.

"I doubt blue devils had anything to do with the words you uttered about my sister," Simon said, offering a brandy when perhaps he should have shown Henry the door.

"I know, and I am ashamed of them," Henry acknowledged. "Look, I need to be honest. I am like a smitten fool around Lady Helena. Which for most of the time, has me acting like an idiot. I want to worship her every day of my life, but I will understand if you send me away after you've boxed my ears for my impertinence!"

Simon frowned. "You did not talk of being smitten. She seemed to have the dubious pleasure of being nothing more than a commodity."

"I know. I suppose I didn't like admitting to you how much she has turned my head. I'd look after her as she deserves if she agreed to be my wife," Henry continued.

"I am pretty certain she doesn't feel the same way about you," Simon cautioned.

"All I am asking for is the chance to plead my case," Henry said. "If she refuses, I'll accept her decision and never mention the subject again."

"I don't want her being put under pressure, Henry!"

"On my honour, I wouldn't dare! Let me court her, but if she rejects me, I will withdraw gracefully. I have been maudlin these last days without you both in my company. I am not going to risk our friendship again."

"You behaved like a cad."

"I did. I'm ashamed of it. Truly, it is not me. Have you never felt completely at a loss and uncertain of your future because of the effects of a beautiful woman? That is how your sister makes me feel. It is terrifying and uplifting at the same time. I promise you, I have only her best interests at heart," Henry said with an unusual amount of sincerity in his words.

Simon could completely understand his feelings as they seemed to reflect some of the inner turmoil he was feeling himself. He wouldn't normally have capitulated quite so easily, but Henry had struck a chord with him, and he relented. "Fine. Good," Simon said.

They continued to chat before Henry turned the subject round to the visitors. "Is our highwayman still under this roof?" he asked.

"Yes. For now. I think they are to return to Scotland in a few days. Helena is organising a small party before they leave."

"I hope I'm invited," Henry said.

"Why would you want to attend when you think I have been out of my mind since that first evening?" Simon asked incredulously.

"If they are a pet-project of Lady Helena's, I'll support her. I will dance with thieves and vagabonds all day if it means she looks more favourably on me!" Henry said.

"You must be smitten!" Simon said with a shake of his head. He accepted Henry's apology, but he would be watching his friend a lot more closely than he had in the past. If he showed any sign of the behaviour he'd shown at the ball, Simon would terminate their acquaintance completely. He'd seen an ugly side to Henry, and he wasn't convinced that it was a one-time lapse of judgement.

*

Lou had explained to Heather and Marianne about their new position in life. Both had been shocked and deeply upset at Duncan's betrayal.

"He's injured us in the worst way possible!" Heather said in disgust.

"Yes. To some extent he has," Lou admitted.

"We need to find positions as companions or governesses," Marianne said. "It's silly the way I planned our futures out. I always presumed we would be settled close to each other, but now we could be hundreds of miles apart."

Lou knew how much the words cost Marianne. The twins had never been separated even when one was ill. The other would insist on staying with her ailing sister whether the condition was infectious or not.

"I don't think Cameron would agree to that scheme. Just yet. He wants us to return to Scotland and keep house for him until he comes home for good. We can leave any big decisions until then," Lou said.

"Oh Lou, we cannot let Cameron keep us!" Marianne said. "Better to start now than to wait until he is struggling to fund everything. I'd hate to be a burden on him."

"As would I," Lou said. "He's already paid for all our new clothes. It must have cost him dearly. It seems so unfair!" she snapped.

"I am glad Cameron drew Duncan's cork!" Heather said with gritted teeth.

"It was a little more than that," Lou admitted. "I doubt Duncan will be fit to be seen for a sennight or more!"

"Good! The scoundrel! That was our money! Our security!" Heather ground out.

"I'm sorry the news is not better. We will return to Scotland after Lady Helena's party. I am afraid there's no hope of a season for any of us."

The way her sisters were crushed at her words made Lou need to escape. It was pouring rain when she eventually excused herself from them, so she couldn't find solace outside. She went instead to the long gallery and walked quickly up and down the long room.

"Should I order new flooring? It seems the current one will wear out earlier than expected," came Simon's voice from behind Lou.

She spun around and faced him. "I wish I could have run Duncan through with a sword! In fact that would have been too quick for him! He deserves a slow and painful death for what he's done!"

"Any particular sword?" Simon asked in amusement. He was concerned for Lou, sympathetic to her plight, but it didn't stop him from being diverted by her outpourings.

"Whilst we're in London, I suppose it would have to be a fencing sword. You are too soft down here to fight with decent weapons," Lou said with derision.

"He's done you all a great disservice," Simon said quietly, becoming serious.

Lou sighed. "I did not expect a great come out. I never have really. Balls are not my idea of a good evening. But Heather and Marianne... " She faltered, choking on the words.

"Is there no hope Lord Glenmire will return any of the money? I have spoken to your brother, and he agreed there's no point in pursuing it through the courts. Perhaps he will find it in his conscience to give you a little?"

"No! He would never do that! He's a complete buffoon! They were not huge dowries, but they were enough to secure a decent marriage. He has condemned them to remain spinsters. He has condemned all of us."

"Not all marriages need dowries," Simon soothed, seeing how much the betrayal was hurting Lou.

"I wanted them to marry decent men. The chances of that happening now are remote at best. I have left them planning what positions they think they are qualified for," Lou said. "I didn't think things could get worse when I came down to London and realised I was completely out of my depth and had no one to turn to, but now, this! I just don't know how to make it right!" She shrugged her shoulders, unable to carry on speaking because of the tears brimming in her eyes.

"Oh, Lou! You can't solve everything by yourself. None of us are invincible," Simon said, moving towards her.

"I thought I was! I was that much of an idiot! I am the biggest fool of us all!" Lou sobbed as the tears that had been bottled up since she'd arrived in London were released.

Simon reached her in one stride and wrapped his arms around her, holding her to himself as she broke down. He knew how strong she usually was and guessed she rarely cried. It pulled at his heart to know how much she must be hurting.

He didn't try to soothe her; she needed to cry, and if it took all day, he was going to let her release her frustration. He held her close, rubbing his hand along her back in a slow, comforting movement. He needed no shallow words that would assure her things would be well. He couldn't give her false platitudes when it was clear the situation was so difficult for them all.

They stood together, his head rested on hers, her head buried in his shoulder. No one disturbed them; no one saw the touching act of support and tenderness.

Eventually Lou's sobs eased, and she rested her face against the damp woollen material of his frock coat. She could hear his heartbeat, strong, steady, and soothing, and for the first time in her life, she allowed herself to feel protected by someone outside her family. It felt right. It felt good and would leave a feeling of loss when she pulled away.

Lou shifted slightly. She had to retake control of the situation. She'd never shown vulnerability to anyone before, and it left her feeling uncertain and unsure. "I'd send your coat to be cleaned if I were you. It has had a torrent of tears on it."

Simon smiled into her hair. "I go to the finest tailors. If the material fails, I'll be demanding a refund!"

"I am sorry," Lou said quietly, not responding to the light-hearted quip.

"Don't be. I know what it must have cost you to finally let go. And it had its benefits… "

"Do not utter another word!" Lou said with a choke. "I want to maintain the illusion of finding one decent man in the world, apart from Cameron!"

Simon chuckled. "In that case, I won't! But please promise me you will seek me out if you need to do that again."

"I won't, but I will promise, nevertheless. I know how fragile a man's self-worth is."

Simon squeezed Lou. "Hoyden!" he said affectionately.

"I do have one problem I hadn't considered," Lou admitted.

"Oh?"

"How to get away from you without you seeing my blotched and swollen face. I was not crying daintily as ladies are expected to do. It will not be a pretty sight."

"You will always be beautiful to me, so just do it," Simon said with a kiss to the top of Lou's head before she moved.

Lou was right, she was blotchy-skinned with swollen eyes, but to Simon she looked as beautiful as she ever had. She looked at Simon wryly. "Thank you. I'm now going to attempt a dignified exit."

"You should attempt an abusive one. It is what I have come to expect," Simon said, purposely lightening the mood.

Lou smiled. "I will let you be today since you've been such a gentleman."

"Praise indeed!" Simon grinned. "But I shan't be foolish enough to let it go to my head!"

"I would not. Normal conditions will be resumed tomorrow," Lou said with a watery smile before leaving Simon alone.

Simon stood looking out the window at the busy street. He longed to be out in the open where he could think everything through. London never seemed to offer him that same peace as the countryside did. He was smitten. He was worse than smitten, but he didn't know what to do about it. If he offered for her, she would presume it was out of pity. The situation was damned sensitive, but the closer it came to her leaving, the less he felt he could face it.

Helena entered the long gallery and seemed surprised to see her brother. "Are you hiding from us all?" she asked joining him at the window.

"No. Just longing for the view from home," Simon answered honestly.

"When the captain and his sisters leave, can we leave London at the same time?" Helena asked.

"Really?" Simon asked in surprise. "I know you said you weren't really enjoying the season, but taking yourself away from it will put you at a disadvantage Helena."

"At this moment, I honestly do not care," Helena said. She was still reeling from what had passed between Cameron and herself.

"There's someone who wishes to marry you, if you would have him," Simon said gently.

"Who?" her heart leapt. Could Cameron have had a change of heart?

"Henry."

The disappointment was almost crushing. "Oh."

"That doesn't sound very hopeful for him. I know you have said before he is a little harsh, but I didn't know whether it was a dislike of him or if you felt a little unsure of him because you are an innocent in the ways of Society," Simon explained.

"I do not like him, Simon, and it has nothing to do with my lack of experience," Helena tried to explain. "He makes me feel uncomfortable, and I don't think he's very nice. He tries to hide it most of the time, but there is a coldness there that frightens me."

Simon thought back to his conversation with Henry in the ballroom and couldn't disagree with Helena's assessment. "I am sorry he makes you feel that way. You've no need to socialise with him if you would rather not. I can keep our acquaintance to when I attend the clubs. I've no need to encourage him as much as I have been doing."

"It is fine, honestly. It would be foolish of me to hide from the acquaintance at this point," Helena assured her brother. "But I am glad you know the truth. It would make things awkward between you if we were to start avoiding him now. But if you could have a word with him I would be grateful. I'd rather not have to go through an embarrassing conversation with him, especially as he would want to do it in private."

"I will choose my moment. Probably after our party; there is no need to cause any upset before it," Simon said. "Don't worry. I'll be more alert to his attentions to you in future if we do return to town. I promise I shall not abandon you to him!"

"Thank you!" Helena said. She didn't think she could face another embarrassing conversation about her marital state. It was going to be a long time before she would be able to peer in her looking glass without cringing in mortification.

Chapter 13

The following morning Helena received some correspondence while the ladies were gathered over breakfast.

"More acceptances to our little soiree!" Helena said.

"How many will be attending?" Heather asked, tucking into thick slices of ham.

"Quite a few," Helena responded, buttering a warm bread roll. "In parties it's usual to have equal numbers of men and women, but I confess there will be slightly more men at our gathering. I decided brothers don't count!"

"Good! Cameron dances like a bull. Not elegant in the slightest," Lou said.

Helena flushed slightly but managed to laugh with the others. She hadn't seen Cameron since her foolish offer, and she was sure she'd give something away if she had to face him. Thankfully, he'd gone out the previous evening, preventing her from the mortification of sitting opposite him at supper.

"There's Lord Ince, who I'm afraid I really do not like, but since he is one of Simon's closest friends, I couldn't avoid inviting him. Then there are the Atkinsons, a lovely family with two eligible sons. I have also invited Maria and Jane Walsh, although at nineteen, they're a little older than we are but perfectly lovely," Helena looked down her list.

"Is Captain Philips attending?" Heather asked, turning a little pink.

"Of course, as is Captain Wilmslow and Mr Bibby and Mr Lucas," Helena responded. "In all we should be about thirty people, most willing to dance! Mrs Atkinson has kindly offered to play the pianoforte for as long as we would wish."

"Her fingers will be sore!" Marianne exclaimed.

"She's a very good sort," Helena smiled. "I am really looking forward to dancing alongside you."

"It's very kind of you to go to all this trouble, especially as we will be leaving two days later," Lou said, once more overwhelmed by the way the family had taken them in and accepted them.

"I wish you could all stay longer, but I understand the urge to see your own home," Helena responded diplomatically. "We shall make sure it is a night to remember!"

Simon entered the breakfast room and looked at Lou. A subtle raise of his brows in an unspoken question and a slight smile from Lou was all that was silently communicated between them, but it was enough to reassure him that she was suffering no lasting effects from the previous day.

"Helena, do you wish to join me on a ride around Hyde Park?" Simon asked. "You have not been out very much these last days."

"That's because I prefer the company indoors to that outdoors," Helena said.

"If I arrange the top down on the carriage would you like to join us, Lady Heather, Lady Marianne?"

"Oh, yes, please!" came the chorus.

"In that case, I will meet you in the hallway in ten minutes," Simon said before leaving the room.

The three girls quickly finished what was on their plates before leaving hurriedly to dress in their finest daywear. Lou was left alone. She smiled at Simon's offer. He hadn't included her, probably because he was aware that she wouldn't have enjoyed the trip as her sisters would.

Cameron entered the room looking amused. "I've just nearly been flattened by the three of them running upstairs. Is there something exciting I should not miss out on?"

"A carriage ride around Hyde Park," Lou said in amusement.

"Ah. I see. I think breakfast is preferable," Cameron said, helping himself to a pile of food.

"Lady Helena is doing everything in her power to make the party something special. It's almost as if she wants us all to receive offers of marriage as a result of it. It seems such a waste of effort since yesterday," Lou said, after nodding to the footman that they could be left alone.

Cameron looked at Lou and smiled. "She is very good."

Lou grinned at her brother. "Are you a little smitten with our hostess?"

Cameron looked uncomfortable. "A little. A lot actually."

"Oh! She is very beautiful," Lou acknowledged. "Are we going to have an announcement after all?"

Cameron paused. "If I tell you the whole, you are not to utter a word or make any of your sharp comments to the girl. I do not want to torture her any more than she's probably already doing to herself."

"Now, I am completely intrigued, which means I give you my firm promise of my discretion. Even though it might kill me," Lou said.

Cameron smiled at his sister's remark, but he couldn't inflict any pain on Helena, even indirectly. "She proposed to me yesterday," he said simply.

Lou looked stunned before choking out, "Lady Helena? Proposed to you?"

"Yes."

"My goodness! I've underestimated her! The girl has spirit!"

"She does."

"And can I ask why, if you say you are enamoured with her, are you not announcing your engagement this morning? I know it's a little unconventional, but well done, Lady Helena!" Lou said admiringly.

"I have said no."

"Now I'm completely confused," Lou responded.

"She wanted me to have her dowry," Cameron admitted.

"Ah. Oh. Blasted Duncan!" Lou cursed.

"Exactly. I could quite happily strangle the fool."

"That was the one thing you didn't do," Lou responded with a slight smile. "It was a kind offer from Lady Helena though. This family have certainly tried to help us. I am not sure other members of London Society would have acted in the same way."

"Nor am I," Cameron agreed.

"You could marry her. Forgetting about the dowry for a moment. If you like her, and let us be honest, she hasn't any faults — which grieves me to say about any human being, as until now, I was convinced everyone was flawed," Lou said.

"Praise indeed! I could wed, but does it make sense that I want to choose my own wife? The money would make our lives easier, but I cannot agree to it. But in addition to that, I cannot allow her to attach herself to me when I'm facing a battle. I have to be aware of the fact that I might not return," Cameron responded.

"I don't like it when you speak so, but I understand completely your hesitation. You would never receive any condemnation from me for not taking the opportunity, but she could be the best person you ever meet. Would you not be afraid of missing out on the opportunity to secure her?"

"Now she's made the offer, there would always be the doubt that I had married her for her money," Cameron admitted. "I do not want to start married life on that footing if I do survive my return to battle."

"In the meantime, she could receive an offer of her own," Lou pointed out gently. "She is beautiful, titled, and wealthy. Tempting in this world. And you'll be in Portugal or Spain."

"That's the thought that kept me awake half the night," Cameron admitted. "But I'm not changing my mind. It is too much to ask of anyone, especially her. I won't have her wasting years of her life on waiting for me. It's not fair."

"Then I hope you don't come to regret your decision," Lou said, standing and moving around to the side of the table where her brother sat. "We could both be considered foolish in recent months. I have had a second chance when I should have been hanging from the gallows. Don't rely on the fact that you might get another opportunity at happiness. We are not that lucky."

*

Heather was delighted when she saw Captain Philips riding towards them in Hyde Park. He was travelling with another gentleman, who looked very dark and exotic. All the women quietly admired the two men approaching them.

"Good morning, ladies, Lord Garswood," Michael Philips said as he approached the group. "I hope you are well?"

After the ladies had welcomed him, he turned to the gentleman at his side. "Please let me introduce my good friend to you. This is Joseph Anderton, he's a captain for one of the finest ships to sail the seas and very rarely home. I couldn't not join him this morning as he will be gone once more next week."

"It is very nice to make your acquaintance," Heather said.

"Captain Anderton, it's a pleasure to meet you," Helena stated. "We are having a small party in two days. If you are not otherwise engaged, we would love for you to come. Your friend is already attending."

Joseph smiled. "That would be lovely, thank you, Lady Helena. My friend is as keen as myself to spend time in company as much as possible whilst still on shore."

"Well, that's settled then!" Helena said happily. "Come prepared to dance, Captain. Before my friends leave for their Scottish home, I've promised them many reels!"

"In that case, could I secure the first two with you, Lady Helena?" Joseph asked smoothly.

"Oh, I didn't speak about dancing to beg for a partner. Please do not think I did! But I will happily accept your offer," Helena said with a flush. She would rather have started the evening with Cameron, but after their exchange, she wasn't even sure he would ask her.

"Might I claim the first two with you, Lady Heather?" Captain Philips asked quickly.

"Yes. Thank you," Heather said, blushing furiously, but looking as pleased as punch.

"Lady Marianne, I'd like to claim my dances if I may?" Simon said quickly, not wishing the young girl to feel left out.

"Of course," Marianne said with pleasure.

The two gentlemen soon rode away, congratulating themselves on securing time with pretty young women and looking forward to an enjoyable evening. As the ladies watched their retreating backs, Simon smiled at his sister.

"Are there going to be any ladies at this gathering apart from the four staying in our home?" he asked with a grin.

"Unfortunately, I could not be so poor a hostess, but I would have preferred it that way," Helena admitted with a smile.

"I thought as much. I am glad I've secured two dances with you Lady Marianne. I feel as host I shall be standing at the side-lines for much of the evening," Simon said.

"Oh, stop!" Helena laughed. "You are too old to be bothered about dancing!"

Simon looked slightly stunned. "I shall remind you about this conversation when you are six and twenty, dear sister."

Chapter 14

Everyone was excited about the entertainments. Helena had experienced the pleasure of seeing Cameron a little put-out when he'd asked for the first two dances and she was able to inform him that she was already taken. She wasn't in any way gloating or vindictive, but it gave her confidence a little boost to appear wanted by another. Cameron had to settle for the third and fourth dances.

Lou dressed carefully for the evening. She had long given up trying to convince herself that she wasn't attracted to the handsome Lord Garswood. He was so much more than the aristocrat she'd growled at in those first few days. She was ashamed to remember her words. She knew her feelings would come to naught. Men had to be careful in choosing their life-partners as much as women did, but she could dream for one night that she had no cares in the world and was just the same as everyone else.

Wearing a pale apple-green dress with darker Pomona green edging, which set-off her colouring perfectly, she fixed her hair in the style she preferred, a tumble of curls cascading from a high bun. Curls on the top of her head gave her extra height. She perhaps should have chosen a lighter colour, still being a debutante, but she was drawn to colour, rather than the white and creams debutantes were expected to wear. It wouldn't matter after tonight, so her choice had been made with consideration as to what suited her.

Smiling into the mirror before she joined the others in the drawing room, she was pleased with the way she looked. It was probably the anticipation of the two dances she was to enjoy with Simon that gave her the sparkling eyes and flushed cheeks. She was determined to relish every moment of their time together. She refused to dwell on their parting. Those maudlin thoughts were for another day.

The drawing room was filled with chatter when Lou entered. It appeared she was one of the last to arrive. Taking in the view, she felt a pang of regret. Heather and Marianne were doing what young girls should be doing at their age: flirting with new acquaintances. It was wrong that they were going to miss out in the future.

Cameron approached her with a knowing look on his face. "Come, Lou. No time for melancholy thoughts tonight."

Lou smiled. "You are right. There isn't. Tonight is for enjoyment; tomorrow can look after itself."

"That's the spirit! Now I hope you are not engaged for the first two. I find myself usurped by the handsome young captain over there," Cameron said, looking at where Helena and Marianne were chatting with the newcomer.

"And you aren't allowed to be jealous of that fact," Lou said primly.

"I am trying my best not to be," Cameron grimaced.

Helena was only standing beside Joseph because of a comment made by Marianne that she liked him. The young girl had voiced that she thought Joseph very handsome, and Helena thought it a perfect opportunity for both of her friends to make good matches. She smiled at Marianne, who for once wasn't being her usual restrained self.

"So, Captain, have you travelled all across the world?" Marianne asked.

"There or thereabouts, Lady Marianne. I'm travelling to North Portugal on my next trip, which is not as far as some of the journeys I have undertaken, but I will be away for some weeks," Joseph responded.

"London is as far as I've travelled, and although there is a huge difference between the highlands and the capital, 'tis nothing compared to your travels!" Marianne said wistfully.

"Scotland is one of the most beautiful places in the world, Lady Marianne. One cannot go wrong with the scenery, the space, and the clean air. I just wish it was slightly warmer! The West Indies are not as breath-taking in my humble opinion but are certainly a pleasanter temperature!"

"Yes. The Scots are a hardy people. We have to be," Marianne said.

They were joined by Henry, who'd also arrived a little later than the others. He approached Helena.

"It's a fine gathering you have organised," Henry said when he'd been introduced to Joseph.

"Thank you. It's been quite nerve-wracking, but hopefully, it will be seen as a success when everyone is reflecting on it tomorrow," Helena said with a smile.

"May I secure the first two dances with you?" Henry asked.

"I am afraid not," Helena responded. "I'm engaged to dance with Captain Anderton."

"I see. Maybe the next two then?" Henry asked.

"I am sorry. Captain Drummond's secured those dances," Helena said.

A look of anger and annoyance crossed Henry's face, but he schooled his features into a false smile. "I shall have to hope to be seated near you at supper then," he said. "Excuse me, I'd like a word with your brother."

Helena chewed her lip as she watched Henry approach Simon.

"Is he to be disappointed further?" Cameron asked, having overheard the exchange between Helena and Henry. Cameron had an innate dislike of Henry, and the urge to protect Helena against him had made him follow Henry when he'd approached Helena, making sure the cad didn't upset their hostess.

Helena looked up in surprise before smiling and blushing at Cameron. "Yes. I never considered sitting him near me. Selfishly, I want to enjoy this evening, but in reality, one should expect long-time acquaintances to fit in wherever it is appropriate for them."

"I agree, and a gentleman would never complain, but I fear he is the type to do so."

"Yes. He will be cutting, I'm sure," Helena sighed.

"If he says anything that upsets you, let me know. I've never liked him and would love an excuse to put him in his place," Cameron ground out.

Helena frowned a little, giving Cameron a sharp look. "Thank you, but if I am in need of assistance, I will inform my brother."

"Ah, yes. I deserved that comment," Cameron acknowledged.

"I do not wish us to fall-out Captain Drummond. I think too highly of you for that. But please be sympathetic to my feelings. I cannot let my mind wander, for the thoughts and feelings aren't reciprocated. I understand that. But I do not wish to appear foolish in turning to you when I have not that right," Helena said quietly, so Marianne and Joseph wouldn't overhear.

"I'm sorry, Lady Helena. I did not mean to upset you. Truly," Cameron said sincerely.

"I'm not vexed in the slightest, and I am looking forward to our dances," Helena smiled.

"As am I," Cameron responded truthfully.

*

Henry approached Simon, his scowl returning once his back had been turned on Helena. He was met part way across the room by his friend, who had seen the set of Henry's face and didn't want anyone to overhear their conversation if at all possible.

"Do I have to battle through the whole of the army and navy before I can dance with your sister?" Henry snarled.

"She's the hostess. Of course she is going to dance with everyone," Simon soothed.

"One doesn't cast-off old friends so easily in my book, but it seems she has had her head turned ever since that blasted night on the heath!" Henry growled.

"Keep your voice down!" Simon snapped. "I really do not know what has got into you these last few weeks!"

"I'm trying to seek favour with your sister; only I appear to be thwarted at every attempt!" Henry said.

"Ah, with regards to that. We need a chat about it, but not tonight," Simon said. There was no point giving Henry false hope.

"You cannot utter those words and expect me to be satisfied!" Henry exclaimed. "I am presuming you won't be wishing me happy if it is a conversation we need in private?"

"I'm afraid Helena just does not see you as a potential husband," Simon said, trying to keep his tone calm. He didn't need an outburst at the start of the evening.

"Well, what the bloody hell am I doing here then? Standing by while she makes doe eyes at every other man in the room except me?" Henry snarled.

"That's enough Henry!" Simon said warningly. "You are here because you are my close friend, but to be honest, the way you have been acting lately, I'm beginning to wonder who you really are. You never used to be so angry and unpleasant!"

"We don't all sail through every day only seeing the best of it like some sort of smitten fool. Some of us have a more realistic take on life. I need to marry, and your sister was my choice. I am not going to be jumping for joy when I've been rejected over some unknown dandy," Henry said with derision.

"There is not some 'unknown dandy', as you put it. She's not intending marrying anyone yet, and I cannot really blame her. There are months of the season left. Why does she need to marry so soon? Be careful Henry. You are in danger of becoming very bitter and self-obsessed," Simon said with a shake of his head. For the second time since becoming friends with Henry, Simon was coming to the conclusion that his friend was more like his own father. It worried him that he'd been attracted to befriend the same sort of character he actually despised.

"I think it is too late for that," Henry said. "I will stay for the meal, but I'll be damned if I will hang around to watch your sister be passed from one fop to another when the dancing takes place!"

"That's your choice, but I am genuinely sorry it has come to this," Simon said. He would not be seeking out Henry after the evening's events. They no longer seemed to have anything in common, if they ever had. Simon wouldn't be upset to end the acquaintance, and it made it an even easier decision to know Helena would be relieved. It seemed his sister had been right about Henry's character after all.

He moved away from Henry, and at the butler's appearance, indicated that the group should move to the dining room. They walked through in pairs, all chattering and looking forward to the evening ahead.

Helena had not seated Cameron on either side of her, not sure she could stop herself constantly apologising for her silly offer. Instead, she'd placed two married gentlemen within the party by each of her seating positions, ensuring that her three friends had a single man on either side of them.

Henry was seated opposite Lou. He watched her closely throughout the meal. His lip curled with bitter amusement that she had the gall to act every inch the lady. She seemed unaware of his scrutiny, even though he was openly glaring at her.

To one side of him was Mrs Atkinson, a pleasant woman, with two very marriageable sons and on his other side was Marianne. Helena had spent an age trying to decide who to put next to Henry and had finally decided that Marianne and Mrs Atkinson both had a soothing presence that would please even the most difficult of guests. She would have preferred to put someone nicer next to Marianne, but at least they would be sat together only for the meal, and on her other side, she had Captain Anderton.

Henry continued to observe Lou and decided he had had enough. He'd been rejected and criticised by people who weren't good enough to be considered his equals. No. It was time Lady Lou was told exactly what she was. He determined to speak to her. He was adamant that she, at least, would not forget the way they had met.

Marianne had noticed Henry's perusal of her sister, and not unreasonably, had come to the conclusion he might admire her.

"My sister is very often the centre of any party," Marianne said with a fond look at Lou.

"She certainly knows how to entertain," Henry said, as Captain Philips laughed loudly at something Lou had just uttered.

"I am usually jealous of her ability to deal with any situation she faces. She is always so confident and poised," Marianne admitted.

"Not in every situation," Henry said.

"I think it's natural to look up to one's siblings, but it is easy to do so when Lou is your older sister," Marianne said with pride.

"Really? That surprises me," Henry said, looking once more at Lou.

"Why should it surprise you?" Marianne asked in confusion. "She is clever, funny, loyal and very loving. What is there not to like?"

"You describe her as almost pious, but I don't consider anything saintly when one breaks the laws of the land," Henry said, his tone slightly rough. "Would you not agree?"

"Well… But I do not understand your meaning, Lord Ince," Marianne said, completely at a loss as to what was being implied.

"So, she has not been honest with you all? I'd presumed she had," Henry said darkly.

"I really do not know to what you are referring. I didn't think you knew my sister before our recent acquaintance," Marianne said.

"Oh, I met her in a way that I am hardly likely to forget, although our hosts are trying their best to pretend it didn't happen," Henry said, once more looking at Lou.

Lou had noticed the constant interest she was attracting and was puzzled by it. She saw the confusion on Marianne's face and would have liked to speak to her sister, but it wasn't polite to speak across the table, so she held her counsel.

Henry smiled slightly when he saw the bewildered look on Lou's face. Yes, let her wonder what he was talking about.

Marianne frowned. She was trying to work out the meaning in Henry's words but could not. She turned to him once more. "I am sorry, My Lord. I've really no idea to what you are alluding. Our hosts cared for my sister when she was ill."

"Have they never explained how they came across your sister?" Henry asked, at last enjoying himself.

"N-no," Marianne said beginning to wonder where the conversation was heading. She was starting to feel decidedly uncomfortable.

"Shall we ask your sister?" Henry said.

"We should not," Marianne said. "Not at the moment." Instinct put Marianne suddenly on edge.

"Let's," Henry said with a smile that barely touched his lips, let alone his eyes. "Lady Lou, your sister is curious to know something," he said across the table.

"I am sure she can wait until the meal is complete," Lou said roughly, her tone brusque because of Henry's bad manners.

"Oh, I don't think she can, can you, Lady Marianne? Let us ask your sister just how she came to know Lord Garswood and his sister," Henry said, pushing his chair away from the table a little and crossing his arms.

Lou had paled at his words and sent a quick look of alarm to Simon. Unfortunately, he was seated far enough away not to have noticed the conversation that was developing at the centre of the table. "I will explain later," she said quickly and turned to Captain Philips, who looked slightly curious at the exchange.

"I think it would be best to explain now, my dear Lady. After all, perhaps the people you are sitting near need to be on the alert. We do have a criminal in our midst, after all," Henry said, his voice rising.

His words were enough to stop the other conversations going on around the table. A sudden stillness developed as everyone looked with curiosity at Henry.

"Lord Ince?" Captain Philips said, looking more concerned at his words. Henry clearly wasn't behaving in a gentlemanly way, but it was a strange accusation to make without foundation.

"Henry, shut the devil up!" Simon snapped from the top of the table. He hadn't heard what Henry had said, but knew it was Henry intent on causing trouble by the gleam in his eye.

"Coming to her rescue again, Garswood?" Henry drawled. "Don't tell me you are still feeling guilty about shooting the chit?"

The chair Cameron was seated on, was flung to one side, as he shot to a standing position. "You damned dog! I will meet you for this!"

"For telling the truth?" Henry laughed, unconcerned that Simon and Cameron had reached his seat. "Tell them, Lady Lou! Tell your sisters, and everyone else here, how we were first introduced to you!"

"I don't know what you're talking about!" Lou said, pale and shaking. She wanted to move from the seat but knew her legs didn't have the strength to propel her from the horrific situation she was now embroiled in. Everyone looked on with a mixture of fascination, horror, and inquisitiveness.

"So, it was not you who Garswood shot on Hampstead Heath a few weeks ago as you were trying to rob us? Your disguise was very good. We did not know the highwayman threatening us was a woman until you had been shot. Don't believe me? Have a look at her shoulder? Oooff!"

Simon punched Henry with such force that Henry flew backwards over his chair and landed in an ungainly heap. Simon indicated that two footmen should grab him.

"Enough of this nonsense, Henry! You insult my guests because I refused to let you pay court to my sister? It seems I was wise in my decision! I never want to see you near any of my family or close friends again! You are no gentleman!" Simon spat at his one-time friend.

Henry glared at Simon. "We'll see what she says when the magistrate visits her! The evidence is there for all to see!"

"You have gone mad, Henry!" Simon said as the footmen dragged Lord Ince out of the room.

Chapter 15

Simon turned to his guests. "I'm so very sorry. I knew Henry was upset about my refusal in giving him permission to court my sister, but I did not realise to what lengths he would go to lash out at me. I am sorry your personal affairs have been aired in public, Helena, and I am sorry you were his victim, My Lady," he said to Lou.

Helena was pale and looked as if she was badly shaken, but she shook her head. "It does not matter. It seems I've had a lucky escape!" she said, going along with Simon's story.

"But why would he pick on Lady Lou rather than Lady Helena?" Captain Philips asked.

Simon sighed and rubbed a hand across his face. His mind raced in an effort to extract them from this dire situation. He hoped to goodness Lou would go along with the only solution he could come up with. He glanced at Cameron who looked about to speak, but Simon shook his head gently. He turned to Lou.

"I am sorry our secret has to come out, my sweet," Simon said with a slight smile.

Lou didn't think she could lose more colour but felt even more blood draining from her face as she anticipated Simon's next words.

"Henry picked on Lady Lou because he knows we are betrothed. We wanted to keep it a secret for a little while, to announce it at the end of this evening. It clearly upset Henry further that I had secured a wife, and yet I had stopped him from marrying Helena. I'm sorry you had to witness this spectacle," Simon said. Not wishing to look at Lou in case the idea of marrying him was worse than facing the magistrate.

Lou and Cameron seemed to physically sag, but they looked gratefully at Simon. Everyone was silent while they processed the information.

Captain Anderton was the first one to speak. "That is certainly a unique way of making a wedding announcement, but I congratulate you," he said to Simon.

"Thank you," Simon responded. "I don't know about everyone else, but I need a drink!"

There were murmurings around the table, and Mr Atkinson stood. "We had best leave you in peace, My Lord," he said with a sympathetic smile. "Have that drink, but let your guests leave you be before you take it. You won't feel like playing the host after that abominable behaviour. Lord Ince was always been a spiteful sort. I pity the wife he does eventually secure!"

There were mutterings of support. "Thank you," Simon said. "We will organise another gathering before too long, and I will make sure Ince is not within a hundred miles of it!"

The visitors moved towards the door, saying their goodbyes in subdued voices. They might feel sympathy for the family, but they certainly would have something to talk about in the coming days. Henry's vindictiveness would be the *on-dit* of the season.

Left in the room were Lou, Heather, Marianne, Cameron, and Helena. Simon returned when the last guests had been shown out. He moved over to the side-table and poured large glasses of wine for everyone. Helena helped to hand them out.

"Drink," Simon instructed. "It's been a shock."

Heather had not taken her eyes off Lou but neither had she spoken. After taking an automatic sip of wine at Simon's request, she put down her glass. "Show me your shoulder," she said to her sister.

Lou looked pained at the request. "Heather… "

"Show me your shoulder," Heather said again.

"There is no need for this," Cameron said gently.

"It is true, isn't it?" Heather asked, staring at Lou. "You were not doing some respectable job. You were being a highwayman?"

"I-It's hard to explain," Lou said, her voice barely a whisper.

"Which bit is hard to explain? That you lied to us? That you stole from innocent people? That you could have hanged? Still could?" Heather asked, her tone rising as she uttered each question.

"Heather! No!" Lou said, standing in response to the pain etched on her sister's face. "I didn't know what to do! We were stranded in London with no-one to turn to! I just wanted to get some money from somewhere to get us home and settled!"

"You are no better than Duncan!" Heather spat. "He cheated people out of their money. In fact, I take that back. You're worse than he is. You held a gun in their faces while you robbed them! At least we didn't know Duncan was attacking us!"

"Do not compare me to him! I always had your best interests at heart!" Lou responded heatedly.

"Do not twist your motivation to commit crime onto our shoulders! I will not take the blame for your actions!" Heather sobbed, unable to keep the tears of anger and shock at bay any longer. "We would've helped if we had been told the truth. We could have gained positions and been respectable if not rich! Duncan ruined us financially, but you've ruined our reputations! We have nothing after this! Absolutely nothing!" Heather shouted, running from the room.

Helena stood. "She does not mean it."

"She does," Lou said covering her face. "I cannot blame her because everything she says is true."

Marianne stood. She turned to Cameron. "I will go to Heather. Please could you arrange for our journey home as soon as possible? I can't stay here," she said quietly.

"We will travel home as soon as we can," Lou said.

"I don't want anything to do with you, Lou. I want to travel home and try to arrange some employment as far away from you as I can possibly get," Marianne said. Her tone was quiet, but her words were as painfully spoken as Heather's had been. "I am ashamed of you."

Marianne left the room. Cameron looked at Simon. "I think he'll send the magistrate," he said simply.

"I agree," Simon said. "We were seen leaving the party late. My staff will be loyal, but we need to make sure our story will tally. I am sorry Helena. I don't like asking you to do this but you were there."

"It doesn't matter. I will do whatever I need to."

"Thank you," Cameron said to her.

"Lou was waiting for us when we returned home. She had been robbed and had come to us because of our previous acquaintance," he said looking at Cameron. "She fell into a fever, so we couldn't ascertain where your sisters were. We went and collected them as soon as we found out. We have to keep this as close to the truth as possible," Simon instructed.

"I have a gun wound," Lou said.

"That is unfortunate, but that's why I'm saying you were robbed on your way here," Simon said. "I do not lie. My reputation is such that I will be believed."

"I wish I had your confidence," Cameron said.

"If we're constant, the story will stand the test," Simon said.

"If that is all, I'll go and check that Mrs Cox is aware of what to expect. The staff will not betray us, but they need to know what they will be facing," Helena said, moving to leave the room. "I have plenty of examples of when Lord Ince was a beast! The magistrate will be under no doubt what sort of man Henry is when I've finished speaking!"

Cameron suppressed a smile at Helena's fiery words. "I am going to check on the girls," he said to Lou.

"They'll never forgive me," Lou said.

"They will. They love you. It has been a shock because they both idolise you. Perhaps it will be a good thing in the long-term. It'll show them that you are not infallible," Cameron said, walking to where his sister sat. He placed a kiss on top of her head. "They will rally."

Lou and Simon were left alone. Cameron closed the door behind him, ignoring propriety. The evening had gone beyond that.

Simon moved around the table. "Try not to worry too much," he said gently, holding one of Lou's hands in his own.

"Why did you tell him?" Lou asked.

"I didn't!" Simon responded quickly.

"Someone had to! How could he have known what I did if you had not told him?"

"Do you not remember that night?" Simon asked.

"Not really. It's a bit of a blur," Lou admitted.

"There were three of us in the carriage that night," Simon said gently.

"Oh. I see," Lou said.

"I presumed you would remember, but it all happened very fast."

"So he was there."

"Yes, but if we stick to our story, it'll work out," Simon assured her.

"I am going to confess," Lou said, looking at Simon for the first time. Her expression was bleak.

Lou's words hit Simon like a punch to the gut. "No!" he almost shouted.

"I've lost everything," Lou said in defeat. "All that risk, and it was for nothing."

"It was not for nothing!" Simon said, refusing to lose hope. "It has worked out well!"

"How can you say that?" Lou asked "Even if we had the money to stay and come out in London, we would be tainted. Even if the magistrate believes our lies, gossip sticks."

Simon knew her words were correct. He could dispute Henry's claim, and some people would believe him, but there would be others who would question why Henry would fabricate such a tall tale. They would likely believe there was truth behind the denials although believing Lou had been a highwayman would stretch the imaginations of most people.

"On that night, I might have wanted you to hang," Simon started, "but I refuse to let you give up now. Your sacrifice will cause even more scandal for your sisters," he finished.

"They could put the blame solely on me," Lou reasoned.

"It doesn't work like that, and you know it. Any shame is attached to every member of the family. I have seen it often enough," Simon said, relieved he seemed to be finally making her realise that confessing wasn't the solution.

"What if the magistrate wants to see my wound?" Lou asked.

"We will not lie about that. You were shot as part of a robbery. Keeping as much to what actually happened means the story we tell is less likely to fail," Simon said.

"I do not like lying. It goes against everything I think is decent," Lou said.

"Neither do I. But it's better than the alternative," Simon said. He sighed. He had to make her see another side of the issue. "I told everyone we would be marrying—"

"But you did not mean it. Don't worry. I won't hold you to it!" Lou interrupted, laughing bitterly.

"You see, that is where I have a little problem," Simon said, standing and reaching out for Lou's hands, so he could gently pull her to her feet. "It's far from the ideal situation, but I do want to marry you, Lou. More than I have ever wanted anything else."

Lou's eyes flicked to Simon's in surprise and shock. "You dislike me for threatening your sister. You have said it enough times!"

Simon smiled. "That was at the beginning. Only at the beginning. I thought it was just curiosity that kept me going along this strange road, but it was not. It was you. Even on that first night, you had started to creep underneath my defences to a place no other woman has ever reached."

Lou thought her head was going to explode with the events of the evening. And now this! She'd dreamed of him declaring his affection to her, but she couldn't let him sacrifice himself, just as he wouldn't let her sacrifice herself.

Simon saw the doubt in her expression but kept on. "I know it's not the ideal time or way to reveal my feelings, but when this has all died down, we are going to marry. I hope. Will you have me?"

"Thank you," Lou said. "Thank you for everything you've done. I do not deserve it. But I cannot marry you. I am sorry. I need to try to repair the damage I've caused to everyone, starting with Heather and Marianne. I do not know if they'll ever forgive me, but I have to try."

"We can marry after that. There is no desperate hurry," Simon soothed, understanding her need to repair the injury done to her relations, but at the same time, not wanting to lose her.

"No. We are not going to marry. It would be a union based on a lie, a falsehood, and I couldn't stand that. You will end up resenting me when half the *ton* start to gossip about your wife and you aren't allowed access to the finest clubs. No. I will return to Scotland, and you will be able to congratulate yourself on having a lucky escape," Lou said firmly.

"You think I would care for the twattling the *ton* would do? You think I cannot face gossip?" Simon asked in disbelief.

"I'm saying you are not going to be put in that position," Lou said.

"You cannot think I have a very strong character!" Simon said, unable to stop bitterness sounding in his voice.

Lou saw her opportunity and took it. "No, I don't. I think you are slightly better than most people I know, but you're a fully-fledged member of the aristocracy and ultimately have never faced anything that has seriously tested you!"

"Says Lady Lou!" Simon said sarcastically.

"I come from an area where life is hard, My Lord. You would not stand two weeks there without your fine assemblies and equally fine ladies swooning behind their fans. Thank you for everything you have done for my family. I'll always be grateful for that, but you stay in your world and let me return to mine! Please excuse me," Lou said. She left the room, knowing without doubt that she would never feel as desolate again in her life.

Chapter 16

Cameron had been unsurprised when he'd entered Heather and Marianne's bedchamber and found them huddled together, each comforting the other while they both cried.

He'd approached them, and in an undignified fashion, had climbed on the bed and wrapped his arms around his younger sisters. They'd embraced him, continuing to sob for half an hour or more.

Eventually, the tears ceased, and Cameron kissed both their heads.

"Why did she do it, Cameron?" Heather asked.

"It was a poor decision, but she felt she had no other choice," Cameron said gently. "She has suffered for it and will continue to do so."

"Good!" Heather responded. "We cannot show our faces again, so why shouldn't she suffer?"

"Do you want to see her hang?" Cameron asked.

"Yes! No! Oh, I don't know! I want her to hurt as much as she has hurt everyone around her," Heather said.

Cameron smiled slightly. Heather was so like Lou. "She is. She is devastated that she's lost your respect and good opinion."

"She could have hurt someone. Or worse," Marianne said with less venom than Heather's tone.

"I know, and so does she. Her crime is the largest, but we have all been at fault through this whole sorry episode. I should not have trusted Duncan. I shouldn't have left you all to your fates. I knew what he was like. Duncan has let us all down," Cameron said.

"Duncan did not go out and put others at risk," Marianne pointed out.

"No, but he has affected us deeply. I'm truly not making excuses for Lou," Cameron said softly. "She did wrong and is ashamed of her foolishness. Her overriding aim was to protect you both. And me to some extent. She didn't want to worry me while I was away. What she failed to think through was that it would have been catastrophic if she'd been caught by anyone other than the Ashtons."

"We really are doomed to be spinsters," Heather said, her anger fading.

"I hope all is not lost," Cameron said.

"Could you see Captain Philips marrying someone with a ruined reputation and no dowry?" Heather asked.

Cameron looked surprised. "Michael? You have feelings for Michael?"

Heather blushed. "For all the good it will do me."

"I'm not sure he is looking for any wife at the moment, what with his father dying and decisions he has to make about leaving the regiment," Cameron said gently. "You are still young yet. There will be others who turn your head."

"Said by an idiotish older brother!" Marianne scolded. "It is not about who turns our heads. It is about who will accept us!"

Cameron smiled sadly. "If they care for you, the dowry and reputation won't matter."

"You've been away for too long!" Heather said. "Even when we were in Hyde Park, we were looked at with curiosity and scorn because our attire was not quite the thing. If we remained here, our lack of fortune and Lord Ince's animosity would soon see us shunned."

"I am sorry you are suffering as a result of your foolish brother and sister," Cameron said. "I can condemn one easier than the other, as their motives were very different."

"They both have stolen," Heather pointed out.

"Yes. They have. Is it wrong of me to not be able to face seeing that Lou gets punished for her crime? It would kill me to see her hanged," Cameron said.

Marianne put her hand on her brother's. "Neither of us wants such a horror for Lou. But we cannot face questioning. Enough lies have been told."

"I agree. I think that's what Lord Garswood meant when he said we need to keep as close to the truth as possible."

"Lord Ince might not inform on Lou," Heather said.

"I am afraid that sneaks-be will have little compunction on tittle-tattling to anyone who will listen. He has been thwarted by Lady Helena and will not take it as a decent man would," Cameron ground out.

"At the moment, I'm not sure I can be much in Lou's company," Heather admitted.

"No. That is understandable. We will go out for the day tomorrow. We can see some of the sights before we go home," Cameron offered.

"Won't you need to stay with Lou?" Marianne asked in surprise.

"If we carry on as normal, it will appear less suspicious. And I am certain Lord Garswood will provide all the protection she needs." Cameron had a sneaking suspicion that Simon cared about his sister, and he approved wholeheartedly.

"He said they were to marry," Marianne pointed out.

"Said in the spur of the moment," Heather responded.

"There's no point in concerning ourselves over that matter at the moment," Cameron said. He could see that it was an announcement made because of the situation. He hoped Simon meant it and Lou would accept it eventually.

"In that case, I would like to be away from this house tomorrow," Heather said, determined.

*

Simon ensconced himself in his study. He was under no illusion that the magistrate wouldn't call. He was surprised he hadn't been knocked up at some ungodly hour during the night. He hoped it was a good sign that he hadn't been.

Half-way through the morning, one of the gentlemen magistrates from Bow Street was admitted into the study. There were a number of men who carried out the role across London. Simon offered him refreshments, which he refused.

"My Lord, I'll give you the courtesy of coming to the point, and I hope you will do the same with me," the magistrate said, sitting opposite Simon.

"Of course," Simon responded.

"Good. You are not surprised at my visit, so I am presuming what Lord Ince has relayed to us is correct." The tone was professional, and although not brusque, was clipped and direct.

"I can only presume that Henry has uttered the same nonsense to you that he spouted to us last night," Simon said.

"He states, that along with your sister, the three of you were accosted on Hampstead Heath on the night of the twelfth. In the skirmish, you shot a high pad and then returned home with same, who you found out to be a female," the magistrate stated. "We've checked the Earl of Gloucester's home, and he confirmed that you left the ball long after most of the other guests."

Damn Henry, Simon thought. He smiled in amusement, his eyebrow quirking. "We were on the heath as you say, and we did leave ridiculously late, but as for the other accusations… Henry is being malicious and using you to seek his revenge."

"I will need to question your staff," the magistrate said.

"Of course. But I must point out, as you'd expect, my staff are loyal, so if Henry's poison was correct, they would likely support my telling of the events rather than his," Simon said amenably.

"Liars make mistakes."

"I hope Henry's were easy to pick out then. Let me tell you a little about Henry," Simon said. "We have been friends for many years. He is one for visiting every gaming hell and brothel this side of the Thames and very often travels to the South Bank if he can't find what he requires over here. It is funny and amusing to observe, and in some cases to take part, but when he started having designs on my sister, things began to change between us."

"A tad hypocritical of you, My Lord," the magistrate pointed out.

"A lot, I would say," Simon responded fairly. "But there we have it. I wasn't very happy with the way he intended his married life to be. In fact, I would not wish it on someone I didn't like, let alone my only sister, so I tried to discourage him. He persisted, and I decided I would seek the view of my sister. After all, she could have held him in affection, whatever my feelings on the matter. Helena was completely against the match. Which I told him at the start of our evening dinner party."

"Not the best time to break the news."

"No. And I would not normally have done so," Simon admitted. "Unfortunately, Henry was in a foul mood and knew me well enough to guess that what I'd wanted to speak to him about was not going to be good news. I admit, I did not expect him to react quite so badly."

"And why would Henry wish to damage the young lady he accused?"

"Because she is the woman I love," Simon said with conviction. He knew without doubt his words were sincere. "He was aiming to hurt me. He knew I am robust enough to withstand any accusations against my person. As I have said, I've known him for years. Anyone hearing him bad-mouth me would take it for a spat between the both of us, but my betrothed is new to London. She was the most vulnerable, yet after Helena, the one most closely connected to me. An easy target for a man without scruples."

"And if your betrothed is new to London, how is it that you are now hosting the whole family?" the magistrate asked. "Even if the affection was quickly formed, moving the family into your own home is a little odd, wouldn't you say?"

Simon looked slightly uncomfortable. "I know the family through Captain Drummond, but I have only recently got to know his sisters. Look, I need your assurance that the information I divulge will not be relayed to Henry, or anyone else, for that matter."

"This is a confidential conversation."

"Good." Simon went on to explain about the wrongs Duncan had done to his sisters and tried to do to Cameron. "I don't want this becoming common knowledge. They have enough to deal with as it is. I was sought out because of my previous friendship with Drummond. Thank God, I was. Lady Lou could've died!"

"Is she available to speak to me?"

"If you need to speak to her, of course," Simon said without hesitation. "The wound and fever have drained her, and she rests quite a lot during the day, but thankfully, she's recovering. Last night was supposed to be an enjoyable evening, their first since we all came together. I will never forgive Henry for this!" he ground out.

The study door opened, and although Simon glanced in alarm at whomever was entering, he smiled in welcome when he saw Helena. She was blushing furiously and looked worried.

"Might I come in?" she asked. Her voice was quiet and demure.

"Of course, my dear, but you do not need to sit through this," Simon said gently.

"I must. I feel I have caused the upset," Helena said, coming into the room and approaching Simon.

Simon turned to the magistrate. "This is my sister, Lady Helena Ashton."

The magistrate stood when Helena entered the room and bobbed his head in a brief bow. "My Lady," he said.

"Please excuse my intrusion, sir," Helena said to the magistrate. "I've had a sleepless night and cannot settle."

"Why so disturbed, My Lady?" the magistrate asked.

"Lord Ince frightens me," Helena admitted. "He always abuses me verbally and ridicules my opinions. His attentions have become — quite — overwhelming to be honest."

"I am sorry I didn't protect you more," Simon said honestly.

Helena smiled shyly at her brother. "You cannot be there all the time." She turned her gaze back to the magistrate. "Lord Ince was becoming openly rude and offensive if I accepted a dance from another. It was very embarrassing for myself and whichever gentleman was requesting a dance. I was getting to the point of disliking going to entertainments."

"My enquiries have raised the fact that you've not been out as much recently," the magistrate confirmed.

Simon realised he hadn't been visited first thing because the man was obviously gathering information about them all. He hoped to goodness their story would be believed. This man was very thorough.

"No. I have asked my brother if we could leave London when our friends return to Scotland. Lord Ince was hard enough to deal with when he was supposedly my friend. Now that I have rejected his proposal, I'm quite afraid!" Helena flushed and looked down at her hands. She looked once more at the magistrate, her eyes full of tears. "You probably think I am being foolish, but I had rather miss the season than be pursued by Lord Ince!"

"There is no need for upset, My Lady," the magistrate said soothingly. Helena's distress was clearly sincere. "You have been unfortunate in meeting a cad so early in the season, but there are a lot of good people out there."

"This is what I keep telling her," Simon said. "I've been reluctant to leave London because it is her first season but after last night…"

"I doubt Lord Ince would be repeating his proposals from what he said when he visited me," the magistrate said.

"No. But if I go on a wedding trip, I am loath to leave Helena in his society. They're bound to come into contact with each other."

"Lady Heather and Lady Marianne have spoken about my visiting them," Helena said to Simon. "I would like to do that if I may? I really cannot face Henry."

"I am so sorry your first entry into Society has led to this," Simon responded gently. He turned to the magistrate. "I could kill Henry for this! She should be enjoying herself not hiding out at the other side of the country!"

"No. I feel in future you'll be more circumspect in whom you introduce to your relations," the magistrate said.

Simon looked shamefaced. "I take my part in the whole sorry episode very seriously. I know I failed, I can assure you."

The magistrate stood. "I've seen enough, My Lord. I shall bid you good-day."

"You do not wish to speak to my betrothed?" Simon asked, hoping to goodness the magistrate wouldn't take him up on his offer.

"No. I can't see any advantage in doing that. I see how things lie here. Lady Helena, I would go to Scotland and return for the next season. Lord Ince will have moved on to another victim by then. Men like that soon seek out another poor thing. Usually one who hasn't the protection you have," the magistrate said gently.

"It seems so very wrong that someone else could be made to feel as I have done," Helena said with sincerity.

"It is, but unfortunately, that's what happens," the magistrate said. "I shall put this down to maliciousness on Lord Ince's part, My Lord. I hope that is to your satisfaction?"

"Of course. I am sorry you've been troubled," Simon said, standing.

"It's my job to make enquiries, but I refuse to be used by one member of the aristocracy against another," the magistrate said. "If I could make one suggestion, My Lord?"

"Of course," Simon said.

"I would advise you and that lady of yours to stay off the heath at night. It's not worth the risk," the magistrate said before leaving the room.

Simon paled at his words, and once the door closed behind the gentleman, Simon sank into his seat.

Helena looked at Simon in horror. When they heard the thud of the front door closing, Helena spoke in barely a whisper. "He knows the truth."

"Yes, or he suspects some of it is true," Simon responded, rubbing his hands over his face. "But for some reason, he's letting it go."

"Why would he do that?"

"I've no idea, but I will be forever grateful that he has," Simon answered. "Perhaps Henry was his usual self and acted the brutish beast? Something must've gone wrong, because he could have questioned anyone he chose, and yet he did not."

'"I hope you didn't mind me interrupting," Helena said. "I wasn't sure I would be able to stop myself making a mistake, but I wanted the magistrate to know what Henry is really like."

"I admit, I was alarmed at first, but then it turned to relief. You were magnificent, and all I feel now is shame," Simon admitted.

"Shame? Why on earth would you feel that?" Helena asked.

"For not seeing what a rogue Henry was earlier. I should've guessed he had designs on you, and yet I was buffleheaded enough not to notice it," Simon responded.

"That does not matter now. I will not be in his company anytime soon."

"Good. Now wish me well when I go and break the news to Lou and try to convince her that she still needs to marry me," Simon smiled.

"Of course she will marry you. She'd be foolish not to," Helena said as loyal as a sibling could be.

Chapter 17

Cameron took his sisters to Vauxhall Gardens. The Gardens opened during the afternoon, and for a few shillings each, people were allowed to wander and admire the walks in the daylight. He had promised them a decadent hot chocolate when they finished walking to their hearts content.

Being used to wide open spaces, Heather and Marianne loved walking through the groves. There were enough people passing through to make the excursion interesting without making them feel inferior as they had when walking through Hyde Park. Realising that you were not up to snuff for the *ton* was a sobering lesson for two girls to learn; until the reality hit home, they had been filled with romantic notions of London Society.

Emerging from an avenue of trees, Marianne stopped suddenly. "Captain Anderton!" she said in surprise and mortification. She hadn't expected to meet her favoured one, and knowing that he'd seen them when all the accusations had been flung at her family, she wasn't sure what reception she would receive.

"Lady Marianne! What a pleasure to see you," Joseph said with a smile. "Lady Heather, Captain Drummond. I see you are taking the air while the day is fresh and sunny."

"Yes. We needed to be outdoors," Marianne admitted, her colour still heightened.

Joseph looked at the prettiest sister with sympathy. She was clearly suffering under the presumption he would snub them after the previous evening. Little did she know he was grateful for anyone in Society taking notice of him. The fewer people who knew his background the better, so he was hardly likely to condemn anyone else, especially when she was as beautiful as Lady Marianne.

"If you have no commitments, perhaps you would like to explore my ship? I remember you expressing an interest at the dinner party, and she is a beauty, even if I do say so myself!" Joseph smiled in encouragement.

"Cameron has promised us hot chocolate," Heather said with a smile.

"I cannot promise that, but I can offer the finest tea and spiced biscuits," Joseph responded.

"Sounds interesting." Cameron joined in the conversation.

"Yes. Cook likes to experiment with the spices we sometimes transport. I have no objection as it reminds me of home," Joseph admitted.

"Are you not from these shores?" Cameron asked.

"No. I was born in India," Joseph admitted. He would acknowledge that much to anyone. Who his parents were was something he kept firmly to himself.

"An exotic place," Marianne sighed. "You must've seen so many interesting places."

"And a lot of countries I would not like to see ever again," Joseph admitted. "It's not all beautiful kingdoms and fascinating people. Everywhere has its dark side, just as London does."

"And poverty," Cameron admitted. "It is hell to see a village decimated by the French who just go in and take what supplies they wish without paying or considering what the locals need. At least Wellesley makes sure we pay for everything we use."

"War brings out the best and worst in people," Joseph said.

"It does, but enough maudlin thoughts!" Cameron said with a laugh. "I want to see this ship of yours as much as my sisters do!"

"Well, let's hail two hackneys and get on our way," Joseph said, offering his arm to Lady Marianne. The journey would take a while to reach the docks from Vauxhall Gardens, and he was determined that Marianne would travel in the hackney with him.

Cameron looked on at Joseph and Marianne with amusement. Marianne's blushes betrayed her, but he'd also noticed the way Joseph looked at his sister. Let her enjoy a flirtation, Cameron thought to himself. It couldn't do any harm.

Cameron offered his arm to Heather, and they trailed behind Marianne and Joseph.

Marianne was enjoying being escorted by Joseph, and although quieter than her sisters, she was determined to speak about what had happened when they'd last met.

"It was a kind service you did to my family, helping to break up the party so sensitively," Marianne stated. She was no longer enjoying the scenery she was walking past, concentrating solely on the feel of her arm on his as Joseph walked by her side.

"Anyone would have done it," Joseph said with a reassuring smile. "I, of all people, know what it's like not to wish for my family business to be discussed in public."

"Are you saying that because it is true, or are you trying to make yourself seem more enigmatic?" Marianne asked.

"More enigmatic? Now, those are two words to warm my soul," Joseph teased.

Marianne flushed, and Joseph placed his free hand on hers.

"Fear not, Lady Marianne. I'm a brute, and I tease," he said reassuringly.

Marianne smiled, but her cheeks seemed to be constantly burning in Joseph's company. "You are, and you do, Captain Anderton! I wish I could parry, but I am afraid you'll find me sadly lacking."

"I find you nothing of the sort!" Joseph scoffed. "It is a welcome relief to meet someone so unaffected who also has beauty, poise, and a sweet nature, and I'm neither being a brute nor teasing in this regard."

"In that case, my cheeks will continue to burn as I thank you for your compliments," Marianne said.

They reached the exit to the gardens, and Joseph whistled loudly for two hackney carriages. He instructed the second one which dock to aim for before taking his place next to Marianne in the front carriage.

"I'm pleased you are willing to see my ship. Every sailor loves his vessel as if it's a living, breathing being," he said to try to put Marianne at ease.

"What is your ship's name?" Marianne asked. The hackney was roomy enough for two people, but Joseph seemed to take up more space than the average person. Marianne felt it sweet torture to be pressed against him in such a manner.

"Her name is *Tara*," Joseph responded.

"That's an unusual name."

"In Hinduism, *Tara* is a goddess. She is one who protects. I thought it was appropriate for a ship that would protect us against the worst the sea can throw at us," Joseph said seriously.

"It's a beautiful name. Is India very exotic?" Marianne asked.

"It is," Joseph said, turning slightly, so he could stare fully into Marianne's wide green eyes. "I cannot explain the colour, the noise, the people. It all seems so much more alive, if that makes sense? I dock in a city like London, and I can't wait to escape. The wealth of the world might be here, but I would always swap it for the vibrancy of India. I've never been to another place that can compete. Even the buildings change colour depending on the time of day, or the position of the sun. Can you imagine stone that turns pink in the evening or yellow buildings that seem to glow golden?"

"You make it sound magical," Marianne said. "Do your family live out there?"

"In a fashion," Joseph responded, turning away slightly and glancing out of the window to his side.

"I have been lucky with my family. It is only my eldest brother who has let us all down. Most of the time, I want to be with the people who are related to me, but I know that isn't always the case," Marianne said gently.

"No."

"Tell me more of your travels, please," she requested quietly. Her question about his family had changed the mood in the carriage, and she regretted speaking about something that was none of her business. She wanted to see Joseph's eyes light up as they had when he'd described India.

Joseph smiled at Marianne. "If the world interests you so, you need to travel yourself one day."

"I am returning to Scotland in the next day or two, and there won't be opportunity for travel after that," Marianne responded. This time it was she who felt discomfited.

"That is a shame," Joseph said, meaning it.

"It is usual for a woman in my situation," Marianne said quietly.

"Would you like to tell me about it?"

"No. Thank you, but I should not. My family is too proud sometimes, but I can't air our story at the moment. It affects us all and can therefore hurt us all if I speak the words," Marianne explained.

"In that case, I shall ask no more. Instead I'll tell you about China and the people who live there," Joseph said, understanding full well what it was like not to wish your family story aired for public scrutiny.

The carriage ride seemed to pass in an instant for Marianne. Joseph was a natural storyteller, and he kept her laughing all the way to the docks as he told her of escapades that he'd been a part of while traveling the world as sailor and then as captain. If she admired him at the start of their acquaintance, she was more than half-way in love with him by the time the journey was over.

They arrived at the dock, and Marianne hesitated before allowing Joseph to help her out of the hackney.

"It's so busy!" she said in surprise.

Joseph smiled. "It is the heart of the city, whatever anyone else says."

Masts from ships seemed almost entwined with each other, there was so many in the dock. Bells clanked mournfully as the vessels rocked slowly with the ebb of the tide. Many were being loaded and unloaded with men swarming around each one, shouting and cursing at the top of their voices.

Joseph grimaced when the sound of cursing wafted over to their location. "Perhaps not one of my finest ideas to bring two young ladies into this maelstrom," he said wryly.

"Don't you dare change your mind!" Marianne said heatedly. She was seeing something she'd never experienced before. Her eyes were round with wonder.

"I could not disappoint you, My Lady," Joseph said seriously.

He led the way to his pride and joy once Cameron and Heather arrived. "Here we are!" he said, opening his arms to take in the large vessel at the dockside.

"It's huge!" Marianne gasped.

"She, Lady Marianne," Joseph said with a smile. "Every ship is a 'she'. Never an 'it'."

"I'm sorry. She's beautiful!" Marianne responded.

"She certainly is," Joseph responded with pride. "Come, let us go on board."

Chapter 18

They were shown around the ship as eager to be impressed as Joseph was to impress them. Marianne and Heather were fascinated by the workings of the vessel. Whilst being shown the Captain's sumptuous accommodation, Marianne turned to her brother.

"Is this the type of ship you will be travelling on when you return to Portugal?"

Cameron nodded. "Yes. Although my cabin will not be as grand as this!"

"But you're a captain!" Heather responded indignantly.

"I am a cavalry officer of his majesty's army. I am nothing special, believe me," Cameron smiled.

"I would like to see all the areas, if that's possible?" Marianne asked Joseph.

Her request was met with a grimace. "Ladies really should not be taken below deck. It's not the nicest of areas," Joseph replied.

"Oh, we don't mind seeing all of this majestic craft," Heather intervened in support of her sister. "We do not need to be cosseted, Captain. We have never had the chance to step on board a ship before. We'd love to visit all the decks."

Joseph glanced at Cameron but received a shrug, which was of no use whatsoever. Now somewhat regretting his invitation, he led his guests to one of the staircases that led into the bowels of the vessel. Thankfully, they weren't to load their cargo until the morrow, so there were few sailors on board.

Stopping at the top of the staircase, Joseph turned to his guests. "For safety's sake, go down the stairs backwards," he said.

"Backwards?" Heather and Marianne both exclaimed.

"Let me show them," Cameron offered, amused at his sisters expressions. He skilfully negotiated the steps.

"A ship's steps aren't as wide as you find with steps on land, so it is safer to descend the way your brother has," Joseph explained. "Another rule is to have two parts of your body in contact with the ship at all times. That way, if the ship should lurch suddenly, there is less chance to fall. Walking around can be dangerous even when it seems the sea is quite calm. One rogue wave can result in fatal injuries."

Heather followed Cameron, gingerly moving down the stairs one step at a time. It wasn't an easy task to perform whilst wearing a dress. Marianne faltered at the top. The stairs looked dangerously steep.

"One moment, Lady Marianne," Joseph said, moving towards the top of the staircase. "I'll go down first in case you stumble."

He climbed lithely on the top stair and positioned his feet on the outer string of the staircase. He seemed to push himself off, and in no more than a second, had reached the bottom of the steps, his hands causing a squeak as they travelled at speed down the bannisters. Joseph looked up to the open stairway with a laugh. "Sometimes we need to descend quickly."

Marianne looked stunned but grinned at Joseph's laugh. "I shall not be trying to copy your method," she said, gripping the bannister firmly.

"Come down at your own speed. I was only showing-off," Joseph responded, watching intently as Marianne took each step. Her brother could quite easily have caught Marianne if she'd slipped, but for some reason, Joseph wanted to be the one to save her. He didn't look at Cameron, afraid he had revealed too much of his favouritism towards Marianne.

Cameron exchanged a smile with Heather at the action and stepped back to allow Joseph room to perform his heroics.

Marianne wasn't incapable and stepped onto the lower deck without any mishap. She smiled at Joseph. "Now we can explore all of the ship."

Joseph shook his head in wonder. "I hope you're not disappointed," he said before leading the way.

Later, returning the party to his room, which was used as dining room, map room and meeting room as each need arose, Joseph encouraged them to sit. A tray had been laid out with tea and biscuits.

"What pretty china!" Marianne said of the dainty pattern of a cuckoo in a tree. The cups were covered in colour, unlike the more restrained patterns that were popular in the fine houses of the *ton*.

"My mother's favourite English bird was a cuckoo, so my father commissioned this set. Its colour reminds me of India. The bird reminds me of England," Joseph explained.

"A perfect mix of the two cultures. I'd be afraid to use them on a ship. What happens in rough seas? Do you not risk losing them?" Marianne asked.

Joseph smiled. "No. They are packed away safely. Everything that can move is secured. We cannot have furniture flying around us while we're trying to deal with an angry sea."

"It sounds treacherous," Marianne said with a frown.

"It can be, but if we see a storm brewing, we do what we can to change course. There's no point putting us all at risk. It is more difficult to outrun trouble in open seas. Sometimes storms just cannot be avoided," Joseph explained.

"I don't know how your family can rest easy while you are away!" Marianne exclaimed.

Joseph smiled. He was pleased at Marianne's response. "I'm the last of my family, so there is no one to worry about me. It's best that way." His words glossed over so much.

A knock on the door interrupted the group. A man only slightly younger than Joseph entered the room. "Sorry to disturb you, Capt'n. Thought you would want to see the papers as soon as they arrived."

"Yes. Thank you, Peter. Leave them on my desk, and I'll attend to them soon," Joseph responded. "Let me introduce you to my new friends. Captain Drummond, Lady Heather Drummond, Lady Marianne, please allow me to introduce you to my first mate, Mr Liptrot."

The young man was handsome with chestnut hair and green eyes. He smiled widely at the group. "A pleasure to meet you all," he said with a bow.

"Are you looking forward to your upcoming journey, Mr Liptrot?" Heather asked.

"I am, My Lady. We will be sailing in three days, and it cannot come soonest for me. I love being out on the open water," Mr Liptrot said.

The young man bowed once more and left the guests to finish their tea. "Do you never tire of always leaving one place then another?" Heather asked, noticing that Marianne had looked crestfallen when being reminded of the departure of her favoured one.

"Never," Joseph admitted. "Some places I'm happier to leave than others, but once the sea is in your blood, it is hard to resist its charms."

"I never thought any of my sisters would leave Scotland, but it seems that might no longer be the case. Who knows where we will go? It could be overseas," Heather said, a touch of melancholy entering her voice.

"Oh?" Joseph asked.

"I think we have imposed on Captain Anderton enough," Cameron interrupted before Heather could respond. He knew full well she would tell Joseph all their troubles with little encouragement, and the fewer people who knew their plight, the better.

Joseph stood along with Cameron. "I shall return with you to Half Moon Street."

"There's really no need. You have work to do here. I will send the girls in one hackney, and I will follow in a second," Cameron said easily, failing to notice the facial expressions fall on two of the party.

"In that case, let me bid you a good day, Captain. Lady Marianne, Lady Heather, it has been a pleasure."

Marianne stepped forward. "Thank you for showing us the *Tara*. I can see why she's your pride and joy."

"She is," Joseph admitted. "I hope I see you again before I set sail."

"As do I," Marianne said quietly. She could see real warmth in Joseph's eyes, and it made the fact that he was leaving so soon even harder to think about.

The party separated at the gang plank, Joseph watching the group until they entered into hackneys and were driven away. Sighing he turned to return to his quarters. Noticing Peter Liptrot waiting for him, loitering at the doorway to Joseph's rooms, he groaned.

"So, which of the pretty ladies is smitten with the captain? Or have you conquered both hearts?" Peter teased, as only an old friend could.

"Haven't you got work to do?" Joseph asked, ignoring the jibe.

"Plenty. All of which will get done as soon as my Captain confesses all to his best friend."

"There is still time to employ a more amenable first mate," Joseph responded.

"None who would have my witty repartee and good looks."

"Thankfully, neither of those traits is a requirement for the role. I would go so far as to say that having them is a distinct disadvantage," Joseph said.

"I have just thought of a new ditty we can sing when raising a sail," Peter continued. "Captain Joe had so many women he didn't know which way to go. One was Marianne, one was Heather, but he couldn't decide which one would be better!"

Joseph turned to Peter. "If you want a flogging by my own hands, continue. Otherwise, not another word."

Peter clamped his mouth shut, but his eyes laughed at Joseph, who continued into his cabin and shut the door firmly. When there was no chance of being overheard, Peter started singing quietly. "Our captain's in love, but who is it to be? It won't be long before he says goodbye to the sea. A lady will tempt him away from us all. He will soon be dancing to her tune at a ball." Chuckling to himself, he walked away from Joseph's cabin.

*

Marianne sighed resignedly when she was seated in the hackney carriage.

Heather squeezed her sister's arm. "I think he likes you," she said quietly. "And I shall be having a word with Cameron. He should have encouraged Captain Anderton's accompanying us. It was poorly done by him."

Marianne smiled a little. "It was, but what's the use anyway? He sails in three days. By the time he returns to these shores, we will be goodness knows where, earning our keep."

"A pity you cannot force him to take you with him. That would be romantic... sailing off into the sunset."

"The only woman on a ship full of sailors," Marianne shuddered. "Not a prospect I would relish!"

Heather rested her head on the back of the seat. "We are going to have to find employment, aren't we? I keep trying not to think about it, but it is there at the back of my mind all the time. I think I'm not going to make a good companion or governess. I cannot seem to be silent or still when the need arises."

"Too long in Lou's company, I fear," Marianne said gently.

Heather turned to face her sister. "I don't know if I will ever be able to forgive her for what she did. I keep thinking back to those five days when we were going out of our minds with worry and she'd put herself at so much risk. If she had died, or been hanged, what would've become of us, Marianne? I had nightmares about it last night."

It was Marianne's turn to squeeze her sister. She grasped Heather's hands gently. "I know. We would have been lost to everyone and everything we know. We would've lost the opportunity to fit into polite Society. There was no chance we would have survived the seedier side of life. We should never have allowed Lou to come to London."

"As if she would have listened to us!" Heather snorted. "She has been too much the one to make decisions while we have been too easy to follow. But, no more! She'll influence me no longer!"

"Nor I," Marianne said. "Although when she marries Lord Garswood, she will be a woman of standing."

"Not while Lord Ince is in London," Heather said darkly. "I doubt he'll be one to forgive and forget what Lou did."

"What if the magistrate has taken her away?" Marianne asked, suddenly realising they could be returning to the news their sister had been arrested.

Heather swallowed. "Then it is best that we will not be in London for many days longer. I could not face being here while she suffered her punishment."

"She'll hang," Marianne whispered.

"I know."

Chapter 19

Simon took the stairs two at a time. He wanted to tell her the good news. He hadn't acknowledged how much he had worried about the meeting with the magistrate until it was over. He couldn't wait to tell her she was safe. He couldn't wait to tell her she had escaped punishment.

Knocking on Lou's bedchamber door, he opened it when he received acknowledgement from inside the room.

Lou was seated on the window seat, looking blindly outside. She'd been like that since the morning, unable to eat or drink anything. She turned to look at Simon, knowing immediately it wasn't bad news.

"How did you convince him?" she asked.

"I think it had more to do with Helena's words than mine. Before she entered, he seemed intent on questioning the servants and yourself, but after Helena had spoken, he changed his mind. If he did not believe me, Helena put enough questions in his mind about Henry's character to persuade him that what he'd been told was not all that it seemed," Simon explained.

Lou's head flopped back onto the window frame in relief. "Thank God for that. I was trying to be brave, but I was terrified."

"As was I," Simon admitted. "I didn't know how, but if he had not believed us, I was determined you were going to leave this house safely. It would probably have resulted in my arrest for imprisoning a magistrate!"

Lou looked at Simon. "Why are you so good?"

Simon blinked and then smiled. "I don't wish to be derogatory about my own character, but if you asked most of my acquaintance, they would respond with astonishment at my being considered good!"

"You have done so much for my family and asked naught in return. I don't understand why you would do that."

Simon seated himself at the edge of the bed. It was clear a flippant response wasn't appropriate. She needed to understand what drove him, and if they were to have a happy marriage, it was only fair he should try to explain himself.

"My father and mother," Simon started, before faltering and sighing. "My father was not a good man. He flaunted his mistresses, invited them into our home. They spent so much time with us. When I was old enough to realise what was going on, I was mortified. My mother hated it. But she stood by and let it go on, even defending it to me once. To be fair to her, there was little she could have done. My father had a temper. The only time he wasn't a cold fish was when he was angry," he finished.

Lou turned towards Simon, almost feeling the pain that was etched on his face. "Was he violent?"

Simon nodded. "To anyone who disagreed with him. I detested him. Another problem I had was that everyone ignored or accepted what he was and what he did. If he had a different mistress hanging from his arm every week, it did not matter. They all just chatted as if it were the most natural thing in the world."

"Your poor mother," Lou said quietly.

"I truly believe it killed her," Simon admitted out loud for the first time. "She just faded away. I hated him and detested the culture we belonged to. I was determined I wasn't going to be anything like him. And I certainly wanted nothing to do with Society and its fickle ways. I acted appallingly so no one would wish to get close to me, and it worked. I was a chip off the old block, so to speak."

"You were acting the part."

"Yes. And I did it well. But then you came along and crept under my skin," Simon smiled slightly.

"I was unconscious for most of the time!" Lou said.

Simon laughed. "Yes, you were. My curiosity was stirred from the moment I realised you were a woman. Then when I saw you dosed with laudanum, I felt a pull like I had never felt before."

Lou raised her hands. "Stop."

"Why?"

"I am more grateful than I've ever been in my life that you were the one to stop my scheme, no matter how you did it. I was foolish in the extreme, and I know I got off lightly for my crimes," Lou said quickly. "But the rest has to stop."

"The rest?" Simon asked, his expression darkening slightly as he guessed what Lou was going to say.

"The marriage proposal. Us. This!" Lou shrugged, not knowing how to eloquently word her rejection.

"We have to marry," Simon said.

"No. We do not. And we are not. I'm not forcing you into a loveless marriage when you've just explained how you hated your parent's marriage," Lou stated.

"That is why I was explaining my feelings. How I was drawn to you," Simon responded. "This is not some sort of idle offer."

"You were drawn to me because I was different. Do not mistake curiosity for love. It's not the same," Lou tried to explain.

"You think I'd get the two mixed up?"

"Don't get defensive. We aren't going to marry. I do not want to," Lou said. If her heart felt like lead as she uttered the words, she pushed the sensation away.

"The party. The guests. Your reputation," Simon stammered, trying to work out a way of convincing her that she was wrong. Again.

"We'll be leaving in a couple of days. I will be soon forgotten, and you'll be free to find a wife who will love you as you should be loved," Lou said, her tone sounding cold and uncaring. "I will let you off with a beating with a broad sword. I will not make you suffer the mortification of defeat."

She'd tried to lighten the mood, but she could see her words hadn't had an impact. Simon looked hurt, and she hated that she'd been the one to inflict pain on him.

"So that's it?" Simon asked, rising to his feet. "I am dismissed with a flippant attempt at humour?" he snapped.

"I was trying to be nice to you," Lou snapped in return. "To save your low feelings of self-worth. I shouldn't have bothered. I am saying no. I do not want to marry you. Is that clear enough?"

"I should not be surprised that you rode roughshod over my proposal. You've done it to your family. Why should I think I would receive different treatment?"

"Oh, don't start a pity fest, for goodness sake!" Lou said. Her defences were firmly in place, which in Lou's case, meant she was intent on self-destruction.

Simon looked at Lou as if seeing her for the first time. He ran his hand through his hair in an act of exasperation, but he continued to glare at her. "I have suddenly realised why your sisters have turned away from you. If you do not get your own way, you are vicious, aren't you? There is no compromise or consideration of anyone or anything else. Henry was right. On that night, you were nothing more than a criminal low-life. My guilty feelings made me see something that wasn't there: decency and love. My God, how wrong have I been! And I have committed perjury for you!"

Simon shook his head and turned away from Lou. He stormed to the bedchamber door but turned back towards Lou. "Please arrange your removal as soon as it's possible. I cannot bear to be near you."

The door slammed as Simon left the room, and Lou crumpled to the floor gasping for breath as the tears flowed in a torrent down her face.

*

An hour after Simon left the room, Cameron found Lou in the same position she'd fallen into on the floor. Cameron had been reluctant to leave his sister to her fate but had realised Heather and Marianne needed to be away from the house.

His stomach lurched when he saw what state Lou was in.

"My God! Lou! What's happened?" Cameron asked as he rushed to his sister's side. "Have they believed Lord Ince's story?"

Lou shook her head, trying to stem her sobs.

"Is that not a reason to celebrate then?" Cameron asked, his heart soaring at the thought that Lou wasn't going to hang.

"It's all gone wrong, Cameron! I've lost everything!" Lou sobbed, being enfolded into her brother's embrace.

Cameron allowed Lou to calm herself before trying to speak to her once more. "I don't understand your words. Did you or did you not convince the magistrate you were innocent?"

Lou took large gulps of air to try to control her sobs. When she had herself under control once more, she was finally able to speak. "Lady Helena was the one to save me. I didn't see the magistrate. After he spoke to her, he did not need to hear or see anything else."

Cameron's good opinion of Helena increased enormously, but he kept his feelings to himself. "So why all this despair?" he asked gently.

"I've refused Lord Garswood and made him detest me, just as Heather and Marianne hate me," Lou said, her tears falling once more.

"Ock, I am sure that's not right," Cameron soothed.

"You did not see it."

"Why have you refused his proposal? I know you like him, Lou. And I can see he likes you."

"How could I accept?" Lou asked incredulously. "He had just told me how fickle and shallow Society was, and then he was willing to bring a criminal into their midst. He'd have been laughed at, Cameron! How could I put him through such censure? I am not good enough for him, and I never will be! I think it's acceptable to steal from people when I am in dire straits! I'm not a good person."

"I will let the self-condemnation lie for the moment. So, you are admitting you do have feelings for him?" Cameron asked, needing to clarify.

"Of course, I do! I would be a halfwit not to love him for what he's done for me. For us all," Lou responded in a tone of voice that was more her usual self.

"Do not confuse gratitude with love," Cameron cautioned.

"It isn't gratitude. I feel that towards Lady Helena. More so after today. But Lord Garswood? No. That is something else completely. But I can't marry him, and the only way I could convince him he did not want to marry me was by making him hate me. Needless to say, I did it in spectacular fashion," Lou said wryly.

Cameron sat back and shook his head. "We are a fine pair, aren't we? I want Lady Helena but refuse either to make her a widow or ask her to wait years for me, and you want Lord Garswood but will not let his reputation be smeared because of your own. Some would say we are foolish in the extreme."

"I'm trying to convince myself that we are being noble," Lou responded.

"I'm not so sure any more," Cameron admitted.

"Oh, and as a result of Lord Garswood despising me, he would like us to leave as soon as possible," Lou said.

"I'll go and speak to him, but I think it is time to leave. I'm going to suggest the day after tomorrow. I want the chance to see Phillips before I return you all to Scotland. I am going to send a letter to start the arrangements for a chaperone," Cameron mused aloud.

"We need to find positions of employment," Lou said, relieved she was able to put her own hurt to one side in order to be practical.

"Eventually, perhaps, but not straight away," Cameron said. "I think some time together as sisters would do you all the world of good, but if I appoint a chaperone before I return to Portugal, I will rest easy knowing that there is someone responsible for you all."

"Yes. After my last great plan, I deserve not to be trusted," Lou acknowledged.

"Phew. That was easier than I expected!" Cameron smirked.

"You got me on a bad day," Lou responded darkly.

"Come. Wash your face. Have a rest. I'll ask for some tea to be sent up while I go speak to Lord Garswood and the girls," Cameron instructed.

"I have hurt them all by my actions," Lou said.

"No more self-pity. It is time to put this all behind us and return home. Look on the positive. At least I arrived home before Duncan had sold Glenloch!" Cameron said as he left Lou alone.

Chapter 20

Cameron spoke to Heather and Marianne and explained that they'd all be travelling to Scotland, he hoped, in two days. He left them alone to seek out Simon and ask for his indulgence once more in accommodating them for a little longer.

"I'm glad Lou is not being punished, but I do not want to be with her," Heather admitted.

"I suppose we have no choice in the matter if she isn't to marry," Marianne said dully.

"I am sorry you will not get to see Captain Anderton again," Heather said, guessing correctly the reason for her sister's despair.

"What am I going to do, Heather?" Marianne almost wailed.

"What can any of us do?" Heather asked rhetorically. "We're hardly able to do anything we wish now. Except of course be at someone's beck and call for the rest of our days."

Marianne covered her face with her hands. "I cannot bear it! Why can't I be with him?"

"I am sorry. There just hasn't been enough time. I do think he likes you," Heather tried to console.

"I think I will go for a lie down," Marianne said. "I feel a headache coming on."

Heather embraced her sister, knowing she was hurting for the loss of possibilities. From the first, Marianne had been smitten with Captain Anderton, and if his looks towards her were any hint, he was halfway in love with Marianne. It was cruel the way events had developed. Heather gritted her teeth. Lou had a lot to answer for!

*

Cameron left the morning room in which Heather and Marianne had ensconced themselves. He approached Simon's study and knocked. Called into the room, he entered but faltered at the door. Simon looked pale and drawn. He acknowledged Cameron with a nod, but there was no welcoming smile or greeting.

"I've come to apologise, yet again, for the difficulties my family has caused you," Cameron said.

"It's best if we end our acquaintance as soon as possible, for all our sakes," Simon responded.

Cameron was surprised at the venom in the words. "I'm sorry for the way Lou rejected your suit. I cannot imagine it was pleasant. She is devastated."

"I doubt that very much," Simon said with derision.

Taking a breath, Cameron squared his shoulders. "She is absolutely crushed by what she has done and by your reaction." Cameron raised his hands in a sign of surrender. "I'm not here to defend her, but I cannot stand by while you believe she is something she is not."

"Bloody minded, stubborn and idiotish?" Simon grumbled.

"She's those without a shadow of a doubt," Cameron admitted readily. "But she is not normally cruel, and if she didn't think her actions were for the best, she would not have hurt you so much."

"So, she decided to make decisions for me?"

"Probably. Yes, definitely. I know my sister, and she has feelings for you. In an odd way she's trying to protect you from making a big mistake."

"I think I am old enough to make my own mistakes," Simon ground out, still unconvinced of Cameron's words.

"Lou couldn't face your being rejected by anyone whom you believed to be your friend."

"If that's all it were, we could easily overcome that. That is of no concern," Simon dismissed Cameron's comments.

"Added to that, she does not feel worthy of you," Cameron continued. "She is not proud of what she did. It was wrong on so many levels. I know she likes you — a lot — but I think she doubts her judgement at the moment. If it were at another time… "

Simon sighed. "I've revealed more to her than I have to anyone else, including Helena. I trusted her. I wanted her to be my wife. But I want a wife who will stand by me when life gets tough not turn against me and push me away. Perhaps in the long-term it is best for both of us."

Cameron wasn't sure he agreed with the sentiment, but enough had been said for one day. "I have come to ask if you will allow us to impose on you for a little while longer. If you can bear us to remain here, I'd like to stay until the day after tomorrow. I have a little business to finish in town, which I can do tomorrow. After that we can remove ourselves to Scotland."

"Of course," Simon said, pushing away the voice that was shouting in his head to use the time to persuade Lou she was wrong. "Forgive me, but I shall keep out of your way as much as possible. You can use the house as you would your home with my blessing."

"Thank you. I don't think you will be in danger of bumping into Lou. I doubt she will be moving much from her chamber. She's in a distressed state, which I have honestly never seen before," Cameron said. Upon getting no real response from Simon, he bade him goodnight and left him alone.

Cameron left the house and entered the garden to the rear of the property. He wanted to feel air on his skin for a moment or two whilst he reordered his thoughts. He hadn't expected to travel to Scotland. He would be away from Portugal for longer than he had anticipated. Not returning as soon as he expected, he felt he was letting down his men, and that made the delay more of an impediment than it would have been in peacetime.

The garden was separated into raised flower beds, creating a little series of pathways around a reasonably small space. He strolled, looking but not seeing the foliage, just pondering on what he was going to do. He turned a corner and started when he saw Helena seated on a stone bench under an arbour.

"You're not a very good military man if I startled you," Helena laughed.

Cameron smiled. "I am not constantly thinking of my three sisters when I am on the battlefield," he admitted.

"Are things really tense? I thought it best to remove myself and let you all sort out things out without interruptions," Helena responded.

Cameron flopped down onto the seat next to Helena without waiting to be invited. "After today, I am not sure if a year would be enough time to reorganise the mess!"

"Is it that bad?" Helena asked, amused at the expression on Cameron's face.

"My sister won't marry your brother because she is not good enough for him, even though she loves him. I am sure of it. Marianne is devastated because she has an affection developing for Captain Anderton, and he is due to set sail in a couple of days. And then there is Heather, who is determined never to forgive Lou and doesn't want to travel to Scotland in the same carriage! Apart from that, life is fine," Cameron said, exasperated.

Helena laughed despite the seriousness of Cameron's words. "I am surprised you aren't running straight back to Portugal if that is the case!"

Cameron smiled, looking at Helena fondly. "I probably should be, but the three termagants who call themselves my sisters require me to act as soother and peacemaker."

"Whilst you would rather be organising a dozen or so unruly soldiers under your command instead," Helena said.

"It would be a sight easier, believe me!" Cameron muttered. He became serious. "I'm glad I came across you. I have you to thank yet again for saving my sister. I've been told how the magistrate believed everything you said."

Helena blushed a sweet pale pink. She could be more confident when the subject did not involve herself. "I actually spoke the truth. I mainly explained how Henry made me feel."

Cameron's cheek twitched as he gritted his teeth. "I would like to meet Lord Ince somewhere we wouldn't be disturbed for a while. He deserves a good beating for hounding you. It is the only fault I think your brother has, not to have seen how uncomfortable his friend made you."

"Simon is a man. He would not understand how someone can be intimidating whilst pretending to be charming," Helena defended her brother.

"I noticed," Cameron said.

"You have three sisters," Helena continued. "You are used to being on the look-out for them. Simon has only me, and it's my first season. I think he presumed that Henry would act like another big brother. In some respects, that was the impression Henry was giving, always making sure I danced the first two with him, leading me in to supper. It was just that no one but me heard what he was saying while we had those dances."

"I feel he deserves a beating even more so," Cameron ground out.

Helena was pleased with the words of protectiveness Cameron was saying, but she knew it would come to naught. Their chance at romance had been slim before the latest upset. She knew without doubt he would be engrossed with his family issues. There was no opportunity for her to try to persuade him to give their flirtation a chance.

"If you would like, I could ask Lady Heather and Marianne to stay with me for a holiday? I've asked my brother if we can leave London soon, and they could come and spend some time at our country home in Berkshire. We will not be entertaining very much, as most people are in Town for the season, but it would prevent you all travelling uncomfortably together," Helena offered.

Cameron swung round and took hold of Helena's gloved hand, raising it to his lips and kissing it. "Thank you," he whispered. "But no. We must overcome this if we are to stay solid as a family."

Helena had burned crimson at the action, but she squeezed Cameron's hand with her own. "As long as you know that you don't have to struggle alone."

Cameron smiled. "Lou is right about one thing. We will always thank the day your brother and you came into our lives. Now with renewed strength and determination, I'll go and face Heather and Marianne. They will have to become accustomed to the idea they'll be holed up with Lou in a carriage for days on end." He stood, and with a look of pure affection and longing, he left Helena alone once more.

"Marianne is not the only one to wish for more time with her chosen captain," Helena said quietly to herself.

Chapter 21

Heather woke to her sister's voice whispering in her ear.

"Wake up! I need to talk to you!" Marianne persisted, as Heather tried to bat her sister away. They shared a room, wishing always to be together since they came out of the crib.

"Can it not wait?" Heather grumbled, trying to burrow her way into the feather pillows.

"No! I've got something important to tell you, but I need your help," Marianne insisted.

Heather blinked a few times to focus her gaze on her sister. "Are you up to no good, Marianne?" she asked in surprise.

"No! Yes!" Marianne responded, her colour heightening.

Heather immediately pushed herself into a sitting position. She rubbed her eyes before smiling at her sister. "This I have to hear!" she said gleefully.

"I don't think you will approve," Marianne admitted.

"Then it must be really bad! You have my full attention, dear sister. Do tell!" Heather responded. Marianne was always the kind, gentle, good one in the family. She had more of Cameron's easy-going, likable nature while Heather should have been twinned with Lou; they were each fiery and impulsive.

"I'm going to stow away on Captain Anderton's ship," Marianne said simply. She was afraid to meet Heather's gaze, half-expecting her sister to laugh at her.

There was an uncomfortable pause, before Heather responded. "You are going to do what?" she asked incredulously.

Marianne flushed deeper red. "I cannot let him leave without me, Heather. If I do, I will never see him again, and I can't let that happen!"

"And when you get found? Because you will," Heather responded, serious for once.

"He will let me stay on his ship, and we will get to know each other better and fall in love," Marianne said.

"You don't think he will be as angry as a trapped wasp?" Heather asked. "He doesn't carry passengers. When he gave us the tour, he said he was happy to carry goods not people."

"I know, but you said yourself you think he likes me!"

"And I believe that. But this is extreme," Heather said. "Marianne, you will be out in open sea with a boat full of sailors. It's not safe!"

"Captain Anderton would not let anyone hurt me," Marianne insisted.

"I admit to not being able to guess what you were going to tell me, but this is madness, Marianne! It cannot work. There are too many things that could go wrong," Heather insisted.

"It doesn't matter. I have to go. I cannot return to Scotland. I won't return!" Marianne said mulishly.

Heather paused. "And what about me?"

"What do you mean?" Marianne asked.

"You're planning on leaving me," Heather said simply. She might be the more outgoing of the twins, but she relied on Marianne as much as her sister relied on her.

"That is the thought that has kept me awake all night," Marianne admitted. "But Heather, we're going to be separated anyway when we find employment. This is going to happen sooner than I thought, but at least I'm deciding what is going to happen to my life."

"Please see the folly of your thoughts," Heather appealed to her sister.

"I need your understanding. I know you think me foolish, but would hate to do something without your support. Even if it is reluctantly given," Marianne said with a sad smile.

Heather's eyes filled with tears. "You are determined to do this, aren't you?"

"Yes," Marianne admitted. "But I can only do it with your help. Please will you assist me, Heather?"

"I'd like to register one last time that this scheme is madness. Just as Lou's was. But, yes, I will help you," Heather said, her heart heavy with the thought that, if their plan worked, she wouldn't be seeing Marianne for goodness knows how long. "You do realise Captain Anderton is due to sail the day after we're leaving for Scotland?"

"Yes, but I am not going to reveal myself until after he's set sail. I want to be far enough out at sea that he cannot change course and return to London," Marianne explained, trying to show she'd thought of everything.

"More importantly, how the heck are you going to get on board?" Heather asked.

"That's where you come in," Marianne said with a smile. "I need to obtain some clothes that look like a sailor's uniform."

"You mean you want me to steal some clothing," Heather said with a huff.

"We can leave some pennies to make-up for the loss of the clothing," Marianne said.

"I am sure that will make all the difference," Heather said sarcastically. "Right. We have to think this through carefully," she said then, getting swept up in the scheme.

*

The hackney came to a stop a little way from the ship it had been directed to find. Marianne turned to Heather; both of them were pale.

"This is it," Marianne said. It had taken them longer than they'd anticipated to organise what was needed and arrange to get out of the house unnoticed.

"You can still change your mind," Heather said.

"If I don't try this, I know I will regret it for the rest of my days," Marianne insisted, but her eyes filled with tears.

"Oh, Marianne! You're the best of sisters, and I am going to miss you so much!" Heather wailed. "Please change your mind and come home!"

"I cannot. Please say you understand," Marianne begged her sister.

"I do. I had thought of persuading Cameron to take me back with him just so I could pursue Captain Philips, but I realised my plan was a foolish one," Heather admitted.

"Promise you will not reveal my absence," Marianne insisted. She'd written a letter but needed as much time to go by as possible before it was found.

"I'll place it on our bed tomorrow morning, as if you have slipped out in the night," Heather said. "Please be careful. I cannot tell you how worried I am about this whole scheme."

"If Lou can turn herself into a highwayman, I am sure I can pass as a sailor," Marianne said, trying to sound more confident than she felt.

"I can't see Cameron returning to Scotland once he discovers your absence, so you can rejoin us if you change your mind." Heather was desperate to reiterate the mantra, to put the seed into Marianne's mind that, if she should have a change of heart, she could return to her family.

Marianne hugged her sister tightly. "I love you, Heather. Please don't be sad."

"I love you too," Heather said, her voice choking. "I wish you all the luck in the world."

"Thank you," Marianne said as she pulled the thick woollen cloak she wore around her shoulders. It hid the male clothing she wore. It had taken some time to secure clothing that resembled a sailor's garb but also fitted her small frame. In the end a stable boy had been persuaded to give up his second set of clothes in exchange for more blunt than he would earn in a year. He'd been more than happy with the swap and had been promised more funds if he kept the secret.

Marianne stepped out onto the dockside. The hackney started to move away with the flick of the driver's reins. This was it. There would be no turning back for her. She hoped she'd not misread

Joseph's feelings or this would be the most embarrassing thing she would ever do.

She stepped behind some boxes piled at the side of a building. Holding her bundle of clothing and provisions close to her, she tried to disappear into the shadows. She couldn't approach the ship directly; there was always someone on duty at the top of the gangplank, but she hoped to spy her chance.

As afternoon progressed into evening, Marianne realised what a foolish chit she was. The night only quietened the docks a little. The hustle and bustle did not stop when the sun set, although without doubt it became more dangerous as the women of the night became more visible and the noise from the drinking hells increased as the effects of cheap alcohol were felt.

The way the women dressed made Marianne shrink into the shadows even further, if that were possible. The doxies were loitering along the dockside. Marianne had never seen sights like it and knew, without doubt, if she were discovered, she'd be ruined, likely in more ways than her panicked mind could imagine.

She watched the sailor on duty on top of the gangplank, willing him to move, but he remained at his post for hour after hour. Captain Anderton had explained that it was important to protect the cargo when they were loaded, so the sailor on duty was fully armed.

Marianne was about to give up hope of ever getting onto the ship when it seemed her luck was about to change. Four or five sailors, clearly very drunk, approached the ship. They shouted good-naturedly to the sailor on duty. Stumbling up the gangplank in the rolling gait that never seemed to change, one sailor was unable to cope with the change of surface and stumbled before falling to his knees. His friends berated him and tried to help him, but their inebriation made their efforts hardly worth the bother.

The sailor on duty cursed his colleagues before barking instructions to them. They were to leave their friend for him to deal with. The drunken sailors made slow progress up the gangplank, with Marianne watching and willing them to hurry.

When they'd moved out of sight, the duty sailor quickly walked to the collapsed sailor and started to lift him. Huffing and puffing he slowly half-carried, half-dragged the almost unconscious man.

Once they were out of sight on the deck of the ship, Marianne had to move. She had no idea if anyone were still on deck, but this was the closest thing to a chance, she'd had all day, and she had to risk it. Grabbing her bundle and holding her cloak closely around her, she ran quietly but quickly up the wooden gangplank. Pausing only slightly at the top, she couldn't see anyone, so she jumped on the deck.

She would be ever grateful that Joseph had been persuaded to take them below decks on their tour. Marianne hadn't been planning her scheme when she'd insisted on seeing the lower decks even though Joseph had explained that the lower decks weren't fit for a lady to see. The information was now vital if she were to secrete herself on board.

Now, with her heart beating loudly, she wondered about her sanity for even considering such a scheme.

The hold was her chosen location to hide. She knew she had no chance of hiding for the whole journey but hoped to remain undiscovered until they were well on their way to Portugal. She longed to travel and that part of the scheme excited her, but there was also the increasing presence of doubts that wouldn't go away. She had to hope that Joseph would not cast her overboard when she eventually revealed herself.

The hold was filled with products being taken to Portugal. Troops needed much equipment if they were going to continue the push into Spain.

Marianne moved quickly to the grill covering the hold and pushed it to one side just enough to fit through it. She clambered over the edge, and throwing down her bag, she let herself fall into the dark space.

She didn't have far to tumble. The hold on this voyage was full of fur from the Americas and Nankeen clothing from the mills of Manchester. It meant it was a soft landing and would provide warmth for Marianne when the ship started to move.

Having no light was a problem at first. Moonlight provided little help, and Marianne had to remain where she landed until her eyes became accustomed to the dark. The smell of the skins was almost overwhelming at first, the different animals having differing odours, even though the fur had been processed. Marianne had retched initially at the aroma but managed to calm her stomach by breathing through her mouth. She would have to become accustomed to the stench.

She wore fur at home. Anyone spending a winter in Scotland appreciated the warmth a fur could bring, but she would have never guessed the effect of having so many in one place.

Eventually, her eyes became used to the almost complete darkness, and she was able to see crates, presumably filled with the nankeen clothing. She was thankful the furs were positioned where they were, or she could've had a far more painful landing.

Pushing herself further into the hold, she was able to make a space behind some of the crates. The hold was extremely full but had a small walkway through it. There was a door that allowed access into the lower decks, but she couldn't risk going that way. There would be too many sailors on board.

She managed to pull one fur off one of the large piles for her to sit on and used another to cover herself. She tried to settle in. Knowing the ship was going to sail on the high tide in two days filled her with nerves. She had brought some bread, ham, and biscuits with her and knew she would have to ration them carefully. Something to drink was more problematic. For the first time in her life she had stolen — two hipflasks from her brother.

She'd filled the flasks with brandy. Not usually a drink she'd choose, she thought it might help her sleep for the journey.

Now all she had to do was be patient and wait.

Chapter 22

Heather hardly slept without Marianne in the same room. She fretted all night about the safety of her gentle sister. On her return to the house, she'd entered without anyone noticing and had said that Marianne was feeling unwell, so she had retired early.

It had been easier to tell the lies with only Cameron being around, as Lou was still keeping to her room. Heather tried to avoid Helena; she didn't like lying to their hostess, especially as she'd been so kind to them all.

Now it was early morning, and Heather would have to lie again. She'd placed Marianne's letter on the pillow the previous evening. At least the first words she uttered were more or less the truth. She had found the letter there when she awoke.

Heather sighed and got out of bed. Cameron was an early riser. It was best to get this over with.

Finding Cameron in the dining room tucking into a large plate of food, she handed him the letter. He tried to smile at Heather but paused when he saw her expression.

"What is it?" he asked, half expecting Heather to refuse to travel in the same carriage as Lou.

"This was on Marianne's side of the bed this morning," Heather said, holding out the letter.

Cameron immediately wiped his mouth and hands on his napkin before reaching for the letter. "Where is Marianne?" he asked, tearing the seal on the letter.

"I don't know," Heather responded. She consoled herself with thinking that she actually didn't know where her sister was.

Cameron skimmed the letter before cursing under his breath and pushing away from the table.

"What is it?" Heather asked.

"Have her things gone?" Cameron demanded, already walking out of the dining room and making his way to the stairs.

"I don't know. What does she write?" Heather asked, genuinely wishing to see what Marianne had penned.

Cameron didn't respond, instead bursting into their bedchamber and making for the drawers. He pulled out each drawer, looking for signs of Marianne, but there weren't any. "Did you not hear anything last night?" he demanded of Heather.

"No. Can I see the letter? What's Marianne written?"

"I need to know if she spoke to Lou," Cameron responded. "Have you any idea where she is?"

"No." Heather would be haunted by the look of pain on Cameron's face for long into the future, but she had to give Marianne this chance, so she squared her shoulders and looked directly at Cameron. "I don't know where she is."

Cameron banged on Lou's chamber door before walking in, Heather following in his wake. "Marianne has disappeared," he said without preamble.

Lou had been sitting on the window seat. The place she had spent the last couple of days, but she swung her legs off the seat when Cameron entered. "What? How?"

"That's what I would like to know," Cameron ground out. "She left this." He handed the letter to his sister.

Lou read the missive, her frown increasing with every word. "What can she be thinking?"

"I want to see the letter!" Heather demanded. "She is my twin, and I am being kept in the dark!"

Lou handed Heather the letter without a word. She'd have normally cursed at Heather, but since they had found out what she'd done, Lou no longer felt able to use the authority of being the elder sister to coerce her younger siblings into doing as she wished.

Heather snatched the parchment and began to read.

Dear Heather, Cameron, and Lou,

I am sorry to have to send this letter and leave the way I have, but I felt there was no other choice open to me.

I cannot face returning to Scotland with you all and then leaving my home once more for goodness knows what fate. I have little to recommend myself for employment, so I have come to the conclusion that it is up to me, and only me, to decide what happens in my future.

I know this will cause you pain, but I feel it is the only way to take back control of my life. Since we left Scotland, events have been out of my control, and I cannot bear it any longer.

Thank you, my lovely family, for everything you have done for me. I am going to miss you more than you could ever realise. Please forgive me, Heather.

I will send a letter once I have settled somewhere.
Yours affectionately,
Marianne

Heather was crying real tears by the time she'd finished the letter. There was no need for falsehoods. She turned to Lou. "You caused this. If anything untoward happens to her, I will blame you until my last breath!"

"Heather… " Cameron started.

Lou shook her head at her brother. "Don't. She's right. I am to blame, and I'm sorry, Heather. I will do everything I can to find her."

"You still don't understand, do you?" Heather snapped. "She doesn't want to be found! She wishes to be as far away from us as she can get, and I can't criticise her! She has the guts to do what I wish for!"

"We will have none of that," Cameron said sternly. "You are remaining here while I try to find Marianne."

"Let her be, Cameron," Heather said sadly.

Cameron shook his head before enfolding Heather into his embrace. "You cannot expect me to do that, surely?" he asked gently. "She is out goodness knows where. I have to find her, Heather. We will work something out when we've found her so that she will be happy to return with us."

"What can you possibly offer that will make everything right again?" Heather sobbed.

"We aren't paupers," Cameron said gently. "We can work something out even if we have to retrench. I could sell our home and buy a smaller place."

"But Papa left you that. It's yours!" Lou intervened.

"And how happy do you think I'll be knowing that you three are employed in some form, whilst I have a secure roof over my head?" Cameron asked. "No. We are sticking together as a family."

"It isn't just about obtaining a position in order to earn a living, though, is it?" Heather asked, looking at her siblings.

"What else is it about?" Cameron asked.

"It's about marriage and the chance of our own families. We will not attract anyone with sense from Society," Heather tried to explain. "And if we try to marry a gentleman farmer, we have no skills to offer. We have been cosseted and are useless!"

"I beg to differ. I have three resourceful sisters, which is why one of you is usually being the bane of my life. I admit, I never thought Marianne would be, but perhaps this is her turn," Cameron said with a small smile.

A tap on the door notified the occupants that Helena and Simon were standing in the doorway. "Is there anything amiss? We heard raised voices," Simon said.

"We have a problem," Cameron said before informing them of what had happened. Helena immediately went to comfort Heather, and although Simon glanced at Lou, he didn't say anything to her.

"We need to organise a search. I will get the butler to gather the footmen and the grooms, and we can cover more places. Have you any idea where she might be?" Simon asked.

"I haven't a clue," Cameron admitted. "She does not know anyone apart from whom she's met through you."

"We will start by checking with them. We'll also check on the stage and coaching inns, to see if she left town," Simon said, being practical.

Cameron nodded. He turned to Lou and Heather. "Please remain here," he instructed.

"But we could help," Lou insisted.

"No. I want to know you're both safe here. I need your promise, Lou," Cameron responded.

Lou nodded, and it was the cue for Simon and Cameron to leave. The room quietened.

Lou turned to Heather, still being held by Helena. "I am sorry, Heather. I truly am."

"But you can't make it right, can you? You started a spiral of events, and now I have lost Marianne! Yet, you have lost nothing!" Heather said, removing herself from Helena's embrace and walking out of the room.

"She is hurting and angry. She does not mean what she says," Helena said gently.

"I don't blame her. I would be twice as angry if our roles were reversed," Lou admitted. "It's such a damned mess!"

Helena winced slightly at the language Lou had used but was used to her enough to understand it was part and parcel of who Lou was. "We will have to hope they find her."

"I'm afraid to think what will happen to her if they do not," Lou said, all bravado gone.

*

Heather hadn't had to fake any of the concern she felt for her sister. She was half hopeful all day they would find Marianne, and it would have nothing to do with a betrayal on her part if that happened. When darkness fell, the servants, along with Cameron and Simon, returned to the house in a dejected state. Heather was as torn as she'd ever been, wanting her sister to have the chance at love and yet at the same time needing her to be home.

She eventually cried herself to sleep. Unhappy and not knowing which way she should react she knew that, if she didn't speak out soon, the chance would be gone.

Cameron had seated himself in the library, pouring a glass of whisky. Taking a large swig, he flushed a little when Simon entered the room. "I'm depleting your stock, I'm afraid. Yet another thing I have to apologise for."

Simon smiled. "That's not necessary. I can only try to imagine what you are feeling." He filled his own glass with a large measure and sat in the vacant chair. It had been a long day for them all. "What are you going to do next?"

"First thing tomorrow, I will find us accommodation and then continue my search. Admittedly, I've no idea where to start, as we appeared to cover every possibility today," Cameron admitted. "But I cannot leave London without her. Lou would survive, of sorts, if she had to remain here, but not Marianne. I'd even rate Heather's chances above her sister's. She is such an innocent, and she is somewhere on the streets of the largest city in the world with little money and even less protection."

"You can stay here as long as you need to," Simon said quickly.

"After what has gone on? No. We've definitely outstayed our welcome," Cameron said dryly.

"I cannot offer much, but I'm insisting you have the use of my home. You can rely on me to do anything that is required. And Helena can help support Lady Heather."

"We can't keep increasing our debt to you in this way," Cameron said.

"There is no debt," Simon responded. "Funnily enough, you have helped me get rid of a friendship that wasn't good for myself or my sister. That is payment enough."

"I am glad he's a great distance from Lady Helena. She deserves better than he," Cameron said forcefully.

"She does," Simon acknowledged. A small nugget of curiosity unfurled as he wondered at the venom in Cameron's words. It was not the appropriate time to question the young man who was rapidly turning into a friend despite the odd circumstances with which they were constantly being faced. "So, it's settled that you will all stay here. If there's anything else, including funds that you require, you have my support."

"I will not be asking you for any blunt!" Cameron exclaimed.

Simon smiled sympathetically. "Forgive my frankness, but a captain's wage is going to be exhausted at some point if you are paying for people to search for Lady Marianne."

Cameron gritted his teeth. "I never thought I'd curse Marianne to the devil. All I hope is that she is well and safe. I cannot face the thought of her in danger."

*

Lou had been updated by Cameron, before he'd gone to bed. She'd paced her bedchamber for over an hour before she decided what she had to do. Still dressed, although her candles had burned low, she left her room. She just knew he'd still be downstairs.

Opening the library door, she felt a slight tug of satisfaction to have guessed correctly. Simon was still in the chair he'd been seated in when sharing whisky with Cameron.

As she'd done before, she just seated herself in the chair next to him without a word.

Simon raised his eyebrows in question when Lou entered the room. They hadn't seen each other properly since their argument, the words of which still rang through his mind.

"I think you have a sleep problem," Lou said quietly.

"I don't. I drink myself into oblivion, and then I sleep. No problem," Simon said flippantly.

"And what keeps a lord of the realm awake at night?" she asked.

"If I knew that, I would not have a large whisky and brandy bill to finance each month," came the dry reply.

"So, it's not since you met me?"

"No. it's not a recent thing. Although you've not helped," he admitted.

Lou grimaced. "That will be my epitaph. Or, the one that says she managed to make an unholy mess every time she tried to sort out her life."

"I did not have you down as one for self-pity," Simon admitted.

"I'd rather say it was being honest with oneself."

"Well you were honest with me," Simon couldn't help mentioning their argument.

"No, I wasn't," Lou admitted.

"I don't think it's the appropriate time to go over our last conversation. I am still smarting from the verbal whipping you gave me," Simon admitted.

Lou sighed. "I seem to be saying this a lot recently, but I am truly sorry. When I'm afraid, I just do not think rationally, and I lash out."

"That is true."

"You aren't going to make this easy, are you?" Lou asked.

"I am not a vindictive person, but I'm also not a fool. I am not about to be taken in again so easily," Simon replied honestly.

Lou blinked quickly before gaining control of her emotions once more. It was her own fault. Of course, he wasn't going to forget what she'd said; no one would. "Believe this. I admire you and like you more than I've ever done with anyone else. And I include my family in that."

"Praise indeed."

"I mean it. I truly do," Lou insisted. "Lord Garswood... Simon... please. If there is a grain of forgiveness within you, please allow it to surface. I do not want your pity, but your poor opinion of me is more than I can stand at the moment. I do not deserve your indulgence. I'm fully aware of that. But I need it," Lou said with a choked voice.

"Why does my opinion matter so much to you?" Simon asked in genuine puzzlement.

Lou took a breath before speaking. The words wouldn't be easily said. "When you saw me in the long gallery that day and I broke down… I was so ashamed at first. I thought it was a sign of weakness on my part, and you would ridicule me for it."

"I would never be so brutish."

"I know. I think I knew then, only I didn't trust my feelings. I've got so much wrong recently. I doubt I will ever recover fully, but one thing I am sure about," Lou said tentatively.

"What's that?" Simon asked, turning so he could look her fully in the face.

"I have never felt so damned safe as I did in your arms. It felt like what was happening around me did not matter. With you holding me, all would be well."

Simon stood and approached the fireplace. He rested his fist on the mantelpiece, almost as if he'd like to punch it. "Lou. I do not think now is the time for this conversation. Your emotions are all over the place because of your sister. Let's forget we ever said anything and just concentrate on bringing your family back together."

Lou visibly sagged at his words. "I have lost you, haven't I?" she asked quietly.

"I think we've lost each other," Simon admitted. "I will assist you all in whatever way I can. And hopefully with the safe return of Lady Marianne, we can all resume our lives as if the last weeks haven't happened."

"I'm not sure I will be able to do that," Lou admitted. She stood. There was no point trying to convince him of her remorse any longer. He'd been very clear in his rejection. As she walked towards the door, she turned back to Simon. "I am truly sorry. If you believe nothing else, please believe that."

"As am I," Simon said as Lou left the room and closed the door.

Once alone, Simon pushed off the mantelpiece as if he were going to follow Lou before checking himself and flopping into one of the vacant chairs. Rubbing his hands over his face, he groaned.

"What the bloody hell did you hope to achieve by pushing her away in her hour of need, you dammed fool," he cursed himself, before reaching for the brandy decanter.

Chapter 23

Captain Joseph Anderton was, for the first time in his life, reluctant to set sail. He'd been at sea since he was a young boy. It had been a perfect choice of profession for a boy wishing to escape his family history.

Born and bred in India, his father a member of the British aristocracy, his mother an Indian mistress, he had never fitted into either world. He would never be recognised as heir to his father's estate in England. After all, the man had a wife and family at home, waiting for his return. If Joseph was questioned about his family, he always said they were dead. It was easiest that way.

His mother's family, although not poor by Indian standards, were not rich by any means. His mother had acted as his father's housekeeper before their relationship had developed into something else.

She'd been set-up as his father's mistress, bringing shame to her Indian family and ensuring any offspring they had would be considered outcasts for the whole of their lives.

Joseph had been given an English name and been brought up in the English fashion. Some of the British people living in India had accepted his father's living arrangements. He wasn't the only British man to adopt an Indian mistress. So Joseph had grown, to some extent, as he would've done had he been a genuine member of the aristocracy.

Looking like his British father, with the darker hair and skin tone of his mother, meant that his darkness could be put down to his chosen occupation of sea captain. Most sailor's complexions were tanned by the sun and salty wind.

His father had close links to the East India Company, and at an early age, Joseph had spent his time around ships. Choosing to remove himself from a life in which he would always be the outsider, he joined a ship's crew as soon as he was able.

The East India Company was rapidly expanding, and a capable, hard-working young man with some connections could rise through the ranks quickly. Joseph had been made captain of his own ship two years before at the young age of two and twenty. Now, through accumulating prize money he owned his own ship and independently sailed the seas.

Now at four and twenty, for the first time, he'd let his foolish heart dream of a life on land with a young woman. Meeting Marianne had been a delightful surprise, and he'd fallen under her spell immediately.

She was everything he couldn't have: a member of the British aristocracy, an auburn-haired, green-eyed Scot, a fine, shy, beautiful, young woman. Unfortunately, his heart wasn't inclined to listen to his head, and within an hour of their first meeting, he was completely smitten.

He'd shown her round his ship like a child showing off a favourite toy, but he'd longed for her approval. She'd looked to him to tell her tales of travel, claiming she'd hardly travelled herself. He could see she was attracted to him, and he'd been half-pleased, half-tortured by the realisation.

If she knew his background, she wouldn't be allowed to speak to him by her protective older brother. Hell, if she was his sister, he wouldn't let her speak to himself, so he couldn't condemn Cameron for it.

To an outsider, he seemed the perfect gentleman sailor; only he knew of his base roots. It was the reason he should set sail and leave British shores. He had to put Lady Marianne completely out of his mind.

Walking across the top deck as soon as they'd left the Thames estuary, he let his face be warmed with the sun. He'd taken control of the wheel as they'd sailed down the river. The sandbanks under the surface could prove problematic, many used pilots to sail down the river, but he'd been taught by the best and could sail down it without mishap. With confidence he had focused on his task, the first time in days his mind had to be emptied in order to concentrate. Reaching the bow of the ship, he took in a deep breath of salty air. This was what he needed: a stiff breeze to give them speed and blow away his melancholy mood.

Joseph smiled as the wind took hold of the sails and the ship seemed to lurch forwards. It would be good to reach the wide open waters of the Atlantic Ocean once the English Channel had been navigated. Sometimes, the Channel could feel as busy as a dock with the amount of shipping that was to-ing and fro-ing around the southern ports.

Peter approached his captain. They had a good relationship, almost like brothers, as they'd served on the same ships for over seven years. As soon as Joseph had gained his own vessel, he'd approached Peter to be his second-in-command.

"You are looking happier than you have done in days," Peter said, also enjoying the wind in his face.

"I'd started to day dream about a life I could not have," Joseph admitted.

"What else ever upsets our balance? There's nothing as damning as what a fair woman does to us. I suggest a hefty measure of rum and a trip to a brothel at the first port we visit. That will take your mind off those we should not touch."

The thought of lying with a woman who wasn't Marianne made bile rise in his throat, something he'd never experienced before. He hid the emotion with a small smile to his friend. "You're right about the rum."

"I am always right," Peter said before sauntering onto the main deck.

*

Marianne was alerted that something was happening with the increased noise level, which seemed to be all encompassing. The ship started to move slowly at first, as if she were reluctant to leave her docking. Marianne couldn't see that the ship had only two sails unfurled, purposely reducing the speed whilst navigating the Thames.

There were voices shouting above her, but she couldn't pick out Joseph's voice. Staying in the hold had proved more difficult than she'd anticipated. There was nowhere in which ablutions could take place. She'd been mortified but had to use a bucket and then try to keep it out of sight. Luckily, no one had come into the hold, and she hoped no one would until they reached their destination.

Unfortunately for Marianne she hadn't considered how her body would react to sea travel; it hadn't occurred immediately. The smooth journey down the Thames had lulled her into a false sense of security. When the ship lurched forward and started to pick up speed, Marianne's stomach had lurched as well, but she tried to push away the sensation, putting it down to excitement.

Within a very short period of time, Marianne knew she was in trouble. She was going to cast up her accounts, and there was nothing she could do about it. Using the bucket at first, she felt more nauseated every time the ship rolled with the waves. She was convinced, that once her stomach was empty of the little she'd eaten, it would settle down.

It wasn't to be the case.

Within three hours, Marianne could hardly move her head as she vomited on the fur that lay underneath her. She had never felt so ill in her life and was crying with the overwhelming feeling of nausea. She tried to cry out to catch someone's attention but hadn't the strength to raise her voice above the noise of the wood that seemed to be constantly creaking all around her. She might have wondered about the safety of the ship, which seemed to object almost vocally to the task that was being demanded of it, but she hadn't the energy to think, let alone worry.

After ten hours, Marianne was barely conscious.

*

Cameron was seated in the library on the third day of Marianne's absence. He was coming to the conclusion that his sister was lost to them forever, and he was struggling to control the waves of despair washing over him.

He was disturbed from his reverie by Simon, entering with the butler and a small boy. Cameron shot a questioning look at Simon.

"Jake here went missing a few days ago. He's a stable boy," Simon started to explain. "It turns out he had come into some money and decided he was going to have a good time with it."

"Oh?" Cameron asked, realising immediately this had something to do with Marianne.

"Yes. It seems that Jake is not as clever as he thought, and a fool and his money are easily parted," Simon continued. "He tried to return to the stables unseen this morning. He has had a beating from the head groom for deserting his post, but in his attempt to avoid punishment, he mentioned how he'd come into the money."

"Marianne?" Cameron asked.

"Yes. It appears she needed to look like a boy, and his clothing was the best fit. He was given more than a year's wage and was promised more if he did not mention to anyone what had happened," Simon said grimly. He knew the information was going to cause even more distress for the Drummond family.

"But how could she get further funds to him?" Cameron asked, before looking angrier than Simon had ever seen him. "Heather!" he exploded before running out of the room and making for the stairs.

The heavy thud of his feet caused Heather, Helena, and Lou to come to the doors of their bedchambers. All thought there was news of Marianne. As Cameron turned onto the upper hallway, he swung around to Heather.

"You knew!" he snarled at his sister.

Heather took a step back in fear. She'd never seen Cameron looking so furious, and it frightened her. "Cameron… I…" she stuttered.

"Tell me I am wrong!" Cameron demanded.

"I… she…" Heather responded, her eyes filling with tears.

"Good God, Heather! We've been out of our minds! We have spent so much time and money, and you knew where she was all this time!" Cameron shouted, all propriety gone.

Simon placed a hand on Cameron's arm. He'd followed upstairs, knowing the situation wasn't going to be easy, but although Cameron was justified with his anger, — Simon could shake the girl himself — he thought it best to try to calm Cameron.

"Let's talk about this," Simon said quietly.

Cameron flashed Simon a look. "I am beyond talking! My sisters are monsters! I used to think Duncan was the worst type of sibling I could ever have, but at least I knew what he was like. My sisters have been cared for, loved dearly by me, and every single one of them has betrayed my trust and love for them. I have had enough!" Cameron said with bitterness. He turned back to Heather. "Tell me where she is, and once I find her, I will return her. I'll give you the funds to get to our Aunt, and then I want nothing more to do with any of you!"

Heather gasped and burst into tears. Lou seemed to sag against the door jamb at her brother's words, but Cameron remained unmoved.

"Where is she?" Cameron bellowed.

"On the... on the... She has gone to Captain Anderton!" Heather wailed.

"He's taken her with him?" Cameron asked in disbelief.

"No! She stowed herself away on board ship!" Heather sobbed.

"A stowaway?" Cameron asked, stunned. "What was she thinking of?"

"S-she wanted to have more time with him. She loves him." Heather crumpled to the floor, sobbing uncontrollably.

Helena went to her friend, lifting her upright. "Captain Drummond, you need to check when Captain Anderton's ship sailed. It might not be too late to find her."

Cameron took a moment for Helena's words to register before turning on his heel and thundering back down the stairs. Simon looked ready to follow Cameron but then he caught sight of Lou's expression.

Lou's eyes were haunted, but she met Simon's gaze. "She will be safe on the ship, won't she?" she asked, barely above a whisper.

Simon nodded. "If she is on the ship with Anderton, she's safe. He is a gentleman," Simon assured her.

Lou covered her mouth with her hand, trying to contain the sobs, but the emotion was too strong. She faltered as if to faint. Simon was by her side in an instant, catching her falling body and lifting her easily into his arms. He glanced at Helena.

"Take Lady Heather to her bed. Give her some brandy," Simon instructed, before carrying Lou into her own chamber.

The butler had followed his master. "My Lord, is there anything I can do?"

"Bring me a few drops of laudanum and some whisky. I think Lady Lou needs to rest. She has had a shock."

The butler nodded and left the room, closing the door behind him.

Simon lay Lou on her bed. She normally had a pale complexion, but now she looked ghostly. Sitting on the edge of the bed, Simon started to rub Lou's hands, trying to increase her blood circulation.

"This is good news," Simon said quietly. "She is ensconced on board a fine ship, if Captain Anderton's description was anything to go by." He was trying to lighten the situation without being glib.

Lou eventually stirred and slowly opened her eyes. She fixed Simon with a stare, as if he were the only person who could save her. "I thought she was dead," she whispered, swallowing hard to control the tumultuous feelings thrashing about her insides.

Simon had also been presuming the same. "Even if your brother is too late and they've set sail, she will return in a few weeks."

"But we will not know for certain if she is aboard," Lou pointed out.

"No. But there is a bigger chance she will be," Simon said reasonably.

They were interrupted by the butler, bringing a tray that contained a decanter, glasses, and a bottle of laudanum. "If you need anything else, My Lord, I can send a maid to sit with My Lady."

"T-that won't be necessary," Lou said. "I will be fine soon." She tried to raise herself higher on the bed, but the movement caused the dizziness to return.

Simon saw her face pale once more and put his hand on her shoulder. "You are going nowhere," he said firmly. "I will stay for a while."

The butler acknowledged the words and left the chamber once more.

Lou acquiesced to Simon's instructions far meeker than she would have done normally. "I do not want laudanum."

"We'll start with the whisky then," Simon said. He brought a full glass, and raising Lou's head slightly, tilted the glass against her lips.

Lou took a sip and then turned her head into the crook of Simon's arm. She sighed.

Simon was able to be pragmatic about caring for Lou. Being so close while he gathered her up to raise her off the pillows had been necessary to tend to her. When she reacted by almost snuggling into him, he swallowed. He could not help but be moved by her action.

"Lou," he said quietly.

"I need you," Lou said in return.

Simon didn't need to be told twice. He moved himself onto the bed and wrapped Lou in a full embrace. Their bodies were fully laid against each other. It was completely inappropriate, and he supposed he was taking advantage of Lou's weakened state, but he wanted to be as close to her as she appeared to want him.

Lou gripped one lapel of his frock coat in her hand, as if to prevent him moving away from her and rested her head on his chest. She was still and quiet for many minutes. Simon presumed she had fallen into an exhausted sleep, but then she stirred.

Forcing herself to move her upper body so that she could look into Simon's eyes, Lou swallowed when she realised how close they were. It was a stupid thought really. She knew how close she was to him, but somehow it had seemed more impersonal when they hadn't been looking at each other. Now, she could see the deep blue of his eyes, the curve of his cheeks, and the way his breath caught as she looked at him.

"I was wrong," she said quietly. It wasn't the time. She wasn't strong enough to face his rejection, but she had to say the words.

"What about?" Simon asked. He was looking at Lou with equal intensity.

"Everything. But especially about my feelings."

"I don't want to fight with you again," Simon said.

"No. Neither do I. But I do not need you as I said," Lou said.

"I see," Simon said. He started to move off the bed, but Lou tugged his frock coat, which she still held grasped in her hand.

"No. You do not," she said. "I want you. I need you in a way I never thought possible."

"Lou. You do not have to say this. I'm here. I'm your friend," Simon said.

"I do not want you as my friend. I want you as my lover, my husband, everything," Lou said, releasing his frock coat in order to tentatively touch Simon's face. "I was so wrong when I rejected you. I cared for you so much, but I could not give myself to you."

"And now?"

Lou took a deep breath. "Now I don't care that I will attach scandal to your name, that I am not nearly as good for you as you deserve. I want you, and I could not bear it if you were with someone else. If Marianne has chased Captain Anderton out of love, I completely understand her reasoning. Will you take me as your wife? Please?"

Simon kissed Lou gently on the lips. "We don't have to do this now."

"I don't understand."

"You've just been through an emotional upheaval," Simon explained. "I realise that. Do not proclaim something to me that might fade once your feelings have had time to settle down."

"They won't. The other night in the library. I wanted to say so much to you, but you would have rejected me. You dismissed what I was trying to say. I have been at a loss as to how I could speak to you in a way that would convince you of my words. You have got to believe me because I've never loved anyone like this, and it is frightening me half to death. It is uncontrollable! Draining and overwhelming. And it won't go away!"

Simon chuckled. "Only you could make a declaration of love sound so inconvenient!"

"I don't like not being in control. It's terrifying," Lou admitted.

"You won't be in control all of the time if we marry," Simon pointed out seriously. "I am not going to do battle with you for every little thing, Lou."

Lou glanced away for a moment. "I know," she said eventually. "I wouldn't want to marry me if I were you. I know I am not going to be the easiest of wives to live with. But trust me in what I say. I love you, and your happiness is so important to me. If that means biting my lip a time or two, I'll learn."

Simon smiled. "That sounds promising, at least."

"Does this mean we are to marry?"

Simon paused with a slight frown marring his features. "Do you know, I think you wanted to marry me all along. You just wanted to be the one doing the asking! I'm right, aren't I?"

Lou laughed despite her earlier despair about Marianne. "No! You are completely wrong!" Simon glared at her, which made her laugh again. "Well, maybe a little wrong."

"God help me! Give me strength to deal with this woman! I am going to need it!" Simon said before kissing the woman who'd caused him nothing but trouble since the day he'd met her.

Eventually, Simon pulled away from Lou. He looked at her with a smile on his face. "Your colour is back, and your lips look completely kissed. I like this version of you."

"Why stop?" Lou said, kissing him once more, but Simon pulled away from her.

"I don't think now is the time to be announcing we are to marry," he said.

Lou's brow clouded. "No, probably not. We need to know Marianne's safe and well. But it doesn't stop me from wanting to marry soon!" Lou half-wailed.

"Well, you are going to have to learn patience," Simon said, consoling her with kisses.

"Will you still spend time with me, alone?" Lou asked.

"Every moment I can, you doxy."

Lou laughed. "In that case, we will wait. But I want to be married as soon as I can. Preferably, the day after we find out Marianne is safe. I don't want you changing your mind."

"I will not be doing that," Simon said with conviction.

Chapter 24

The afternoon was coming to an end on the second day of sailing, and Joseph was walking along one of the lower decks when he was nearly bowled over by one of his able seamen. The boy looked mortified at barrelling into his captain, but he was obviously agitated about something. Joseph watched the boy with some sympathy; he'd been terrified of his higher ranking officers when he'd been that age.

"What is it, Wallis?" Joseph asked.

"I'm sorry, Capt'n," Wallis responded, looking back over his shoulder.

"Take a breath and tell me what is the matter," Joseph responded.

"I have to check the hold on every other watch. I just make sure everything is secure and no crates have fallen," Wallis started. "Yesterday, I thought there was a smell in there."

"Furs have an odour," Joseph pointed out.

"Yes, Capt'n. But this smell was different, and it was worse today," Wallis continued. "I decided to find out what it was."

"And?" Joseph prompted, wishing the boy would get to the point.

"You had best come and see, Capt'n," Wallis finished.

"Lead on," Joseph said resignedly.

Wallis led the way through the small gap in the product being carried. Joseph had to admit there was an unpleasant odour in the space. Wallis stopped in front of a pile of crates and pointed behind them.

"We've got a stowaway, Capt'n," he said, gaining courage now that he could show he wasn't babbling nonsense to his superior officer.

"What?" Joseph said, stepping so he could see what was hidden behind the crates. He faltered at the sight that faced him.

"What shall we do, Capt'n?" Wallis asked, nervous that his captain hadn't spoken on seeing the stowaway.

The frown on Joseph's face was interpreted by the boy as anger about finding a stowaway, but the reality was that Joseph couldn't believe what he was seeing.

Marianne's hair covering had fallen off, and her rich auburn locks cascaded about her shoulders. Joseph had dreamed about that luscious hair but to see it in the hold of his ship? No. It couldn't be her.

After a moment or two, Joseph's mind was able to convince itself that indeed it was her, but not only that, she was in trouble.

He dropped to his knees, ignoring the mess that covered Marianne. Gently brushing her hair away from her face, he whispered her name. There was no response.

Joseph looked around to try to ascertain what ailed her, and it didn't take him long to realise at least some of what was wrong.

"Get the first mate. Now!" Joseph commanded.

Wallis ran at Joseph's words, leaving Joseph kneeling down at the side of a recumbent Marianne.

"Dear God, Lady Marianne! What has happened? What brought you here?"

Joseph's words weren't really questions, as Marianne was unconscious and unresponsive. She was in a state as bad as any Joseph had ever seen, and the stench was almost overwhelming. He felt for signs of breathing and released a heartfelt prayer of thanks when he confirmed she was breathing, albeit shallowly.

Peter arrived in the shortest of time and approached Joseph before stepping back, gagging at the smell. "Good God! What happened?" he asked.

"It seems we have an unexpected visitor," Joseph said, trying to work out how best to convey Marianne out of the hold.

"Who on earth is it?" Peter had seen Marianne only the once, and she was vastly changed from the young lady who'd taken tea on the day they'd met.

"It is Lady Marianne," Joseph said. "Wallis, get the tub filled in my cabin. She needs to be cleaned."

Wallis exited once more, his curiosity increased now that he'd heard the stowaway was a lady and not some waif trying to escape the streets of London.

"Help me to wrap her in a clean fur," Joseph said to Peter. "I will carry her to my cabin. She needs to be cleaned up, and then we need to get some fluid down her. Goodness knows how long she's been unconscious."

"Dear Lord! What a state she's in!" Peter said. "What can have possessed her to try to obtain free passage in this way?"

"I have no idea. She looks to not have had enough provisions for the short time she has been here. And look how unresponsive her skin is." Joseph gently pinched a little skin on Marianne's arm; it seemed to have lost its elasticity. Lack of fluid was always at the forefront of any sailor's mind; it could cause an unpleasant death. "I can't see any sign of a water jug, and it appears she's not a good sailor," Joseph guessed correctly.

Peter had grabbed an unused fur. "Those furs are going to take some cleaning," he said, looking at the two Marianne had used.

"They can be thrown overboard for all I care," Joseph responded.

They worked together to wrap Marianne in the clean covering. Joseph wanted to shield her from prying eyes as they moved through the ship. There would be speculation enough without giving the sailors a peep show.

"Capt'n, how are you going to bathe her?" Peter asked. Normally, he wouldn't be so hesitant about the need to undress a woman, but a doxy was one thing; a Lady was something else.

"The best I can," Joseph said through gritted teeth. "My first worry is that I hope to God she's not beyond help."

Wrapping Marianne in the fur, Joseph lifted her into his arms. She was light and unresponsive to the movement, which increased Joseph's concern tenfold. He had to get some liquid inside her. Soon.

His chest felt tight with the emotion of seeing her in such a poor state, but he knew if he gave in to his feelings he'd be of no use to Marianne. Gritting his teeth he left the hold.

Joseph's cabin was a flurry of activity by the time he reached it. Word had travelled fast, and the tin bath had been carried through and placed behind a screen. It was being filled with water by a number of the sailors carrying pans or pots from the galley, where all the heat was being used to provide warm water.

When the bath was filled, Joseph dismissed everyone and laid Marianne on his bed, still encased in the fur. He'd kept her in his arms whilst the line of people were to-ing and fro-ing, keeping her covered from prying eyes.

Peter offered to stay. "For your protection more than hers," he said, not unreasonably.

"No. I know her character enough to know she would be mortified if you remained. I will care for her," Joseph responded.

Peter shrugged. It was a difficult situation, and whichever way Marianne was cared for, she was effectively compromised.

"You take over command. I don't know how long this will take, but I am not leaving her side until she is well on the way to recovery," Joseph said.

Peter nodded. "Yes, Capt'n," he said, exiting the room.

A large earthen jug and cup had been brought in, and it was Joseph's first task to try to get some fluid into Marianne. He laid her on his bed, and after pouring some water into the cup, he raised her head a little. Struggling to open her cracked lips with the cup, he resorted to squeezing a cloth soaked in the water into her mouth.

Not convinced her body was receiving enough liquid, Joseph kept sponging the water onto her lips. When they were moist enough to move more easily, he reverted to using the cup.

Marianne started to choke when the water reached the back of her throat, but at least it meant her body was getting some much needed fluid. She tried to push away the cup in her half-conscious state, but Joseph soothed her.

"Marianne, no. You need to drink. Shhh, don't distress yourself. I am here. I am here. You are safe," Joseph repeated over and over. It was through being ill because of the seasickness that her symptoms were so far advanced and not just because of lack of water.

When the ship moved, Marianne groaned and grasped her stomach.

"So, we know you are no sailor," Joseph said with a grimace. "I'm going to leave you for a moment, but I will be back."

Joseph went to his cabin door and opened it. His cabin boy was waiting outside for instructions. "I need lots of cold ginger tea and tell Mr Liptrot I need to see him," Joseph commanded.

"Yes, Capt'n!" the boy responded before dashing off to the galley.

Joseph returned to Marianne, and although he held her, he only put the cloth to her lips, rather than continuing with the cup. There was no point trying to force her to drink when it was likely she'd cast up her accounts as soon as something hit her stomach.

A tap on the door, brought Peter into the room.

"She's a bad sailor," Joseph said without preamble. "I have ordered ginger tea, but I need an even keel until I get some in her."

"That will delay us," Peter pointed out. "We have a fine wind at the moment."

"A delay is irrelevant," Joseph said. "I need to stabilise her, then we can think about speed."

"Aye, aye, Capt'n," Peter said. There was no point in arguing. Peter had seen the way Joseph had been with Marianne on the visit. Now that she was ill, Joseph would put her first. Peter couldn't criticise his captain for his actions. A decent man was honourable in every respect, which was why Joseph instilled loyalty into his sailors of all ranks.

Joseph was brought a second jug by the cabin boy, this one smelling of ginger. It was a tried and tested solution that most new sailors relied on until they gained their sea legs.

He filled a cup and once more raised Marianne's head. "Come," he encouraged. "This will ease your stomach, and then you can bathe."

Marianne spluttered again, and although she turned her head away at first, with Joseph's persuasion, she drank some of the cool liquid. Joseph fed her slowly. It was clear her stomach was very delicate and wouldn't be able to cope with excess volume.

He glanced out of a port hole when he felt the ship come to a natural halt. Peter had given the order to furl the sails, and as the sea was calm, there was little movement.

After what seemed like an age of Joseph slowly feeding tiny amounts of liquid, Marianne moaned slightly. Three hours had passed since she'd been found. The groan sounded like relief.

"What is it?" Joseph asked gently.

Marianne didn't open her eyes but managed to croak out. "Not moving. So glad."

Joseph smiled despite their dreadful state. "Yes, we've stopped for now. Marianne, can you open your eyes?"

Marianne seemed to struggle, but eventually she blinked and tried to focus on Joseph.

"That's better. I like my stowaways to be conscious," he said with a gentle smile. "You need to have a bath."

Marianne turned her head slightly into Joseph's chest. The action made Joseph's heart swell with protectiveness, but he had to be practical.

"We both of us stink to high heaven," he said softly. "But I am going to need to help you."

Marianne looked in alarm at Joseph. "No. I-I can manage," she croaked. Even though Joseph was still feeding her sips of ginger tea every few moments, her throat felt raw.

"You cannot. But trust me. I only want to help you. Do you believe me?" Joseph asked.

Marianne nodded. She was lifted from the bed and carried over to the bath.

"This will be cooler than I'd like, but first of all I had to get some fluid inside you," Joseph explained. "I am going to put you in the water fully clothed."

Slowly he lowered Marianne into the water, allowing her time to get used to the temperature before easing her in further. He didn't want her body going into shock from any sudden surprise. Once she was seated, he removed his hands from underneath her. He was soaked through, but it didn't matter, his clothing was covered in everything Marianne had been soaked in anyway. He gave Marianne a bar of soap.

"I will have to wash your hair, but I suggest, you wash yourself, both over the clothing and underneath. I will look away but I need to remain close. I'm sorry if it causes you embarrassment, but I cannot risk leaving you alone," he explained.

Marianne quietly accepted Joseph's words. She wasn't in any position to argue. Conscious thought was returning by the minute, and she was mortified at her state. Slowly, she did as she was bid, effectively washing her clothes and herself. When she stilled, Joseph took over, drenching her hair with water before lathering the soap and carefully washing Marianne's hair.

It was the most intimate thing Marianne had ever experienced, and although she still felt very woozy, her cheeks burned with the effect of having Joseph tend her.

When Joseph was sure her hair was thoroughly washed, he rinsed it through. He hadn't said a word through the whole experience, not sure he could speak when his heart was pounding in such a way as to convince him Marianne must be able to hear it.

When he was finished, he gathered a large linen cloth. "Take off your wet clothes and then I can wrap you in this. When you're dry we will sort out some other clothing," Joseph instructed.

"I-I brought a change of clothes," Marianne said. She started to undress, but her cheeks burned each time the water sloshed when she removed an item. Joseph was being the perfect gentleman, but it didn't lessen her discomfort.

"I'll send for them to be cleaned. They probably did not come away unscathed," Joseph smiled. "Until then, you can wear something else."

Marianne managed to stand in the water and accept the linen towel from Joseph's outstretched hand. His head was turned away. When she was covered, Joseph offered his hand and held onto her whilst she stepped out onto the wooden floor of the cabin.

"Sit in this chair and keep drinking the ginger tea while I get cleaned up," Joseph instructed.

Once Marianne was securely seated, he disappeared behind the screen, stripping off his clothing and throwing it into the bath on top of Marianne's discarded items. He washed with his bowl and jug. It wasn't ideal, but it would have to do for the time being. The water in the bath wasn't suitable for a second person.

Drying himself behind the screen to save Marianne's blushes he dressed in breeches and a shirt, leaving the shirt open. There was no need for formality when he wouldn't be leaving his room for a while.

Pushing the screen to the side of the room, he smiled at Marianne. "You're definitely looking a little better."

"We have stopped moving," Marianne said in explanation.

"Yes. We are going to have to start again soon, but I'm hoping the potion will have done the trick. I want to get some food into you, once you are dressed."

"Oh, no! I could not!" Marianne said, aghast at the thought.

Joseph smiled. "Trust me on this. I have dealt with more seasickness than I care to recall. There is a perfect spot on deck where you can watch the horizon. You'll be fine."

Marianne didn't look completely convinced, but that had more to do with her not wishing to go through a horrific experience again rather than her lack of faith in Joseph.

The bag that Marianne had brought on board with her had actually survived unscathed, so she was able to dress in one of the two cotton day dresses she'd packed. When she was clothed and had secured her hair loosely with a ribbon, as there were no hair clips to secure it properly, Joseph smiled at her.

"Are you feeling more the thing?" he asked.

"Yes, thank you," Marianne replied. "Though I still feel very weak."

"Yes. You were in a sorry state," Joseph admitted. "You need to eat, and we need to start moving again. Sitting adrift in the ocean won't do you or us any good in the long-term."

Marianne grimaced slightly at Joseph's words, but she took a breath before saying what she had to say. "I am sure you are waiting for an explanation from me."

"My curiosity is certainly awash with possibilities, but let's get you above board, and then we can worry about the purpose for your visit later."

"Your men will despise all the work I have caused," Marianne, said looking around the cabin, which was more dishevelled than she'd seen on her first visit.

"My men have not had anything to do this last few hours. The break will compensate for any work in here that needs to be done," Joseph said with a shrug.

"I'm sorry for my actions," Marianne said quietly.

"You obviously had your reasons," Joseph said. "Come. You need to sit in the fresh air."

Joseph led the way, having linked Marianne's arm through his. He wasn't sure how steady she was on her feet as yet, and although the movement of the ship had greatly reduced, there was still some motion caused by the gentle swell. He was thankful for a dry, bright day. Her recovery would have been slower and more problematic if the weather had been inclement.

A seat had been fixed into a small gap on the helm. It was where Joseph or Peter very often sat, when they wanted to enjoy the view without interfering with daily life. It was sheltered and perfect for Marianne to watch the horizon.

Joseph instructed one of his men to visit the galley and obtain specific food. At the moment he wished Marianne to eat only dry crackers. She needed sustenance, but a small amount at a time gave her the best chance of recovery.

Once Marianne was settled, Joseph approached Peter and gave the order for the unfurling of the sails. He had put Marianne before his journey, but now he needed to make up the time. The ship's company jumped into action, no longer able to speculate about their unexpected passenger.

When the ship was skimming the waves once more, Joseph approached Peter.

The first mate smiled at his captain. "Do we know anything of interest as yet?"

"No. I thought it best to get her cleaned up and fed first," Joseph admitted. "There is going to be enough time yet to hear the whys and wherefores."

"Which poses another question," Peter said.

"I know," Joseph admitted. "It looks like you'll be sharing your cabin with your captain until we return home."

Peter groaned. "Could the sweet Lady Marianne not have my cabin? I would much rather share the biggest cabin on board!"

Joseph smiled. "Ever the gentleman, Peter?"

"When it's appropriate, yes, of course," Peter grinned. "As I can see no benefit to me in this scheme, I would rather not be put out."

Shaking his head, Joseph ignored Peter's remark. It was typical of his friend to be so self-adsorbed.

"We'll be sharing yours, especially as anyone has to pass your cabin to approach mine. I do not want anyone thinking she's unprotected."

"Oh, I think only a fool would think that."

"Unfortunately, there are a few of those on board," Joseph responded.

Chapter 25

Cameron returned and went immediately to the library. He poured himself a large drink and sat down near the fire. Resting the glass on his forehead he sighed. He'd never felt so angry in his life, and although the initial burst of anger had subsided, he still couldn't face going to speak to either of his sisters.

He'd seen how his words had hurt them. Normally, he'd have walked barefoot over hot coals rather than cause distress to those he loved, but these last weeks had stretched his forbearance to the limit.

His head was pounding, and he just wanted done with it. He had come to a decision when he'd found out the *Tara* had sailed.

Helena entered the room. She'd asked to be notified as soon as Cameron had returned but had left him to settle in before she'd joined him.

"Captain Drummond, is there any news?" she asked tentatively.

Cameron looked up. He was touched that she was hesitant in disturbing him, yet it was her home and not his. "No. The ship has sailed. No one can confirm whether it left with or without a stowaway on board."

Helena moved into the room and sat next to Cameron. "In that case, she must have been on board."

"I'm hoping so. I asked around. No one seems to have seen anyone resembling Marianne, so perhaps she succeeded, but we will not know until the ship arrives In Portugal."

"Surely, you'll find out when it returns here?" Helena asked.

"No. I have arranged my passage. I'm going back to Wellesley. I will check the port in Portugal on my arrival. Hopefully, Captain Anderton won't have set sail on his return journey by the time I arrive," Cameron responded.

Helena had tears in her eyes. "You should not be returning at this time! You said yourself, it's not good to be distracted!"

Cameron sighed. "I want to be as far away from my sisters as I possibly can be. I am not disowning them, or I wouldn't seek out

Marianne when I reach Portugal, but I cannot be around them at the moment. I haven't the energy."

"They are both very sorry. And I know Marianne would not have undertaken her course of action lightly," Helena said gently, in defence of her new friends.

"But they still do exactly as they wish without thought of anyone other than themselves," Cameron said bleakly. "I'm afraid they are more like Duncan than I have previously seen."

"I doubt that, if the way Lady Heather cried herself to sleep is anything to go by," Helena said. "It's been a hard few days. Rest awhile and see if you feel differently then."

"I am afraid it's too late for that. I've booked my passage for dawn in the morning. I have returned to collect my clothes and say goodbye to your brother and you."

"Oh. I shall be so sorry to see you leave," Helena admitted.

Cameron turned to Helena and grasped her hands in his. "I wish things could have been different. I truly do. Lady Helena, you above everyone, will be the one I will miss the most."

Helena swallowed. She knew he had affection for her but also knew without doubt he would push her away if she started speaking of heartfelt emotions. "And I you, Captain Drummond. I wish there was something I could do to make you wish to stay, but I realise there is not."

Cameron closed his eyes for a moment. A vision of taking Helena into his arms and kissing her, making love to her, flashed before his mind's eye, but he pushed the thought aside. He was in the cavalry, and that came before anything else.

Looking at Helena once more, he smiled. "Believe that your image will help to comfort me when the nights are at their coldest or the enemy is at its most brutal."

"Please don't say that," Helena said with a shudder. "Can I ask one thing of you?"

"Of course."

"Say goodbye to your sisters," Helena said.

"I can't do that. I'm sorry," Cameron responded. He smiled. "I thought it was to give you a farewell kiss, but I should have known you would put others before yourself. A lesson my sisters would be wise to learn."

Helena smiled slightly and stood. "I am sorry you feel so strongly about settling matters between you all. I think it would be best, even for you, but I understand you are still angry. I should leave you now to prepare for your journey. Be safe, Captain Drummond. I will be eager to hear of your safe return home."

Cameron was disappointed he hadn't managed to kiss her. He wanted to wrap her in his arms, but she'd made it clear she wasn't about to let that happen. In a way, he admired her for it. He hadn't given her any encouragement as such, so why should she risk her reputation on a cad like himself.

He stood and bowed, watching as she approached the door.

Helena paused as she twisted the door handle and turned back to Cameron. She saw the longing in his eyes and faltered. "I'll notify my brother of your leaving," she said.

"Thank you," Cameron responded.

"Oh, blast it!" Helena said before running across the room and flinging herself into Cameron's open arms. "Please come back!" she pleaded.

Cameron didn't respond. He pressed his lips to hers and took the kiss he'd been longing for.

Eventually, Helena pulled away. She ran her hands through Cameron's hair and gripped it, forcing his forehead onto hers. "Why will you not admit what is in your heart?" she asked, frustrated.

"I won't ask you to wait for me," Cameron said.

Helena realised what the meaning was behind his words. Though she was young, she understood what his reluctance was.

"I do not want you to," she said. "But hear this. Every morning when I wake, I shall be thinking of you. And during the day and as I fall asleep, you will be in my thoughts. I ask nothing from you but to return safely. If then you cannot return my feelings, I will ask nothing more."

Cameron almost moaned with the emotion in her words. "I shall return. But if you should find another, I underst—"

"I won't," Helena said firmly.

They kissed once more, sealing their commitment to each other. Neither wanted to plan too far ahead; it would make the heartbreak even worse if it didn't come to pass.

*

Simon eventually left Lou when she'd fallen asleep. She'd been exhausted by the exertions and emotional turbulence of the day. Simon would have loved to have stayed by her side, watching her sleep — probably the only time Lou looked restful — but as yet, he hadn't the right.

Closing her door softly, he made his way downstairs. He was in time to see Cameron's portmanteau being loaded onto a carriage.

"You're leaving?" Simon asked in surprise.

"Yes. I am to return to Portugal. There's nothing more for me here," Cameron responded. "It will enable me to see if Marianne was in fact on the *Tara*. We are bound for the same port."

"I'm sorry to see you go. There is something I would like to speak to you about," Simon said.

"Oh?"

"I would rather do it in private."

Cameron reluctantly followed Simon into his study. He presumed Simon was going to defend his sisters, and he wasn't in the frame of mind to respond kindly to any suggestion his host might have.

"I'll come to the point," Simon started. "Your sister has asked for my hand in marriage, and I have agreed," he finished.

Cameron looked in astonishment at Simon. "Lou has proposed to you?"

"Yes. Are you really surprised? You know how she likes to be in control. I've explained I cannot go through married life if she needs to win every discussion or difference of opinion. I am besotted, but not stupid." Simon smiled slightly.

"You are a braver man than I am!" Cameron said. He wondered whether to mention his feelings about Helena, but quickly decided against it. They'd made promises, but both had the opportunity to have a change of heart, although he knew he wouldn't.

"Do we have your blessing?" Simon asked.

"You do not need it. Lou is of age," Cameron pointed out.

"But she, and I, would like it," Simon persisted.

"If you are looking for me to forgive my sisters, I'm afraid I cannot do that at the moment," Cameron said seriously. "But I like you and would be happy to call you brother."

"Thank you. For now, that's all I can ask," Simon responded. "Do know that she is mortified that you are so upset. She will be devastated you've gone without saying goodbye, as will Lady Heather."

"They should have thought about that before dismissing the impact of their foolhardy scheming," Cameron said with a shrug. He would eventually forgive his sisters, and he knew leaving them in such a way was foolhardy on his part. He might never return, and yet he was prepared to leave his sisters without resolving their argument. The burden he'd been struggling with prevented him from seeking them out. He'd tried to do his best by his family even though the responsibility had weighed heavy, but their actions had pushed him too far. He knew the distance would restore his good opinion and resolved to send them all letters. For now, he had to leave.

"I do understand why you are angry. I would be too."

"Yes. I have a long journey to mull over the faults of my family, but that doesn't mean to say I am not fully aware of the service you have done for my sisters and myself," Cameron said. "I thank you sincerely."

"You are welcome, especially as it has led me to Lou," Simon said, unable to prevent the smile from touching his lips.

"I need to take my leave," Cameron said. "I leave in your debt and can only wish you every happiness and patience for the future!"

Simon laughed. "Have a safe trip and keep your head low on the battlefield. We don't need any rogue musket balls finding their mark!"

"I will do my best," Cameron said.

The pair walked into the hallway. Shaking hands at the open doorway, they reiterated their goodbyes.

Cameron walked down the three steps that led to the pavement and quickly stepped into the carriage. As the door slammed, he looked out the window to the second floor and touched his hand to his lips.

Simon had returned inside the house and didn't see Cameron blowing Helena a last kiss.

Chapter 26

Marianne watched the sea as it gently undulated, the grey-blue looking brighter every day. Over the last few days, it seemed her sea legs were indeed getting stronger, although she did still drink warmed ginger tea prior to going to bed and when she awoke in the morning. Joseph had told her they were having a smooth crossing. She didn't want to imagine a rough one.

She'd had plenty of time — in some respects too much — to consider what she'd done and how foolish she'd been. If she hadn't been discovered there wouldn't have been a happy ending. She would have died in the hold through lack of water and food. It shocked her to think back on just how quickly she'd deteriorated.

The work and inconvenience she'd caused everyone, but especially Joseph, made her blush every time she caught anyone's eye. She was mortified. She'd thought she was so clever, when in fact, all she'd done was create a mess and prove how immature she was.

Each day, she sat on what had soon become known as Lady Marianne's seat. It kept her tucked out of the way. She couldn't face the thought of causing even more inconvenience than she already had.

Her mortification had increased ten-fold when they'd passed another ship. Everyone had been interested to find out which port the ship was bound for.

"Ahoy! Who are you and where are you headed?" Joseph had shouted across when the ships had come in close to each other.

"We are the *Laconia* and bound for London! And you?" came the answering call.

"Viana Do Castelo, Portugal!" Joseph responded. "Will you report we are safe and well?"

"We will! Safe trip!"

"Wait! Will you deliver a letter if we row it across?" Joseph shouted.

"Yes!"

Joseph gave the order for a rowing boat to be lowered. He disappeared into his cabin and returned with a sealed letter. Giving it to one of the two sailors who were to row between the ships, he watched as the men climbed over the side of the ship.

It took some time for the men to row across the water and then for one of them to climb up the other ship before returning to his rowing boat, and taking an oar, to return to the *Tara*. Joseph slapped both sailors on the back when they eventually climbed on board and the two ships could part.

Marianne had watched the process with fascination. Later, when Joseph joined her, which he did regularly, she had questioned him about it.

"We always shout to each passing ship," Joseph explained. "They can report where they saw us. It is the perfect way of tracking our progress."

"Do you often swap correspondence?" Marianne asked.

"No. Not unless it's important," Joseph confessed. "I have had the letter written since we found you. In readiness for seeing a ship going to London."

"Me? Have you reported me to the authorities?" Marianne asked, panicked.

Joseph laughed. "No! Why would I do that? I've written to your family to let them know you are safe. I would imagine they will be worried sick."

Marianne blushed. "Yes. They will. I will regret my actions for many years to come. I don't know what I was thinking."

"You spoke of being envious of my travels. I did not know you'd go to such extremes to have travels of your own!" Joseph smiled. He couldn't help enjoying her company. He knew it would come to an end, but he could indulge in his dreams whilst she was on board.

Marianne glanced away. "I was extremely stupid," she admitted. She'd been a fool. Joseph had been everything that was gentlemanly and a perfect host, but she'd detected no feelings of affection or love.

"It does not matter. You have discovered you aren't made for sea travel and had an adventure to boot. It will be something you can tell your grandchildren," Joseph said blithely.

"When I return home I have to find employment," Marianne admitted. "I doubt I shall have a husband or children."

Joseph felt such a sense of need it almost took his breath away. Would being married to him be preferable to a life in service, he wondered. Perhaps. But then if they had children and the children resembled his mother, it would bring shame on her family. His blood was impure. He'd best remember that.

He sighed. "Fate would not be so cruel," he said quietly. "I am sure there's someone out there who would treasure you, Lady Marianne."

She smiled, but it was a forced action. He could speak of her being with another man. She'd fallen in love with a man who cared nothing for her, and she'd taken the biggest risk of all. Who would believe when she returned home that she hadn't been compromised when she was the only woman on a ship full of men? The fact that they'd all treated her with such kindness and respect was irrelevant. She'd ruined her reputation, and for naught. And possibly her chances of employment. As a ruined woman, it would be hard for her to find work.

One evening when Joseph and Peter joined Marianne for an evening meal, Peter made Marianne laugh by forcing Joseph to perform a traditional toast of the navy.

"We are not in the navy," Joseph pointed out.

"But we steal some of their traditions," Peter grinned.

"It is not appropriate in front of a Lady," Joseph persisted, clearly discomfited by Peter's request.

"Perhaps today's isn't what one would wish a lady to hear, but it is important that she learn all aspects of a seafaring life," Peter laughed.

"Please go ahead with the toast," Marianne urged.

Joseph rolled his eyes. "Are you ready?" he asked Peter. His first mate raised his glass of rum in preparation. "To our wives and sweethearts," Joseph said.

"And may they never meet!" Peter finished before swallowing the tot of rum in one gulp and banged his glass onto the table, as was the ritual.

Marianne had laughed at the toast even though Joseph had been correct that she'd not really liked it. It hinted at a side of life she didn't want to consider Joseph a part of.

"That is the worst of the seven toasts," Joseph explained. "A different one for each day of the week."

"There seem to be many traditions," Marianne said.

"They help us develop life-long friendships," Peter explained. "We need to know, that if we were to be attacked or shipwrecked, our fellow sailors would do everything they could to aid us. We literally rely on each other for our lives and our livelihoods."

"That does not take away the fact that sometimes we wish to kill each other, especially on long trips," Joseph pointed out.

"Aw Capt'n, I never want to kill you!" Peter teased.

"If only the feeling were mutual," Joseph ground out.

"Captain Anderton! I am surprised you can be so cruel. Mr Liptrot has been nothing but amenable for this whole trip," Marianne scolded gently.

"It is because he is making a spectacle of himself. He's like a peacock, strutting around with his feathered tail. It is all show and no substance," Joseph said with a look at his friend.

"I'm hurt," Peter laughed, pretending to grip his heart. "Such an attack would have me respond in kind, Capt'n."

"Do!" Marianne said, enjoying the banter.

"I could tell you lots of his secrets," Peter said, lowering his voice.

"I refuse to stay where you torment me. Lady Marianne, please excuse me. I need to check on the watch," Joseph said, rising from his chair and heading to the door.

"If you are not willing to stay and defend yourself, I could say absolutely anything," Peter pointed out.

"You would do that whether I was present or not," Joseph said wryly before leaving the room.

"Have you offended him?" Marianne asked.

"No! Not at all!" Peter said with confidence. "He's not a touchy soul. Just a frightened one."

"Why would he be frightened? Are your stories so bad?" Marianne asked in disbelief.

"I tell you this in the strictest of confidence, My Lady. My Capt'n does not need to realise I know this," Peter said.

"Oh, please don't!" Marianne said quickly. "If it is a secret that should not be told, please refrain from uttering the words!"

Peter smiled. "That puts me in a dilemma, My Lady," he started.

"Why?"

"You see, I watch you both staring at each other longingly when you think the other is not looking. I know unrequited love when I see it," Peter finished, his teasing tone gone.

Marianne blushed furiously. "Captain Anderton is the perfect gentleman."

"Ah, you see, that's where he would beg to differ. Our good captain has a secret he thinks no one knows. But I like to find out about my senior officers before I put my life in their hands," Peter explained. "There is one thing that is keeping him from being open about his feelings towards you."

"And what is that?" Marianne could no longer urge restraint when she had the opportunity of finding out something so important.

"His birth is not that of a gentleman."

"I don't understand."

"His mother is of Indian descent," Peter explained.

"Oh. I see," Marianne said, a little shocked at the information.

"His father acknowledges his son whilst he is in India and has given him the best opportunities in life, but there is a wife and family in England. So, our captain would not be accepted into the *ton* quite as easily as he's accepted by those who know him and know his character and worth," Peter said in defence of his friend. He had only spoken out of friendship but there was a slight chance that Marianne could reject Joseph as a potential suitor when she found out about his background.

"I won't be welcomed into polite Society as a penniless spinster!" Marianne exclaimed.

"Then those who consider themselves above everyone else are fools!" Peter smiled. "After all, a captain can earn a lot during a year. Enough to keep a modest young lady in all the finery she desires."

"Nice clothes are not the most important things in the world. Having a good husband is worth more," Marianne responded.

"Well said, Lady Marianne. I hope you treat my information with delicacy. I think a lot of my captain, despite my teasing of him. I wouldn't like to see him hurt," Peter cautioned.

"Neither would I."

"Then we are of the same mind. I shall leave you to your thoughts, Lady Marianne. Good luck with whatever venture you embark on to persuade our friend he can rely on some people to treat him as he deserves," Peter said. He rose, and with a bow and a smile, he left Marianne to her ruminations.

She was not alone for very long before Joseph returned. He looked surprised to see her alone.

"Has Peter retired?"

"Yes. I think I'm too much of a country innocent to be able to interest Mr Liptrot for long," Marianne admitted with a smile.

"Long might that continue!" Joseph said before recollecting himself and sitting opposite Marianne once more. He'd actually remained out of the room longer than necessary, secreting himself in Peter's cabin. Being near Marianne was torture, and he'd needed a while to get his feelings under control. "We need to decide what is to happen when we reach port. The fine weather and good wind is making our journey short. We should be arriving tomorrow."

"Really? So soon?" Marianne asked.

"I suggest we employ a chaperone to accompany you on your journey home."

"Am I not to travel with you?" Marianne asked in alarm. This was so sudden. She'd never thought to ask when they would arrive. It had seemed so far in the future. She was enjoying each day now that the sickness had receded.

"If there's another ship returning sooner than we are, I would advise you to join them. As long as we can find a suitable chaperone of course," Joseph said. He wasn't uttering the words to be cruel. He wanted her more than he'd wanted anything ever before, and those included legitimacy, credibility, or acceptance. But he couldn't have her, so having her return with someone else was for the best. He was near breaking point with her so close. He was not sure he could be so circumspect on the journey home.

"I should have listened to Heather. She didn't want me to come on this trip, and she was right!" Marianne said with distress. "Nothing has gone to plan!"

Joseph smiled. "I doubt anyone could have foreseen what you experienced those first few days."

"Have you ever wanted something so much it hurt?" Marianne asked.

"Yes," Joseph replied quietly.

"Yet, you do nothing to relieve your hurt, and because of that, I cannot do anything about my feelings." She was being forward, but the realisation she might no longer be in his company was making her panic.

"Lady Marianne, I— "

They were distracted by noises from the deck. They paused to listen but weren't kept in suspense for long. Peter entered the room with only a slight knock of warning.

"Capt'n, you're needed on deck."

"What is it?" Joseph asked, standing. Peter wasn't one to disturb Joseph over a trifling matter.

"Another ship has been spotted. It's appeared out of the sea mist a lot closer than it should be. It's aiming to intercept us," Peter said.

"Flag?"

"No colours showing."

"Damn it!" Joseph said. "I will be there in a moment. Get everyone ready to man the sails."

"Yes, Capt'n," Peter responded and left the room.

"What is it?" Marianne asked.

"I might be mistaken, but it could be pirates," Joseph explained quickly.

"Pirates? No! They don't exist anymore, do they?" Marianne asked.

"There are still a few rogues out there, trying their luck," Joseph said. "I need you to lock this door behind me, and no matter what sounds you hear, you have to promise to hide in here. Do not be tempted to come outside. I will show you the false back on the cupboard that will offer you some protection as it's in the centre of the cabin."

Joseph led Marianne over to what look like a normal wardrobe. Inside the structure, there was a false back, which Joseph pressed in one corner, and it opened to show a small space inside.

"You do not need to secrete yourself in here yet, but if you watch out of the window and see the other ship come alongside, I want you to promise me you'll hide yourself inside and stay there whatever sounds you hear. Do you understand?" Joseph demanded.

Marianne paled but nodded her head. "I promise."

"Good. I need to know you are safe."

"What about you?" Marianne asked, unable to mask the panic in her voice.

"I have to try to outrun them."

"Please be careful."

"I will. I have precious cargo on board," Joseph responded with a smile.

Marianne wasn't quite sure if he meant her or his actual cargo but didn't wish to ask for clarification.

Joseph walked to the door. "Lock this behind me. If we are boarded, my men will do their damnedest to get you to safety."

Marianne followed him to the door. Just as she was closing it with shaking hands, Joseph turned back.

"Lady Marianne?"

"Yes?"

"The journey is going to get very rough," Joseph said before disappearing around the corridor.

Chapter 27

Marianne was terrified. She'd immediately locked the door and then crossed to the porthole, looking outside. The ship bearing down on them was certainly travelling at speed. The *Laconia* had approached them in a far more sedate manner.

She tried to see what was going on above her head, but she couldn't see anything. Considering opening the door and peeking out to see if that provided her with more information, Marianne almost lost her balance when the ship suddenly lurched to one side. Catching hold of the table, she quickly sat as it felt as if the ship had jumped forward. Within moments, the speed at which they were travelling had increased dramatically.

Making her way carefully to the window, Marianne peered out. She could see they had changed course with the direction of the wake, and straining to look to the bow, she saw how fiercely the ship was ploughing through the waves. The pursuing ship was changing course to match theirs. Marianne swallowed, and the effects of the increased speed made her stomach roil.

On deck, Joseph was steering for survival. He had no wish to die, but on this journey, he refused to be boarded by men who had no code of conduct to live by, who just took what they wished. He would fight to the death to save Marianne from being handed over.

He was working with Peter and his second mate. They were shouting commands to the sailors while Joseph dictated the course. He had to keep ahead of the bounty hunters. He had no interest in who they were or what they wanted. The only time a ship didn't show its colours was for nefarious reasons, and he wasn't about to stay within their proximity to find out which clandestine group they were.

The sails were used to catch every whisper of wind in order to give them maximum speed, but he used the waves and an altered course to prevent the other ship coming alongside. He'd seen pirates ram another ship in order to board it. Joseph wasn't going to let the *Tara* be treated in such a way.

Spinning the wheel as if it were a child's toy, Joseph changed course again and again, out-manoeuvring the other ship. As long as they had the wind, they could maintain the pace. Joseph had chosen his ship carefully, having years of experience by the time he acquired her. She wasn't the biggest in the ocean, but she had extra sails, which gave her the speed they so desperately needed.

"Captain, they're gaining!" Peter shouted.

"Keep going!" Joseph shouted in return. He wanted to reach the mist bank the ship had used as cover to gain advantage over them. He risked the wind easing but thought the extra cover could be used to advantage.

The men twisted, pulled, turned, and yanked ropes, pulleys, and other material in order to alter sails to catch the wind.

Joseph glanced behind him, and his heart sank to see the bowsprit of the other ship passing the stern of the *Tara*. Any closer, and they'd be boarded.

"Jem! Cover the stern!" Joseph shouted.

The second mate picked up his musket and indicated that two sailors were to follow him. A lower ranking sailor took his place, shouting orders out to the sailors working the sails on the starboard side. Peter was still working on the port side.

Gunfire was soon echoing around them as the sailors on the *Tara* opened fire on their opponent.

*

Marianne had watched the approach of the boat with increasing terror. All sea sickness was forgotten in the melee. The captain's cabin was to the rear of the ship, so although she'd been looking out at the stern, when the ship started edging closer to the *Tara*, the shadow had darkened the cabin.

Her instinct was to run to Joseph. She knew he'd make her feel safe, but she couldn't distract him. Of that, she was certain. Watching the progress of the other ship, she managed to stir herself enough to approach the wardrobe. She had no idea what would happen if they were boarded, but she had started to pray that Joseph wouldn't be killed. In her heart she knew the captain of a ship would not likely be treated well. Tears sprang into her eyes at the thought of him being injured, or worse.

About to climb into the wardrobe, Marianne flung herself to the floor at the sound of shattering glass. A musket ball hit the wardrobe she had been about to climb into.

A sob escaped her lips before Marianne managed to gather her wits about her, and she sat on the floor. Gun shots could be heard clearly now along with the thud of musket balls hitting their targets. Once more she sent up a prayer that no one on the *Tara* got hurt.

It was clear the shot that had smashed its way into the captain's quarters was not aimed specifically for her, but she no longer felt secure in the room.

Crawling to the door, she reached up and unlocked it. Getting into a crouching position, Marianne half-crawled, half-fell through the now open door. The cabin wasn't safe. She had to find somewhere else.

Standing, she moved quickly along the corridor, keeping to the wall as the ship was still being thrown about the water like a bobbing ball. There were three steps leading up to the open deck and Joseph, but Marianne turned away. One sighting of her, and Joseph would be distracted; she knew that.

Not having explored the lower parts of the ship since the day she'd had the tour, Marianne moved slowly, looking for anywhere to hide herself.

She eventually came to a door that was locked from the outside. Turning the key, she immediately recognised that she'd rediscovered the hold. She had forgotten there was a door leading into it, being barely conscious when she'd been carried out and deeming it too risky to use when she'd first boarded the ship. Moving into the space, she locked the door behind her and pocketed the key. She wasn't where Joseph had instructed, but at least she was behind a locked door for now.

She knew the hold would be of interest to any attacker, but Marianne reasoned that, if they reached so far into the ship, they'd find her no matter where she was. Clambering over the furs, she secreted herself towards the front of the ship to keep herself as far away from musket balls as she could.

She could still hear dull thuds, but they were in the distance. It wasn't clear whether it was gun fire from the *Tara* or shots hitting the *Tara*.

There were no signs that Marianne had spent an eventful few days in the hold. All had been cleaned. If she wasn't half terrified out of her wits, she'd have felt embarrassment at what had happened, but at the moment, she was desperately praying for something to save them all but especially Joseph.

Curling into a ball, she closed her eyes. Trying to think of her sisters and how they would feel to hear news that she was safe, only to find out that she'd been hurt or killed in an attack, filled her with sadness. She'd never been away from her family for so long. Being with Joseph had alleviated any deep feelings of homesickness. It had felt as if she were in a different world. Now though, she longed to see Heather's face, even if she was scolding her, as she often did. A wry look from Lou would have been as welcome as anything just at that moment.

Marianne tried to be brave. She was a young woman who was old enough to have had her come out this year. She was old enough to be married and starting a family. She'd grown-up in Scotland, a harsh environment with hard winters and short summers. She was sturdy, hardy even.

Wrapping her arms around herself, she allowed the tears to fall. Despite the harshness of her homeland, she was not made for heroics; she was just a country girl who longed for a quiet life with the man who was trying to save his ship and his crew.

Letting out a sob, she turned her face into a fur and let her fear surface.

*

Joseph was gritting his teeth so hard his jaw was aching. The pirates were gaining on them. It was happening slowly; so far they weren't quite close enough to send a boarding party over, but if nothing changed, it would happen before too long.

Everyone was working at full speed; no one was letting his pace falter, and he was proud of them all. They were all fighting to their full capacity. The shots were sometimes dangerously close. At least one man was injured, and he had no idea what was going on behind him. He just hoped he could stay at the helm without being shot. He knew he was a key target.

"Peter, one last attempt to turn portside!" Joseph shouted. He was going to try twisting the ship away from danger. If the other ship matched the turn, there was nothing else they could do, and the focus would change from sailing to shooting and hand-to-hand combat.

A thought of Marianne flitted into his mind, and he ground down on his jaw even harder. He would not have her hurt. He could not.

A shout from the bow caught his attention. One of the sailors was pointing. Joseph immediately saw it and almost sagged with relief. A shadow was emerging from the mist a little ahead of them.

If they were lucky, it would be a friend. If they'd run out of luck…

Joseph twisted the wheel as he'd planned. He had to keep up the pressure. All hands moved as one to make the most of the wind, and the ship lurched forward a little way.

"It has given us some separation!" Peter shouted in encouragement.

Joseph couldn't ask if it was enough. His muscles were screaming in pain as he maintained the position.

"It's a British ship!" was shouted from the bow.

Joseph let out a long breath. If it was showing colours, it was likely legitimate unless they were part of some grand attack, but the second ship would have appeared sooner if that had been the case.

"Course to starboard!" Joseph shouted, as the wind changed slightly, and he turned the ship to intercept their potential ally. Once more all the crew worked together to make the most of the wind.

The ship that had just emerged had obviously seen what was going on and had raised more sails and was bearing down on the location of the skirmish.

"It's pulling back!" Peter shouted, glancing at Joseph. The first mate looked back at the pirate ship to see it withdraw slightly.

"Are you sure?" Joseph bellowed.

"Yes. There is space between us!" Peter shouted back.

Joseph risked a glance back and could see that the bowsprit was no longer near the stern. He relaxed slightly although not completely. They weren't necessarily out of danger.

Still aiming for the British frigate, Joseph felt a moment of panic. Even at the distance they were from the pirate ship, he could see cannon sticking out of the side and one to the front of the British ship. The cannon located in the bow of the British frigate gave a vessel an advantage as it could fire a shot when approaching a ship, not needing to go broadside. For a moment, Joseph thought they might be aiming at the *Tara*, but when the gun fired, it was clear the ship being aimed at was their attacker.

The men of the *Tara* let up a cheer as their attacker immediately started to turn away from the new pursuer. At first it seemed the British ship was going to give chase, but the pirate ship soon veered off and aimed for the mist once more.

Joseph gave the order, and many of the sails were furled, as the ship slowed down to greet its rescuer. The British ship did the same. When it came properly into view, the name could be seen clearly. The *Bridget* had been their rescuer.

Coming alongside, they exchanged 'ahoys' on either side. The captain on the *Bridget* explained that the ship who'd been chasing them was being hunted because of its recent activity in the area. Joseph was advised to pay for escort until out of range on his return journey.

The ships soon parted, the *Bridget* keen to lie in wait for the rogue ship, and the *Tara* wishing to dock in the safety of port as soon as possible.

Once Joseph had thanked his men for their efforts and checked on the ones exchanging musket fire, he found that only one had been injured, and he was being tended. Joseph handed over control of the ship to Peter.

"I need to check to see if Lady Marianne is well. The turbulence wouldn't have done her insides any good," Joseph said wryly. His heart was still pounding at the thought of how close they'd come to being boarded, which would have put Marianne in real danger.

Walking down to his cabin, he rapped on the door. "My Lady, 'tis me. 'Tis safe to come out," Joseph said, the adrenaline making him almost giddy with relief.

On receiving no reply, Joseph knocked again, this time more urgently and called out again. When there was still no response, he groaned. His door would have to be forced open, which was unnecessary damage to a fine teak door.

As he used his shoulder to charge the door, the catch sprang open, having not been locked once Marianne had left the cabin. Joseph had been half-laughing on entry, but his smile died on his lips as he saw the destruction in his cabin. Three windows were shattered with musket fire. Glass was scattered everywhere. When Joseph instinctively turned to where he'd instructed Marianne to hide, his legs buckled underneath him, and he grabbed the back of a chair to steady himself. A hole the size of a musket ball had penetrated the secret door right through the middle.

Joseph's ears were ringing. He'd given her clear instructions, and her safe place had been shot.

"Peter!" Joseph bellowed, louder than he'd ever shouted, whilst at the same time he ran to the cupboard. Forcing the false back off the wardrobe, he stared at the space unable to process what he was seeing.

Behind him, Peter entered the room, almost screeching to a halt. "What is it?" his second-in-command demanded. "Bloody hell! What an unholy mess!"

"The wardrobe has been shot," Joseph said unnecessarily.

"Damnit!" Peter cursed but came over to see the evidence. "Where is she?" There was clearly no sign of Marianne.

"Could they have boarded us?" Joseph asked, looking back at the broken windows.

"No. There would have been sightings of them on board, and we certainly would have heard the efforts of trying to kidnap a young woman," Peter reasoned, knowing the ever controlled Joseph was in a blind panic.

"Where is she?"

"At the moment, I've no idea, but there is no sign of blood," Peter said. Realising that Joseph hadn't registered his words, he stood in front of his captain. "Joseph, there is no blood."

"I have to find her."

"Yes. Shall I start a search?"

"No. I want to find her. I said I would protect her, and this damned room is shot to pieces!" Joseph growled out.

"We aren't usually chased from behind," Peter pointed out. "It is one of the safest places to be when we are alongside."

"I should have thought of that," Joseph insisted. "But I was so keen to get on deck."

"And if you hadn't been, we would have been captured. Go and find your lady," Peter instructed. He knew Joseph was reacting out of guilt, love, and fear, but the sooner he found Marianne the better.

Joseph started a search of the decks. It quickly dawned on him where she might be: the place she'd picked out as the safest place to hide.

When he reached the lower decks and realised the door to the hold was locked, he refrained from knocking down this door. Returning to his cabin, he grabbed the ring of keys that were kept in his room for times when sailors lost or misplaced keys.

Unlocking the hold door, he entered. "Marianne?" he called out, dispensing with her formal title. He was too anxious to think straight.

"I am here!" came Marianne's quiet, frightened voice.

Joseph moved so swiftly towards her that he almost fell onto her when he crouched down at her side. Uttering no words, he pulled her to him, enfolding her in his arms.

"You're safe! Thank God you are safe!" Joseph choked out.

Marianne was shaking, but clung to Joseph, sobbing. "Are you hurt?" she managed to squeeze out.

"Me? No! We got off far lighter than I was expecting," Joseph said, kissing the top of Marianne's head. "I thought you'd been shot."

"I was watching the ship gaining, and then the shooting started. I was terrified," Marianne admitted. "I had to get out of your cabin. I know you told me to stay, and I'm sorry I disobeyed your order. I realise I should always obey the captain."

Joseph smiled into her hair despite his remaining feelings of fear. "I will be forever grateful you did. I am sorry you were put through this."

"It has all been my doing," Marianne said. "I thought I was so clever, but in reality, I'm nothing more than a foolish chit."

Joseph laughed before becoming serious and tilting Marianne's chin so he could look into her eyes. "I need to know you will get home safely. I will see if I can arrange passage on one of the Naval ships. They have guns to blast rogues like the one we faced out of the water."

Marianne's eyes became moist. "I don't want to leave you," she said quietly.

"Oh, my darling Marianne. I do not want you to go. But I can't have you, and this journey has been nothing but sweet torture. I am not the one for you," Joseph said gently. After what had happened, all he wanted to do was kiss her senseless, but he was not about to bring her to his low level.

Marianne took a breath and with a shaking hand, touched his hair. "It's very black," she said quietly.

Joseph stiffened at her touch.

"I think it must be like your mother's hair," she said gently.

"What are you saying?" Joseph asked.

"I know who your mother and father are," Marianne said, looking into Joseph's eyes. She was afraid he was going to pull away from her, and all would be lost.

"How?"

"Before I fall in love with someone, I like to know of their background," she responded, using a version of Peter's words to her advantage. She didn't want to reveal her source in case it spoiled the friendship between the two men.

"No one knows," Joseph said.

"I do, and I don't care. Nor will my family," Marianne said.

"It matters."

"To whom? To the likes of my eldest brother who is an Earl but is willing to cheat the rest of his family out of their home and inheritance? If you seek the good opinion of men like Duncan then perhaps I misjudged you."

"Any wife I take should not be put through the censure of Society. I don't want my children besmirched by my low birth," Joseph responded.

"Any wife?" Marianne asked indignantly.

Joseph smiled. "You know what I mean."

"I do not!" Marianne said, pushing herself away from Joseph. Her frustration at Joseph's reluctance to believe they were a perfect match making her lose her temper. "That toast obviously means more to the way you live than I thought!"

"I could kill Peter!"

"I should thank him for opening my eyes to how foolish I've been!" Marianne snapped, scrambling into a standing position. She stood, hands on hips, breathing deeply, as Joseph stood to face her.

"You have not been foolish!" He didn't know whether to laugh at her or coax her out of her sudden temper.

"I see the error of my ways. He was giving me the hint, wasn't he? Trying to point out your true character! Perhaps Mr Liptrot will provide escort for my homeward journey! He seems to have been the only one with my best interests at heart," Marianne said in a huff. She was offended at Joseph's words but not quite as much as she was making out. She was trying a last-ditch attempt to make Joseph realise he wanted her as much as she wanted him.

"He damn well will not escort you home!" Joseph shot back.

"Language, Captain! If you'll excuse me, I would like to prepare for when I leave this ship," Marianne said, trying to step around Joseph.

"I haven't got a wife or a sweetheart! Why are you making the nonsense of a foolish toast into a drama?" Joseph asked.

"I'm not. I am going to turn this to my advantage. You're right: I do need a chaperone with all the soldiers passing through the port. Perhaps I will stay for a few days before heading home."

"You're talking about throwing yourself at Peter and now unknown soldiers! What on earth has got into you?" Joseph asked in disbelief. This was so out of character for Marianne. He was as jealous as hell towards unknown servicemen and as for what he was going to do with Peter when he got out of the hold—

"I have decided that trying to convince an imbecile of a captain that I love him has failed. I have nothing left to lose. I've ruined my reputation the moment I boarded this ship. So, I either return home wed — to anyone who will have me — or I can never be seen in polite company again," Marianne said quickly.

"You are prepared to wed anyone? Why would you value yourself so low?"

"You don't want me, so why should that concern you?"

"Marianne! Stop!" Joseph said heatedly. He gripped her shoulders. "It is not as straightforward as you make out. Sometimes we can't have what we want."

"That is true. I want you," Marianne said with a shrug.

"Oh, By God! You are killing me! I thought young ladies didn't have wiles, but the words you are uttering… "

Marianne sighed. "If I mistook your flirting for real feeling when we were in London, I'm truly sorry," she said, finally admitting defeat and giving up on the notion of trying to goad Joseph into acting. "I will not be throwing myself at anyone else. I would not have the first clue how to do it. I tried with you and failed miserably! We can part amenably in port. I am deeply sorry my feelings ran away with me, and I imagined you felt more than you do. This has all been an adventure. Not always a nice one, but at least we are safe."

Joseph took a moment to speak. The kindly Marianne who faced him now was almost as difficult to face as the angry one of moments before. He took a breath. What she'd said reminded him of when he'd first broken into his cabin. He'd almost collapsed because he thought she was lost to him. No. He couldn't face life without her.

"It was real feeling," Joseph finally said.

"Was it?"

"Yes. From the moment I saw you, there was no one else for me. But I knew I could not have you. Or I would not let myself have you."

"That's a shame. It means we are both to be unhappy."

"I do not ever want to see you unhappy," Joseph admitted. "When I thought you had been shot, it felt like my world had ended."

Marianne touched Joseph's face. "I felt the same when you were above deck, and I didn't know if you had been hurt."

"I just wanted to kiss you when I found you."

"Yet you did not. More's the pity."

Joseph smiled at her words. "What I can offer you, is not enough— "

"A loving marriage? Is that what it would be?" Marianne interrupted. "Or do I ask too much?"

"No. You don't. But I— "

"No buts, please," Marianne again interrupted. "Ifs, buts, and maybes are for other people. We just have certainties."

"Do we?"

"Yes. I'm certain I love you, and I'm certain you are the only one who can make me happy. I need no other guarantees in this world," Marianne said.

"There is another certainty."

"What is that?"

"That I am going to kiss you senseless after all," Joseph said. He fell onto the furs, pulling Marianne down with him, wrapping her in his arms and showing her exactly how senseless senseless was.

Chapter 28

Lou was seated in the morning room with Heather and Helena. All three had been subdued since Cameron's departure. Heather had been very withdrawn, prone to burst into tears at any opportunity. Helena was pining for a lost love.

While Lou had her moments with Simon to console her and make her feel happy, the situation was marred because she was unable to share it with her family. For once, her heart was singing, but it really wasn't the time to express her news.

The butler interrupted the three ladies. He approached Lou. "My Lady, a letter has arrived addressed to your brother. It has come from the port. I thought you had better see it."

Lou immediately took the letter, and thanking the butler, she turned to the others. "It could be news of Marianne!"

"But Cameron has been gone for days. No one is looking for her now," Heather pointed out.

Lou had already broken the seal and was reading the letter at speed. "Oh my goodness!" she said, her hand to her mouth.

"What is it?" Heather and Helena chorused.

Lou took a breath. "She is safe! Marianne is on board the *Tara* with Captain Anderton!"

"Oh, thank goodness!" Heather said with a sob. "I didn't know if she had managed to get aboard, and it has been haunting me since she left!"

"She did and managed to hide herself in the hold!" Lou continued. "She was found only because she had been very seasick and was quite ill for a few days. She's well on the way to recovery, ensconced in the Captain's cabin, alone but supervised appropriately. A chaperone will be appointed when they dock in port, and if a quicker route home is found, she will be placed on it."

"Oh dear, that doesn't sound as if Captain Anderton has declared his feelings for Marianne," Helena said with distress.

"She had no evidence he even had feelings for her before she left," Lou said with derision.

"We saw him on the ship. He was smitten," Heather defended her sister.

"Being attracted to a young lady is far different from being in love with one. It was a foolish action," Lou said sternly.

"And you know all about those!" Heather snapped in return.

"Ladies! We must be thankful she is safe!" Helena intervened. "This is the best news in days. Will you send a note to your brother?"

"I think I'll ask your brother to write it. Mine is likely to see my handwriting and burn the missive," Lou said.

"What am I writing?" Simon asked, walking through the door.

Lou smiled at her betrothed before telling him the news of Marianne.

"That is excellent news!" Simon said.

"I am so glad she's safe," Lou said. "I don't know how I would have faced life if she hadn't been." Her words only hinted at the anguish she'd felt every night. It was only with Simon's arms wrapped around her that she'd found some sort of outlet for the feelings she kept in a tight grip during the day.

"And this means I can arrange a special licence," Simon said with a grin at Lou. "There's no other reason to wait, is there? Unless you want to wait for Marianne's return?"

"Special licence? Are you saying what I think you are saying, brother?" Helena asked.

Simon turned to his sister. "Lou has agreed to be my wife. We didn't think it was the right time to announce our engagement with Marianne missing, but now there is no need for delay. I want to marry this fiend before she has time to change her mind!"

Helena squealed and ran to her brother, embracing him before running to Lou to enfold her in a hug. Lou looked a little surprised but laughed at the action.

"Does this mean you do not mind me as a sister?" Lou teased.

"You are the perfect woman for my brother!" Helena gushed. "Oh! A wedding! How wonderful!"

"Congratulations," Heather said, but remained seated.

"I would like to wait for Marianne, but after everything that has happened, I just want to marry as soon as possible. I don't want any more delays. I am sure Marianne would understand. Cameron is aware of our engagement and has no objections to it," Lou explained to Heather.

"As she had the gumption to remove herself from this family, I am not sure she'll pine too much about missing your wedding," Heather said, her anger coming out in cruelty.

Lou blanched at the words, but before she could say anything, Simon crossed to Heather and placed his hand on her shoulder.

"I understand your anger towards Lou, but throughout all of this, she has had your and Marianne's best interests at heart," Simon said seriously.

"Yet she put all our futures at risk," Heather responded.

"I didn't say she went about it the right way, but the motivation was admirable. She was calling out your names when she was barely conscious. Her need to protect you was that great."

Heather looked down at hearing Simon's words.

"If your eldest brother had been more circumspect with his inheritance, none of this would have happened," Simon continued. "As one who's glad it did, I have seen some benefits. You have gained lifelong friends and relations, and our marriage means you will have a come out and a dowry."

"Will I?" Heather asked, the hope in her expression making Lou's heart ache. The older sister knew Heather's anger was partly because she'd been robbed of the future she'd been expecting — what they'd all been expecting.

"Of course. You are my sister once we are married," Simon said with a shrug and a smile.

"Oh! Thank you!" Heather said, flinging her arms around Simon in the way only a young woman could do after she's been given a second chance at obtaining a good match.

Lou walked across to the pair. When Heather released Simon, Lou took her sister's hands. "I am sincerely sorry for the upset I caused. It is my biggest regret. Please, let's just forget the last few weeks and start afresh."

"We have all said so many things," Heather pointed out.

"It doesn't matter. I'm happy. I want you to be happy. The past is forgotten," Lou said.

"I have hated all the upset," Heather admitted. "But Cameron despises us."

"He won't. He will calm down, just as we have done," Lou said. "It's the red hair. We are too quick to anger, but we recover from it quickly."

"I don't want to argue anymore."

"I'm not sure I can promise never to argue with you!" Lou laughed. "But I can certainly promise to forget what's been happening between us. I only ever want what is best for you and Marianne."

Heather was wrapped in an embrace and clung to her sister. They had missed the closeness they'd shared until they'd come to London.

"This wedding is going to be a fresh start," Lou said, smiling at Simon. "I think it is time you sent an announcement to the Times!"

"It is already written," Simon admitted. "This afternoon I'm going to secure a special licence."

"Three days is no time to organise a wedding! I thought you were funning when you mentioned a special licence," Helena exclaimed.

"No. We want to be married as soon as possible. Too much time has been lost," Lou admitted. "Apart from Cameron and

Marianne, the people I want at the wedding are in this room. We do not need anyone else."

"If you're sure," Helena said.

Lou walked over to Simon, and in a brazen act, wrapped her hands around his neck and kissed him full on the lips. "I want to be married to this man as soon as can be. He makes me a better person, and I love him so very much. It takes my breath away."

Helena smiled at her brother, who had looked pleased at Lou's actions, but his cheeks had reddened slightly. "In that case, we had best start making arrangements!"

*

Two days later, Lou was ensconced with Heather and Helena. They were all in a far better frame of mind, chattering and looking forward to the celebration they were to have the following day.

They were surprised when they were disturbed by the butler to announce that Lord and Lady Glenmire were here to pay their respects. The information managed to silence all three ladies at once. The butler made no reaction to the shocked expressions on his audience, but he would smile once out of sight. It wasn't often that one could silence a gaggle of young ladies.

"Should I advise him that you are not at home, My Lady?" the butler asked.

"No! I've no inclination to see him, but he obviously wants something, so let him come in," Lou said. "Just don't be too far away from the door in case I need you to throw him out!"

"Yes, My Lady," came the deadpan response as the butler bowed and left the room.

"What can Duncan want?" Heather hissed at Lou.

"We are about to find out," Lou said, as she stood to welcome her brother and sister-in-law. "Good afternoon. Please be seated. Could we have some refreshments for our guests, please?" Lou welcomed and instructed with as much grace and dignity as any drawing room would require.

"Lou, we had to come and offer our felicitations on your upcoming nuptials," Duncan started immediately the butler left the room. "We were delighted to see the announcement," he added, "but I was surprised your betrothed didn't seek me out to ask my permission."

"I am of age, Duncan, and he sought Cameron's approval, which he received, if any approval were needed," Lou responded, trying not to show that her teeth were already gritted.

"Duncan is the head of the family," Fanny responded, her tone utterly patronising.

Lou didn't respond to the comment. Duncan nodded in agreement at his wife's words.

"With that in mind, I feel that the wedding should be held at our home. I'm sure Lord Garswood would be happy to pay for the wedding breakfast as part of his wedding gift to you, my dear sister. We have drawn up a list of who we think would be suitable to attend your wedding. It is a perfect opportunity to launch you in Society," Duncan said.

"I could have saved you the trouble," Lou said.

"It was no trouble. We are already intimate with many of the people. It needs to be an event that says the Drummonds are the family to befriend," Duncan continued, ignoring Lou's obvious animosity.

"We are to marry tomorrow," Lou said simply.

"What? Why? That is too soon!" Duncan expostulated.

"As I turned down his first proposal out of sheer bloody-mindedness, it is not too soon. It can't come quickly enough," Lou said, amused at Duncan's reaction.

"But your wedding trousseau!" Fanny said. "It cannot be ready in such a short time!"

"It won't be. I haven't ordered one," Lou said with a shrug. "Cameron ensured we had a new wardrobe when he arrived. I have all I need."

"You are joining two fine families together. There are standards to maintain," Duncan said.

"Are those the standards that resulted in your spending our inheritance?" Lou challenged.

Duncan waved his hand. "It all worked out in the end. I have checked. Lord Garswood has enough funds to support the whole family."

"I beg your pardon?" Lou asked darkly.

"Lou, you are being excessively obtuse today," Duncan tsked. "When you marry into a family, there are responsibilities that attach themselves. I'm sure Lord Garswood is fully aware of this and is willing to help his new family in any way he can."

"Yes. He mentioned funding the court case to seek recompense for the money we no longer have," Lou lied.

Fanny looked horrified. "That would cause a scandal!"

"Not for us. We did nothing wrong." Lou shrugged.

"It could take years!" Duncan pooh-poohed.

"Only if you defend your case. That would be very expensive. But my darling future husband has deep pockets and has promised he will spend whatever it takes," Lou said, sighing dramatically.

Helena and Heather looked at Lou, both half-horrified at how she was tormenting her brother. Neither would have had the gall. Lou caught their eyes and her mouth twitched slightly.

Duncan seemed to ponder Lou's words. "I don't think there is any need to take this to court. As I said to Cameron, I will rally."

"And as Cameron said to you, you could sell one of your houses or give it to us instead of handing over the money," Lou said.

"We cannot do that!" Fanny cried.

"Now, my dear," Duncan soothed. "We don't wish our names to be dragged through the courts, do we? If we handed over the house in Bath, it could be seen as a very generous wedding present. Bath isn't so popular anymore. It is not worth what we paid for it. No. I think there is a solution that would make us all happy. What say you, Lou?"

"I think I'd like a house in Bath, or at least a third share in one," Lou responded, her face serious. "What is the address?"

"It is on Gay Street," Duncan said. "An easy walk into the centre. Most people were leasing when we visited, but we decided to buy. It cost us a good deal."

"I am sure it did. But handing it over would save you such a lot of funds. You would no longer need to pay for the staff or the upkeep," Lou said.

"Yes. I think you're right," Duncan said. "How generous our friends will consider us that we gave a house as a wedding gift!" he looked at his wife with glee.

"If you could send the paperwork over as soon as possible and make out the house to Heather, Marianne and myself, I would be obliged," Lou pushed.

"Where is Marianne?" Fanny asked.

Heather looked alarmed, but Lou never flinched. "She is out at the moment. She is enjoying lots of fresh air."

"Really? I find the streets rather crowded at this time of year," Fanny said.

"Duncan, you must excuse us. We have visits to make. We need to let everyone know what a benevolent brother we have."

"Of course!" Duncan said, standing. "I'll send the paperwork over as soon as I have arranged the details with my solicitor."

"Thank you. We would appreciate it. As soon as we receive the deeds, I will instruct Lord Garswood that his solicitors no longer need to pursue the claim," Lou said.

"They are working on the case now?" Duncan asked in alarm.

"There didn't seem any point in delaying," Lou pointed out. "The sooner it is registered at the court the better from our point of view."

"But we don't want the papers getting wind of a hint of a scandal between family members," Duncan said quickly. "None of us would wish our names to become the source of ridicule and speculation!"

"Not at all. Which is why I shall anticipate a rapid delivery of the deeds," Lou said with a sweet smile.

"Yes. Yes. Of course. As soon as possible. Come my dear. We must make haste!" Duncan said, forgetting to bow as he exited the room.

Lou waited until they heard the front door close before she let out a peal of laughter. "Oh, that was so funny!"

"Lou! How on earth did you manage to convince him to hand over a house? A whole house!" Heather asked in disbelief.

It took Lou a moment to regain her composure. "Oh! I wish Cameron could've seen it! Duncan was positively squirming!"

"I do not understand what changed his mind into being so amenable," Heather persisted.

"It's easy," Lou said. "Duncan is all about show and reputation. He knew when I visited with Cameron that we hadn't the blunt to pursue any claim however much we wanted to. But with my marrying a man of wealth and funds, suddenly Duncan isn't untouchable anymore!"

"A house! A whole house!" Heather said with glee.

"I will be handing over my share to be split between Marianne and yourself," Lou said.

"But he spent your inheritance as well," Heather pointed out.

"I do not need it now," Lou said. "I know Simon said he is to give you a dowry, but half a house in Bath will certainly help your prospects. Just because it isn't worth as much as Duncan paid for it, does not mean it's worthless. As he has shown time and again, he is useless with money."

"Thank you, Lou," Heather said. "A dowry, however small, and a home of our own, makes me feel so much more secure. I can't wait to tell Marianne of our good luck! She is not going to be the only one with a tale to tell!"

"I'd better go and inform Simon that he will receive a visit from Duncan's solicitor before too long. I am sure he will be horrified to hear how willing I was to commit his funds to an unwinnable court case!" Lou said.

"You were impressive, Lou," Helena said.

"I am just glad I didn't spoil it by laughing," Lou admitted. "I could not believe how much Duncan was falling over himself to be accommodating. When you have your season, Heather, and all three of you are settled with husbands, I want to move to the country and never see Duncan and his wife ever again!"

*

Sitting on Simon's knee in his study, Lou had informed him of the events of the day. He'd laughed along with Lou at her audacity and kissed her as punishment for pretending to be willing to spend his last penny.

When they'd become breathless with need, they stopped kissing while each allowed the other to calm a little.

"I cannot wait to be married," Lou whispered.

"Neither can I," Simon said, kissing the end of her nose. "There is one thing we need to sort out though before we marry."

"What's that?" Lou asked.

"It's best I show you," Simon said, putting his hands on Lou's waist and lifting her off his lap. When he stood, he kept his hands on her middle for longer than he needed to, enjoying the feel of her. It had been a long few days. He couldn't wait until they were joined as man and wife and he could enjoy relations with her fully.

Eventually holding out his hand, he gripped hers and walked out of the door, leading her upstairs.

"Simon, what are you doing?" Lou hissed, wondering if her husband had decided a further day's wait was too long.

"You will see," Simon responded, cheerfully.

He led the way into the long gallery and came to a stop at one of the window seats.

Lou looked down and started to laugh. "What can you be thinking?"

Simon grinned at his wife-to-be, his eyes alight with laughter, his lips still bruised from kissing, and his hand firmly wrapped around Lou's. She had never seen him look so appealing.

"You once said that you'd beat me with a broadsword. I think it is something we should sort out before you agree to honour and obey," Simon said, pleased that Lou was amused by his actions.

On the window seat, were two large, bulky broadswords, placed across each other.

"Have you ever fought with one of these?" Lou said, picking up one of the weapons and laying the blade across her palm as if assessing the weight.

"That is for you to find out, you angry Scot," Simon said, picking up the second weapon and walking to the middle of the gallery.

"Oh, you English fool!" Lou laughed.

"Don't worry. I have already changed my will, so you'll be very wealthy if an accident should happen," Simon grinned.

"Nice to know," Lou said, before smiling at Simon. "En garde, My Lord! En garde!"

Epilogue

Lou married her unhurt Lord a day after he had beaten her in his broadsword challenge. She was to admit she'd misjudged him far too many times since she'd met him, so she would have to learn not to underestimate her husband.

Simon was just glad the weeks of specialised lessons had paid off.

The bride looked fine in a mint green dress, which was embroidered with orange flowers. Her bonnet matched the dress, being covered in the green with a jaunty orange feather at the front. The mixture of colours might not have sounded compatible, but they matched Lou's colouring and enhanced her petite features perfectly.

Lou was to experience true happiness with Simon. They did move permanently to the countryside as the new Lady Garswood never really took to London. They eventually sold their London home. Duncan would bemoan that his sister had no real class, but during the following year, he moved to the Continent to live more economically and avoid the more persistent of his creditors. He would occasionally write to Lou asking for funds, but never received a reply.

Henry had mocked the news that Simon and Lou were to marry. To anyone who would listen, he would tell his story about the female highwayman who'd escaped hanging. When Lou and Simon moved to the countryside, they became less important to the *ton*, who wanted a constant supply of up-to-the minute gossip and scandal. Henry was greeted with bored looks and mutterings. Without Simon by his side forcing him to attend the more civilised side of Society, he withdrew further into the deviant side. Eventually succumbing to a disease he'd caught from one of his less-salubrious lightskirts, his was an early, unpleasant death.

The happy couple were to be parents of six healthy boys. Simon despaired that it was Lou very often tearing a dress because of climbing a tree or one or more of them would fall into the lake because of Lou's attempts at sailing. He was just thankful they hadn't had girls. He could only cope with one hoyden in the family, and he loved her dearly.

*

Marianne married in Portugal. Joseph and she stayed in port until the wedding could be arranged. Until the event happened, Joseph tried time and again to persuade Marianne that she was too good for him, but she patiently reassured him that he was the only one for her.

There was a little sadness on Marianne's part when she thought her wedding was going to take place without her family being present, but much to her delight, Cameron arrived before the wedding happened.

Cameron and Marianne had a very difficult conversation at first, but eventually, Cameron forgave his sister enough to meet her betrothed. Joseph had been frank and honest in his interview with Cameron. The fact that Joseph was a good friend to Captain Philips went some way to mollify Cameron, who thought highly of their mutual friend.

He agreed to give Marianne away on her wedding day, and although the plain cotton gown was cleaned, it was not the fine gown Joseph wished his bride to have. Marianne dismissed his protestations that she should spend his money on a new wardrobe, only purchasing enough to enable her to live comfortably on her journey home.

Joseph hired an escort for their return journey until they left the waters that were considered dangerous. He was not risking the life of his new bride even though it reduced his profit on that particular journey.

Marianne would never be able to travel far on board ship. She was a fair-weather sailor at best. Joseph eventually hung up his captain's hat and worked on land in one of the large shipping offices. He had amassed enough wealth to live comfortably, but he couldn't be idle so took on the new challenge with relish, eventually owning his own shipping office and amassing even more wealth.

Neither sought the higher echelons of Society. Marianne never used her title, much preferring to be known as Mrs Anderton. They surrounded themselves with sailing people who knew how to cherish friendships, whatever the background of the person.

*

And what happened to Helena and Heather? Well their stories aren't quite finished yet……

Read on for an excerpt of Saving Captain Drummond, the second part in the Drummond series.

About this book

For years, Lou, my Canadian friend, who I met in 2009, at the Jane Austen Festival in Bath kept saying she wanted to be a highwayman in one of my novels. As she also has had lessons with broadswords, I had a character who I was quite happy to develop.

Saying that, it's harder than it first seemed to write someone whom I knew into a story. Even though I've used a lot of artistic licence, there is still a responsibility there to do justice to the character. I also needed to keep my character alive, something that often proved too difficult for the real knights of the road. They were feared by travellers but were not invincible. So, Lou looks like Lady Lou and is has funny as she is, but everything else is from my imagination!

The Peninsular War has fascinated me for a long time. I have referred it in other stories and will probably keep on doing so! It was a war fought differently than we are used to today. There was a lot of spare time between battles. Wellesley, very often went out hunting for the day if there wasn't a battle on. He would take a crust of bread and a boiled egg in his pocket for his lunch and off he would go! I think we always presume war is ongoing day after day, but it certainly wasn't in this case. That doesn't mean it wasn't bloody and brutal when the fighting did happen.

I've been fortunate to travel to some of the sites of the battles of the Peninsular War. There are a few that remain unchanged. What struck me most was that the terrain was so flat. I do wonder how there were any survivors from these battles without any scrubland, woods, and undulating land to provide cover. I thought the site of the battle at Salamanca was particularly open. It was very moving even so many years later.

This book contains pirates. Pirate attacks had reduced in the time period of this story, but they hadn't disappeared completely. Barbary pirates still operated off the coast of Africa and targeted the coasts of Spain, Portugal, and the Mediterranean. They not only took ships and cargo, but they also took the sailors and passengers of the ships and sold them as Christian slaves to the Ottoman Empire. It's estimated that between the sixteenth and nineteenth centuries, over one and a quarter million people were enslaved.

A fate I couldn't have Marianne be subjected to!

About the Author

I have had the fortune to live a dream. I've always wanted to write, but life got in the way as it so often does until a few years ago. Then a change in circumstance enabled me to do what I loved: sit down to write. Now writing has taken over my life, holidays being based around research, so much so that no matter where we go, my long-suffering husband says, 'And what connection to the Regency period has this building/town/garden got?'

That dream became a little more surreal when in 2018, I became an Amazon StorytellerUK Finalist with Lord Livesey's Bluestocking. A Regency Romance in the top five of an all-genre competition! It was a truly wonderful experience, I didn't expect to win, but I had a ball at the awards ceremony.

I do appreciate it when readers get in touch, especially if they love the characters as much as I do. Those first few weeks after release is a trying time; I desperately want everyone to love my characters that take months and months of work to bring to life.

If you enjoy the books please would you take the time to write a review on Amazon? Reviews are vital for an author who is just starting out, although I admit to bad ones being crushing. Selfishly I want readers to love my stories!

I can be contacted for any comments you may have, via my website:

www.audreyharrison.co.uk

or

www.facebook.com/AudreyHarrisonAuthor

Please sign-up for email/newsletter – only sent out when there is something to say!

www.audreyharrison.co.uk

You'll receive a free copy of The Unwilling Earl in mobi format for signing-up as a thank you!

Read on for an excerpt from Saving Captain Drummond!
Novels by Audrey Harrison
Regency Romances – newest release first

Lord Livesey's Bluestocking (Amazon Storyteller Finalist 2018)
Return to the Regency – A Regency Time-travel novel
My Foundlings:-
The Foundling Duke – The Foundlings Book 1
The Foundling Lady – The Foundlings Book 2
Mr Bailey's Lady
The Spy Series:-
My Lord the Spy
My Earl the Spy
The Captain's Wallflower
The Four Sisters' Series:-
Rosalind – Book 1
Annabelle – Book 2
Grace – Book 3
Eleanor – Book 4
The Inconvenient Trilogy:-
The Inconvenient Ward – Book 1
The Inconvenient Wife – Book 2
The Inconvenient Companion – Book 3
The Complicated Earl
The Unwilling Earl (Novella)
Other Eras
A Very Modern Lord
Years Apart

About the Proofreader

Joan Kelley fell in love with words at about 8 months of age and has been using them and correcting them ever since. She's had a 20-year career in U.S. Army public affairs spent mostly writing: speeches for Army generals, safety publications and videos, and has had one awesome book published, *Every Day a New Adventure: Caregivers Look at Alzheimer's Disease*, a really riveting and compelling look at five patients, including her own mother. It is available through Publishamerica.com. She also edits books because she loves correcting other people's use of language. What's to say? She's good at it. She lives in a small town near Atlanta, Georgia, in the American South with one long-haired cat to whom she is allergic and her grandson to whom she is not. If you need her, you may reach her at oh1kelley@gmail.com.

Saving Captain Drummond
Chapter 1
Talavera, Spain July 1809

The shout went up, and the horses and riders surged forward. It didn't matter that the men were hungry and tired, and the horses could have been in better condition, the battle cry had been heard. A mass of snorting animal flesh charged towards the enemy, their riders shouting battle cries and leading with their sabres. It was a scene of noise, dust, and mayhem.

Barely seconds passed before another sound was added to the melee: the unmistakable reverberation of exploding gunpowder, sending musket and cannon balls bouncing through the air, as the enemy responded to the attack. Screams of injured men and animals all too soon added to the noise, but the charge continued.

Cameron hunched down over his horse, making himself a smaller target. His knees dug into his mount's flesh as he urged the charger on. Now was not the time for hesitation. In a tight line, there would have been little opportunity for any other action for the beast than to go forward, but nevertheless, Cameron urged more speed.

The dirt of the dry sandy earth was kicked up in a whirlpool of stone, sand, and soil. It reduced immediate visibility, clouds of dry earth billowing into the faces and mouths of men and horses. Reduced sight wasn't necessarily a bad thing when in the middle of battle.

Gun fire was being aimed in a random fashion. The enemy shot in the general area of the attacking army, wanting to make each shot count, but knowing firing at speed was the priority. The fact that so many were charging towards them made it almost guaranteed that their shot would reach a target of some sort. The enemy concentrated on loading and shooting three balls per minute, the maximum they could achieve. Many failed to reach their maximum shooting speed; nerves made the hands shake in all but the hardiest of soldiers at the formidable wall of horses and cavalrymen bearing down on them.

When the two sides met, the amount of movement slowed slightly, but the clash of steel and cries of battle and pain increased as the opposing sides fought for survival.

Using his sabre, Cameron swung time and again, the power of his attack meeting equal force from his opponents. Sweat ran down his face unnoticed as the heat and movement increased.

When the blow came, it was as if time stopped. Cameron's mouth opened in shock, but no sound was uttered. He didn't feel the pain as such, but he knew he'd been hit. A second shot exploded into the top of his arm, and Cameron rolled off his horse in an effort to save his life. He'd lost his sabre with the first hit, his grip loosened with the effects of a high speed ball connecting with his flesh. There was danger on the ground of being trampled on by a horse, but if he'd stayed seated, a third hit would have been fatal.

Hitting the arid ground, Cameron forced himself to roll away from the hooves that surrounded him. He was not about to be crushed to death by an animal from his own regiment if he could help it. Gritting his teeth, his sheer bloody-mindedness kept his momentum going away from the animals until he reached a boulder to the rear of the line, which offered a modicum of protection.

Holding his right arm in an effort to stem the bleeding, he glanced around. He had to make it back to the medical station just beyond the British line. Gritting his teeth once more, he stumbled, crouching close to the ground, making his way from the battle. There was still danger from fire aimed beyond the cavalry charge, but although pausing and sometimes diving to the ground to try to dodge danger, Cameron maintained his progress. Bodies of animals and men littered the ground. Cameron was in no state to help the injured. He was bleeding profusely and in danger of losing consciousness. He tried to shake off the feelings of faintness threatening to hinder his progress; he had to force himself on.

It felt like hours until he reached the relative safety of the support lines. Crashing to his knees, he fought the dizziness overwhelming him. He needed medical attention or he would bleed to death. A soldier ran to him and helped him once more to his feet. With the stranger's support, Cameron moved slightly faster, being half-carried, half-dragged across the harsh terrain.

An image of his three sisters filled Cameron's vision as if they were there by his side. Their flowing red and auburn hair framed their faces while laughing green eyes gazed at him. Closing his eyes in pain whilst he was still being propelled forwards, he saw another face smiling at him. It was the most beautiful face he'd ever seen, and it belonged to the woman to whom he'd lost his heart. Her perfect porcelain complexion was framed with golden curls. Her blue eyes sparkled and seemed to draw him to her. He wanted to reach her; he knew instinctively she would soothe him. With her, he could smile. She would ease his pain.

Slumping forward into unconsciousness, Cameron uttered one word. "Helena."

*

The soldier stumbled under the weight of a body in a dead faint. Cursing slightly, he shifted the captain and continued on his journey towards the hospital. Soldiers were left on the battlefield until after the battle had ended, but an officer was helped whenever possible. Unbeknownst to Cameron an officer in the infantry had ordered one of his men to help him.

The scene of the after-effects of battle was like something out of a picture of hell — injured officers being carried in from all directions and regular ranks doing the best they could to drag themselves to safety and medical help. It didn't stir confidence for a young inexperienced soldier. James Pike, a newly arrived infantry man, had seen the captain emerge and had been instructed by his senior officer to help the wounded man. James had no time to consider that his own life might be extended because of his present duty, taking him away from the fight; all he could do was concentrate on keeping the unconscious captain moving forwards.

The pair reached the medical station, and James lay Cameron on the floor of the large tent. It was a structure ill-suited for the purpose of accepting and treating the number of men being brought to it.

Cameron stirred a little as a medical man finally approached the pair. He winced as his wounds were examined.

"Amputation is not necessary at the moment in this case," the assistant surgeon said. The senior doctor was farther away from the battle, in a more substantial building. "You are a lucky man. The shots have missed your bones."

Cameron felt anything but lucky.

"I'm going to have to remove the balls and any bits of clothing that are inside," the doctor said.

Cameron gritted his teeth as searing pain shot through his whole body at the invasive, but necessary, procedure. Fainting as his wound was being probed, the captain didn't know James had stepped forward in concern.

"Is he dead?" the soldier asked.

"No. But it is better he's not conscious for this," the doctor responded, not looking up from his work. Every second counted, for there were many other men needing help. He finished his task and rinsed out the two wounds with water. He was satisfied with his work. Neither musket ball had lodged in the bone. There was a strong chance of survival for this one.

"Has he accommodation in the town?" the doctor asked James.

"I don't know."

The doctor shook the patient. "Wake up. It is over, but we need to know where you are staying."

Cameron reluctantly regained consciousness, his focus on the pain more so than anything around him. He nodded when asked again about his accommodation.

"Take him to his lodgings," the doctor instructed James. "Hopefully, he will have help there to nurse him."

"Can he not stay in the hospital? Surely that's the best place for him?" James asked, wary that a badly injured man would be sent away from medical help.

"It doesn't need further treatment. I have done everything that can be done. If he develops a fever, seek help," the doctor explained, eager to move on to the next patient. "For his sake, pray gangrene does not set-in, or two French musket balls will be the least of his worries."

The young soldier was left alone, inexperienced and unsure of what to do. He crouched by the side of Cameron. "Captain, I need to know what address you're residing at," he said, not sure if Cameron was hearing anything of what was going on around him.

It took James three attempts before Cameron was able to focus enough to answer him. "Lodgings near the church," he croaked out. "Señora Calvo."

James nodded, and with difficulty, raised Cameron and once more started their unconventional walk in the direction of the church.

Cameron kept fading in and out of blackness. His arm burned with pain every time he moved and he had lost a lot of blood. All he wanted to do was to lie down and let the blackness engulf him. His protector kept asking questions: Was it this church? Was it this street? What number was it? It felt an inordinate amount of time before he was eventually placed on the bed in his lodgings.

James stepped back with a sigh of relief. The owner of the house was an older woman. She'd remained in the town thinking she was too old for any invading army to wish to ravage and was still able enough that she could remain in the house in the hope, that once the nightmare was over, her family could return to its home, and she could preserve it mostly intact.

She had immediately started to fuss around Cameron. He'd been a gentleman while staying with her and reminded her of one of her grandsons. Through broken English and a lot of gesticulating, she managed to convey what she wanted James to do.

Cameron was undressed by the soldier as gently as he could, but it was not easy. James had cut off Cameron's shirt and stock after making the captain faint when he'd removed his outer coat.

James had blanched at the sight of the blood. The assistant surgeon had secured the holes with bandages, but the journey home had meant the white material was bloodied. He swallowed, trying to regain control of his insides. Faltering now wouldn't do any good. He would likely face worse when he left the captain. Suddenly, battle didn't seem quite as glorious as it had on the journey from England.

Señora Calvo returned to the room with a bowl of vinegar and water and a towel. She looked in concern at the red bandages, but hadn't the same distressing reaction as the young soldier. Removing them, she cast them aside, and placing the bowl on a bedside chest of drawers, she soaked the towel and laid it across the wound.

"You. Do this," she said, indicating to James to continue with the task, every time the towel warmed because of contact with the hot skin.

"I have to get back," James protested.

"You. Sit. Enough death today," she responded firmly. There was no question in her voice. She'd given a command, and she expected it to be carried out. Her family would have recognised the tone of voice; they could have informed James, that at that point, there was no benefit in trying to argue.

James obeyed, more afraid at that moment of the matriarch than he was of his commanding officer.

An hour passed before Cameron's batman returned to the lodging. Thomas was quickly apprised of what was happening, and he readily replaced James in caring for Cameron.

"I thank you on the captain's behalf. He will be indebted to you for the service you have done him today," Thomas said warmly to James.

"I didn't think battle would be so overwhelming," James said, admitting some of his shock at the sights he'd seen.

"There is nothing thrilling about two sides trying to kill each other," Thomas said sagely. "Keep your head down and don't panic. That is the surest way to stay alive."

"I'll try not to panic," James said, not convinced he had the bravery inside him to do what Cameron had done, along with the others in his regiment. "It's time I must return to my own regiment. I have been away far longer than I supposed I would be."

"Take this," Thomas rummaged in the large wooden box that contained Cameron's belongings. He gave the young man a bottle of fortified wine and some bread. Food was short, but the young man deserved some reward for his efforts.

"Thank you," James responded. "I hope he recovers."

"Whatever happens, his war is over now," Thomas responded.

*

Berkshire, England, August 1809

Lady Helena Ashton walked into the breakfast room at her ancestral home. She was a beautiful young lady of almost nineteen years. Having a gentle nature, pretty blond hair, blue eyes, and a decent fortune, she was always welcomed in any home in polite society. She smiled at her older brother who was already seated at the dining table.

"Is Lou having breakfast in her chamber?" Helena asked of her new sister-in-law.

"Yes. This sickness is not helping her morning mood." Lord Simon Ashton, Earl of Garswood, grimaced at his sister. He was a man who, until meeting the young woman who was to become his wife, had been an aloof member of society. His own father's behaviour and his conviction of the shallowness of the people surrounding him prevented him from forming close attachments with almost everyone. That is, until Lou had entered his life. He was an attractive man, darker blonde than his sister, similar blue eyes. Lou had presumed him a sapscull when she'd first met him; Simon was anything but.

She was now his wife of six months, increasing and not happy with the unexpected side-effects of the first few months of pregnancy.

"I feel for her. It cannot be pleasant, but I shall delay my visit to her room until after noon," Helena said, not quite used to the cursing of her new sister-in-law when things weren't going to plan. There was no malice in Lou, but Helena very often felt extremely unworldly when Lou was at her most vociferous. Lou would have been mortified to realise that she slightly intimidated her sister-in-law, but Helena kept the fact from her, knowing that it had more to do with her own very sheltered upbringing than a problem with the new member of her family.

"Probably wise. Have you any arrangements planned with Heather today?" Simon asked, tucking into his breakfast with a gusto that would have repulsed his wife, the way she was feeling. She could barely stomach dry crackers.

Helena nodded. "We're going to go for a day's shopping in Woodly," Helena explained. The Ashton family home was just outside the village of Twyford a few miles from Woodly, a larger town in the county of Berkshire.

"I pity the footman who is charged with accompanying you!"

Helena smiled. "We'll make sure we do not visit too many shops."

"Ha! If he believes that, he's a fool!" Simon scoffed.

"That is no way to talk about your servants," Helen chided. "Heather and I are not that bad."

"Aren't we?" Lady Heather Drummond asked, as she entered the smaller of the two dining rooms in the house. She was very like her sister with red hair and clear green eyes and had often tried to emulate Lou.

Helena smiled at her friend. The way the two families had met had been the strangest of circumstances. Heather's eldest sister, Lou, had been acting as a highwayman and had held up the carriage containing the Ashtons. Simon had shot the thief before realising he'd shot a woman. Not willing to walk away as he would have done if the offender had been a man, he'd returned home with the offender in his carriage. Lou had developed a fever and had been forced to reveal her two sisters were alone and vulnerable in London.

Helena had taken her brother to find the young girls. Unable to leave the girls, friendless and in a less salubrious area of London, Simon and his sister took in the family who turned out to have been cheated out of their fortune by their eldest brother. It had seemed the family faced one disaster after another in those early days.

Simon had been drawn to the spirited woman they'd met on Hampstead Heath, although initially, he'd been willing to call in the magistrate for threatening his only sister, his friend, and himself as they rode in his carriage late at night. After a very shaky start, an unlikely romance had developed between Simon and Lou. It had been a difficult time for them all mainly because of the actions of Lou's half-brother, but eventually a deep and strong love had grown between Lou and Simon, which resulted in a wedding taking place.

"We must try harder to be interestingly different," Heather said, joining the pair at the table. She was more outgoing than Helena, which Simon had welcomed once the initial obstacles facing the two families had been overcome.

"God help me!" Simon groaned.

"I've received a letter from Marianne," Heather continued, smiling at Simon. She liked her brother-in-law and had seen how he'd mellowed the fiery Lou, making her elder sister truly happy. "Marianne is settling into life as a captain's wife, although she writes that Joseph might not be at sea for much longer. He has been approached about a position working in the dock offices."

"Marianne will be happy about that," Helena said. "I doubt she'd have liked being separated for too long from Captain Anderton."

A family who had experienced worry, financial ruin, and the uncertainty of a brother at war in the Peninsular had been under extreme strain. When the reality of Lou's madcap scheme of providing funds by acting as a highwayman had been revealed, it had caused the biggest family fall-out the sisters had ever experienced.

Heather's twin sister, Marianne, had managed to secure a husband in even more unusual circumstances than Lou. Marianne had not wished to return to the family home in Scotland, having started to form an attachment with a captain who owned his own ship and was based in London. In a desperate attempt not to be separated from the man she loved, Marianne had stowed away on Captain Joseph Anderton's ship. She'd failed to consider that she might be seasick, and as a result, had been very ill. Her scheme had seemed to fail, the captain not showing any feelings towards her even after she was so ill. Marianne didn't know it was his own background keeping him from declaring himself. It was only when the ship was under attack that Joseph had realised his own less-than-perfect family history was not insurmountable when wanting to marry the lady he loved.

The newly married pair had settled in London, wishing to be in easy travelling distance to the docks. Heather missed her twin daily; they'd never spent a day apart until Marianne had boarded the ship those few months before, but Heather was happy her sister was well settled with the man she loved.

"I shall write to her when we have had our day out shopping and I can advise her of my new purchases," Heather said.

"Surely you must have enough for the season by now?" Simon teased his new sister.

It had seemed Heather and Marianne wouldn't have a come out because of their eldest brother's actions, but once Lou had married Simon, he'd settled a dowry on Heather, and she was looking forward to the upcoming season. Lou's pregnancy was to cause them a little problem, for she would not be able to chaperone Helena and Heather, but Simon had promised to employ a suitable protectress. He was not about to volunteer himself; he'd made a mistake with the company he'd kept on the previous season, exposing his only sister to a cad. It could still bring him out in a cold sweat when he thought about how close Helena had come to marrying the worst kind of rake. He wasn't going to risk that again.

Helena had been keen to leave London during her first season. A pretty, wealthy, young woman, she'd quickly become disillusioned with society. Escaping to her country home had been a welcome reprieve and a place where she could reflect on her life and on her affection for Heather and Lou's second brother, Captain Cameron Drummond of the 14th Regiment of (Light) Dragoons. She had fallen in love with the dashing captain, and hoped daily for his return from the war.

"Is there ever such a thing as too much when we're discussing ribbons, combs, and fabric?" Heather asked.

"Obviously not," Simon smiled. Heather had been an angry ball of attitude with no restraint when divulging family secrets when she'd first met the Ashtons. Trying to imitate her elder sister, Lou, she'd had a hard time when she'd realised Lou was as flawed as everyone else, and the sisters had argued in spectacular fashion. Now reconciled, Heather was allowing herself to develop her own character.

Although to everyone, she appeared confident and outgoing, no one really knew her inner doubts and the lack of confidence she suffered. She had always been under the shadow of Lou and Marianne, and only now that the dynamics had changed was she beginning to realise she could be her own person, although she could still give a scowl her eldest sister would be proud of when the situation called for it.

The group separated after breakfast. Simon was loath to be away from his wife for very long, especially as he was the only one with whom she felt completely comfortable. The fact that it didn't stop her cursing him to the devil most of the time was beside the point. They were a couple deeply in love and perfectly suited.

Helena joined Heather in the hallway when they were both dressed in pelisses and bonnets. Helena had never had a sister and was enjoying the relationship she shared with the new sisters in her life. Heather, in particular, was becoming her closest of friends.

"Are you ready for a serious day's shopping?" she asked Heather.

"Always!" Heather said. "And if we can turn some heads in the process, it will have been a successful day all 'round!"

Helena laughed as they climbed into the coach. Heather had already expressed that she was determined to have a good time and wanted to become an expert at flirting. They didn't socialise to a great extent, but when they did, Heather was always the one with the most attention. Helena presumed it was because Heather didn't wish to settle down any time soon, determined instead to enjoy the upcoming season as much as possible because it had so nearly been snatched away from her.

Unfortunately, it was Heather's self-doubt and feeling of not quite fitting into her life that was making her wear the mask of the fickle debutante. She couldn't reveal to anyone her innermost fears or feelings, not to her family nor her new friend.

*

Seated in the drawing room after their evening meal, Helena and Heather were recounting their day to Lou, who was only fully able to take part in family socialising later in the day.

She grimaced at Simon. "I curse you for giving these two more money than they have sense!"

"My sister has changed since your sister joined the family," Simon defended Helena.

"I could easily start comparing Duncan more favourably to you!" Heather said indignantly, comparing Simon to her wastrel of an elder half-brother.

"Now there's a fate I'd rail against!" Simon laughed.

"Will Duncan be in London for the season?" Heather asked Lou.

"Probably. He lives in London, after all," Lou responded dryly.

"Do we have to see him?"

Lou laughed. "I doubt he will want to see us any more than we want to see him. Especially as the last time we saw him, he agreed to handing over one of his houses!" It had been amazing to watch Lou persuade her self-absorbed half-brother to give them one of the homes he owned. As he had probably purchased it with the money from his sister's inheritances that he'd squandered, Lou's contrivance gave them some sense of justification. She had guessed right about Duncan's character: Whilst he was the head of the family, he'd thought himself invincible, but once Lou had become engaged to Simon, his sisters were no longer unprotected. They could carry out the threat of an expensive court case. Duncan had capitulated and offered his house in Bath as recompense.

"I don't know how one can be related to someone and dislike him so much!" Heather exclaimed.

"There are no guarantees we'll like our siblings," Simon smiled.

"I certainly have no affection for one of mine," Lou scowled.

"He's probably not overly fond of you. You did draw his cork," Heather pointed out.

"A pity I only did it the once!" Lou responded. "Although Cameron gave him a good beating when he admitted to spending our inheritance." She would never forget the sight of her normally mild brother, dishing out a punishment which Duncan would not soon forget.

The group were disturbed by the entrance of the butler, who announced that Simon had a visitor.

"At this time of night? Who the devil is disturbing us?" Lou asked.

"It is a Captain Philips, My Lady," the butler responded, used to his mistress' outbursts by now. None of her words were delivered with spite or anger, so it was quite easy to school his features into one of bland servitude until out of sight of his employers. Then and only then, would he allow himself a quiet chuckle at some of Lou's direct speeches.

"Captain Philips! Show him in!" Lou said, quickly changing her cursing to a genuine welcome.

"Yes, please do," Simon agreed. "And get the man some refreshments. What is he doing travelling so late at night?"

The butler disappeared and returned a few moments later. Lou had exchanged looks with Helena and Heather. The youngest of the group had sat up straighter the moment Captain Philips' name was mentioned; she'd been very attracted to him when she'd met him before the summer. But then again, who wouldn't be moved by a tall, dark-haired, brown-eyed, military man? Certainly, an innocent young woman like Heather couldn't remain unaffected.

Captain Michael Philips walked into the large drawing room with some apprehension. Simon was seated near his wife on one sofa, and sitting opposite on a second sofa were Heather and Helena. It was a scene of happy family life and contentment. Michael inwardly groaned. He should have stressed that he wanted to speak to Simon alone, but he was unaware that Simon's wife would do anything to put her youngest sister in his way again. She knew of the attraction Heather felt, and it was Lou's way of promoting her sister, which she was motivated to do, more so since their family argument. Lou had always been the one in charge, the one the others looked up to. It had shocked them all to find out their adored sister was as infallible as they were and how close her actions had come to destroying their family. The events had shaken Lou as much as it had her sisters, and she wanted to make things right between her youngest sister and herself, and if that involved welcoming Captain Philips late in the evening, so be it.

The group exchanged greetings and invited Michael to sit. He looked slightly uncomfortable, being on a single chair between the two sofas where the four could ask questions of him. He answered the queries being fired at him as best he could.

"We thought you were abroad, Captain!"

"Have you been travelling long?"

"This is a late hour to be on the roads, Captain!"

"Is Cameron in England?"

Michael couldn't help laughing gently, despite his discomfort and raised his hands in defeat. "I have been travelling so late because I wanted to get here as soon as I could. I'm afraid I have not been back to Portugal since we last met. My mother took a turn for the worse, so I have been working in London recently."

Simon was the first to pick up on the first response Michael had given. "You have news for us?" he asked quietly, but the others realised the meaning behind his words and suddenly became silent.

"Yes," Michael responded. He had hoped not to inflict pain on the sisters, but he took a breath. There was nothing for it. "Cameron has been hurt." There was no point being anything but direct.

There were various exclamations of distress, but Simon called the others to order. "Tell us all you know, Captain Philips."

Michael nodded. "There was a push at Talavera. Not completely successful from all accounts and great losses on both sides. But

Cameron is alive!" he said quickly, as he saw three already pale faces blanch at his words. "He was hurt in one of the cavalry charges," Michael continued. "We receive dispatches a lot sooner than letters home have the time to get through. As soon as I heard he was injured, I sent extra funds for him to use should he need them. There have been delays in payments to the troops, so I wanted to make sure he could buy whatever he might require. I immediately arranged to set out for here to let you know as soon as I possibly could. I didn't want to send an express. I know Cameron would do me the same service if our roles were reversed."

"Thank you," Simon said, standing to pour the man a brandy. "You probably need this."

Helena had stood and walked towards the curtained window. Pulling the thick, heavy fabric aside, she gazed blindly out into the dark night. She felt as if she couldn't breathe. He was hurt and so far away! Cameron and she had a secret understanding. He'd not wanted to ask her to wait for him when he was fighting with Wellesley, but they'd declared their feelings for each other in private. Their relationship had had a complicated start, and Helena had told no one. Marianne and Heather had known of her attraction to their brother, but they didn't know to what level the romance had developed.

She turned to the group. There was only one thing she could do. "I'm going to him," she said simply.

Printed in Great Britain
by Amazon